MONSTERS AMONG US

MONSTERS AMONG US

MONICA RODDEN

EMBER

Text copyright © 2021 by Monica Rodden
Cover and interior photograph © 2021 by plainpicture/visual2020vision
Cover background used under license from Shutterstock.com
Cover design by Casey Moses

All rights reserved. Published in the United States by Ember, an imprint of Random House Children's Books, a division of Penguin Random House LLC, New York. Originally published in hardcover in the United States by Crown Books for Young Readers, an imprint of Random House Children's Books, a division of Penguin Random House LLC, New York, in 2021.

Ember and the E colophon are registered trademarks of Penguin Random House LLC.

Visit us on the Web! GetUnderlined.com

Educators and librarians, for a variety of teaching tools, visit us at RHTeachersLibrarians.com

The Library of Congress has cataloged the hardcover edition of this work as follows:
Names: Rodden, Monica, author.
Title: Monsters among us / Monica Rodden.
Description: First edition. | New York: Crown Books for Young Readers, [2021] | Audience: Ages 14 & up. | Audience: Grades 10–12. | Summary: Recovering at home after a dorm-room rape she can barely remember, Catherine is devastated when a neighbor girl is murdered, and turns to childhood friend, Henry, for help.
Identifiers: LCCN 2019040863 (print) | LCCN 2019040864 (ebook) | ISBN 978-0-593-12586-1 (hardcover) | ISBN 978-0-593-12587-8 (library binding) | ISBN 978-0-593-12588-5 (epub)
Subjects: CYAC: Rape—Fiction. | Murder—Fiction. | Family life—Washington (State)—Fiction. | Washington (State)—Fiction.
Classification: LCC PZ7.1.R63953 Mon 2020 (print) | LCC PZ7.1.R63953 (ebook) | DDC [Fic]—dc23

ISBN 978-0-593-12589-2 (paperback)

Printed in the United States of America
10 9 8 7 6 5 4 3 2 1
First Ember Edition 2022

For those who have met with monsters, and lived.

And for those who did not: you are more alive,
even now, than they ever were.

PART ONE

THE WOODS OF THE SELF-MURDERERS

May she wake in torment!

–EMILY BRONTË, *WUTHERING HEIGHTS*

CHAPTER ONE

Catherine stared out the window of her bedroom and thought about throwing herself out of it.

She could do it, too. There was a screen, but she could unlatch it, or kick it out the way people did in movies. Or cut through it with a knife the way the serial killers did in movies. She'd crawl out like a cat onto the roof, the tiles hard and gritty under her palms, then she'd stand up, breathe in the gray winter air, and run until that was all there was under her bare feet.

"Catherine?"

She turned, dropping her duffel and stepping away from the window. Her mother was in the doorway, all soft blond hair and wide eyes. Her sweater was overlong and swallowed her wrists.

My mom is smaller than I am, Catherine thought. *When did that happen?*

"I wanted to see if you needed anything," her mother said, taking one small step into the room.

Catherine shook her head.

"Your father could have gotten that for you." A gesture toward the bag at Catherine's feet.

Yes, Catherine thought, he could have. But that might have

required him to look at her, and he didn't seem able to do that since she came home. So different from just Thanksgiving break last month, drinking cider on the couch, small dessert plates balanced on their laps, all of them laughing at a car commercial for some reason she couldn't remember. But now there was something between them all, a wall her mother touched with outstretched fingers, making patting and smoothing motions without actually reaching her. But her father made no attempt at all, seeming grateful, in fact, for the barrier.

"It's fine," Catherine said. "I think I'm going to sleep."

"Of course." Her mother, after a brief hesitation, crossed the room, hands reaching out. A nurse's hands, slightly rough, used to dealing with emergencies that weren't her own. "Can I . . . ?"

"Oh." Catherine swallowed. "Sure."

Her mother hugged her. "I'm so sorry, dear."

Catherine nodded against her mother's neck, her eyes fixed on the flat of her bed, the stark white coverlet, dotted with gold and silver suns, moons, and stars.

"Hey, Mom?"

Her mother pulled away, wiping her eyes, which were a little darker blue than Catherine's. A little more beautiful. "I'm sorry. I shouldn't."

Catherine shook her head. "No, it's just . . . can you not tell anyone?"

Her mother stared at her blankly, eyelashes wet.

"About what happened," Catherine added unhelpfully.

"I wouldn't—"

"No, I know. I just wanted to—"

"Right—"

"I just don't want to talk about it. Whatever it was."

"Of course not." A pause. "Do you remember anything more?"

"No."

Catherine walked toward the bed and crawled under the sheets. They were cold. She made herself smile at her mother.

"The curtains?" Her mother made to draw them closed.

"No," Catherine said, a little too quickly, then—"Sorry. No. Leave them. And the light, too. Please."

Her mother left. Catherine turned where she lay and looked out the window. It was a typical Washington afternoon, low gray light and the promise of rain. Trees everywhere, the ones not bare such a lush green they looked painted. She'd been studying William Blake at the university: his poetry and his art. One of his works, a depiction of Dante's hell, was called *The Woods of the Self-Murderers*. Suicides were damned to the seventh circle and entombed in trees—trees that Blake drew hunched and brittle-brown, so unlike the tall, healthy ones outside her window. Catherine noticed something in that painting, something you had to look at closely to see: human forms traced inside each trunk. A man was hidden in the right tree, but she had eyes only for the woman on the left, who was trapped *upside down*, her hair spilling over the roots, her feet lost in the branches above.

"They are the only souls in hell with no possibility of

redemption," Professor Graham had explained in the dim light of the classroom, the watercolor projected massively on the wall, "as they rejected God's gift of life."

Catherine twisted away from the window now, eyes screwed shut.

Do you remember anything more?

I was still, she thought. *Couldn't move. There was laughter. Pain. Like hell.*

Like I deserved it.

———

She didn't think she'd slept at all, but when she finally sat up the clock on her nightstand read two in the morning. She got up, wrapped herself in a thick bathrobe, and felt her way along the dark hallway to the stairs. When she reached the kitchen, she flipped the switch that turned on the light just above the sink; turn the other switch and the whole kitchen would light up like a spotlight and there would be no shadows at all.

She poured herself a glass of water and went onto the porch, but she stilled as soon as she opened the door.

Her father was sitting on one of the porch rocking chairs, eyes staring out into the darkness.

"Catherine," he said, turning to her.

"I was just getting water."

He nodded, leaned back in his chair. "It's cold."

She didn't know what else to do, so she took a sip of water.

"Smells like snow, doesn't it?" he said.

Catherine had no idea what snow smelled like; it barely snowed at all in West Falls, just a few inches each year. She drank again, trying to drain the glass so she could make an excuse to get more and then go back upstairs.

Her father looked smaller than usual in the rocking chair, as though he'd lost weight. His dark hair was thinner too, his eyes just as dark behind those wire frames. She remembered seeing a picture of him once without them, when he'd been much younger. She hadn't recognized him, so straight-backed, his hair thick and glossy. He was the kind of man who looked like he'd been born middle-aged, with glasses and a slightly rounded spine, but then, maybe all children saw their parents like that.

He taught history at the alternative high school on the edge of town, talking endlessly of wars and commanders and laws created and amended. He even had a table of antiques upstairs, collectables from years of infrequent, all-day auctions, him coming back with wrapped packages, carefully unfurling brown paper at the kitchen table, his eyes alight with excitement. "Your father's Christmas," her mother had called it.

Catherine blinked at the night, trying to get her father into focus. "It's cold. I think I'll go back upstairs."

He nodded. She heard the creak of the rocking chair. He was right; the air did sort of smell like snow. Or maybe it just *felt* like snow, a heaviness to the air, a potential energy waiting to fall from the sky.

The facts were these and she was not proud of them.

One: she'd gone to the party. Sigma something. Maybe a Psi in there as well. Two: her dress was yellow and short and thin cotton that danced when she moved, her blond hair curled at the ends to brush her collarbone. And she did move—three—dancing and spinning. Four: she drank. Cheap boxed wine and then something green-blue that burned. No drugs in the drinks—she thought, then tried not to think about that at all. Just too many of them. Strangely, she felt guiltier for that. So much on her shoulders, her choices all her own.

Five: blackness.

Or was that with four? Levels of drinking. All of them wrong but some more wrong than others, like Dante's circles of hell, a punishment to fit the crime and she was a woman upside down in a tree, damned, her hair tangled in the tree's roots, all the blood rushing there as though the tree were feeding off her blood instead of rain.

He fed off her too. She didn't know who. She didn't even remember getting to the dorms back on campus, much less who the room belonged to. The one she woke up in hours later, before the sun was up, a dark room with a tall figure standing over her. He'd been hard to see without any lights on and the window showing only a black sky. He was shaking her.

She tried to push him off, turn over, into the cool covers, but the covers weren't cool and she smelled smoke and turned the other way, coughing. She shoved at the hand on her.

"I'm up," she managed, pulling herself into a sitting position.

"Doesn't look like it."

She wiped her eyes, swallowed. Her throat was so dry it hurt and she wanted to cough but was almost afraid to. "Water," she said without thinking. Her dress felt twisted around her.

A sigh. Footsteps. The tall shadow in front of her walked to the other side of the room. She heard a tap run and then shut off seconds later.

"Here." A cup in front of her face. She could just make out the edge of the rim. She took the cup, feeling for the first time a shiver of unease, but she was thirsty so she drank. It was just enough for a mouthful.

"Thanks," she said. "Where—?" But she broke off. She'd righted herself a little more, shifting against the mattress, and an awareness of her body flung itself into her mind like a blow. She froze where she was, not moving at all, her mouth half open as her lungs inhaled sharply, burning her raw throat, which the water had not helped.

Fear came like a blackout, sudden and complete. A terror out of nowhere.

Now she noticed the height of the shadow—*person, man, stranger*—before her, how he was just inches away, looking down with a featureless face. The cup dropped from her hand and clattered—plastic—onto the floor. She heard every time it hit the floor. Five times, before it rolled away with the sound of grinding pebbles.

"Get up," he said.

She hesitated for a moment, then stood. She tugged at the

hem of her dress. The collar felt all wrong, too high against her neck. Backward, she realized. It was on backward.

Shoes, she thought, because that thought was safe. She felt for them on the floor, crouching like a child. Ankle boots with a low heel. She pulled them on. Her toes hit something hard in the right one. Her cell phone. She took it out and put the shoe on.

There were other thoughts in her mind—not cell phones and not shoes—struggling to get to the front, but she was stiff-arming them to the back like a no-nonsense hall monitor.

"Go."

She looked at the shadow. She was slick all over, her skin twitching and sweating so much it was like it was trying to slide right off her bones.

Fear again, breathing at the place behind her ears.

She went.

CHAPTER TWO

Her sleep was a broken thing she couldn't put back together. But she did try—over-the-counter sleeping pills: white and chalky. When she went back upstairs after talking to her father, she took one. Then another an hour later, her eyes dazedly scanning the back of the box; what was the max dosage? Did it matter? Her mind was thick with slow thoughts that scraped against the inside of her skull.

Don't think.

I don't want to think.

Slowly she fell into blackness and woke coated in a thin sheen of sweat. She smelled. When she sat up she realized she'd kicked the covers off her bed and that the room was lit gold from the sun through the thin, closed curtains. Her clock read three in the afternoon.

She stayed in bed for two more hours, watching random things on YouTube, letting the next video play without clicking, not even bothering to skip the ads. Her mom came in to check on her. Brought her saltines as though she were recovering from the flu.

"Can I get you anything else?"

"No. I'm okay."

But her mom brought her tea, then ice water, then a small bowl of spaghetti shiny with butter. Catherine ate it while watching a documentary about steroids in the Olympics on Netflix. When she heard her parents' bedroom door close just after ten, she got out of bed.

She splashed cold water on her face in the bathroom and saw it catch on her eyelashes. She didn't recognize the girl looking back at her: a mess, her blond hair dirty, the careful highlights barely noticeable under the grime. She had bruises: one at her neck, another on the inside of her right knee. They seemed to hurt more, the longer she looked at them.

She remembered seeing those bruises for the first time in the hall bathroom two days ago, a pulsing sort of heartbeat under the color. Her hands had gone to touch them, then had slid away, her feet moving almost of their own accord, to the showers. She'd stood under the water in her dress until she couldn't feel her skin anymore, then took the dress off, her hands shaking on the zipper at her throat, her fingers slipping on the slick fabric. When she was done, she took the soaking dress and shoved it in the trash can, just as her RA, Cordelia, came in, wearing sweat pants and an irritable expression. She took one look at Catherine and rolled her eyes.

"You know you can't throw away your own trash in here." She pointed to the sign on the wall. "See? No nonbathroom trash. It's already too full."

Catherine said nothing.

Cordelia sighed. "Look, just take it outside to the dumpster if—"

"I'm not going outside."

Raised eyebrows. "Suit yourself then." And to Catherine's disbelief, Cordelia started to take the dress herself, picking it up with her fingers like it was something gross.

"This is soaking. Holy crap. What did you do, go swimming in it?" Her eyes, suddenly searching, caused a dull foreboding to prick at the back of Catherine's neck. She dropped the dress back into the trash. "Catherine? Catherine? Are you okay?"

She closed her eyes, shutting out the memory, telling herself she wasn't there, that she was home and safe and fine. She tried to think of how to pass the time. She didn't think she could sleep any more, and the idea of scrolling through her Netflix recommendations made her twitch. It seemed to take her brain a long time to come up with something, but then she remembered with a little jolt that in two days, it would be Christmas Eve.

She wrapped herself in sweats and a bathrobe and tied her dirty hair in a low ponytail. The hardwood of the stairs was cold under her feet, the kitchen air chilled. Outside the window, the night was dark, but the porch light was on, and she could see that her father had been right: it was snowing. Light, drifting. She sat at the kitchen table and looked at the two gifts she'd brought down: a book for her dad, a paint set for her mother. She'd gotten the paints on Etsy, had paid extra to make sure the set shipped to the university before she left. She remembered getting a notice that she had a package, the day before the night it had happened.

Her parents still kept the scissors and tape in that long, narrow drawer to the left of the oven. She slid the scissors through the wrapping paper. It made a sound like a snake and she closed her eyes. When she opened them again, there was someone outside the kitchen window.

She could just make him out by the glow of the porch light on his blond hair. He was walking a chocolate Lab that was sniffing a tree in Catherine's front yard. The boy seemed to sense somebody watching him, because he turned slowly, head tilted a little, and met her eyes. He raised a hand in greeting and after a moment, Catherine waved back. They looked at each other for another moment and the dog began to wag its tail madly, straining at the leash; unable to help herself, she got up and went to the door. When she opened it, the dog barked and jerked the boy forward with its enthusiasm to get to Catherine.

She knelt down and stroked the dog's head. "Hey, Molly," she said. The dog was somehow cold and warm at the same time, her muzzle grayer than Catherine had ever seen it. Catherine stood up and half smiled at the boy in the doorway.

"Henry," she said. "You need a hat."

He ran a hand through his short hair with a grimace. "No one told me about the snow."

"Yeah, I know." She took a step back, letting both him and

the dog inside, and closed the door. She leaned against it, arms crossed, looking at him a little wonderingly.

They'd been seven years old the summer he moved in down the street. Both of them blond-haired, blue-eyed children who blistered in the rare Washington sun. It had been hotter than usual, but they discovered a shared love of the outdoors: running wild through tall, damp grass; coming home for dinner with cuts and grime up and down their bare, skinny calves; Henry pulling splinters from her palms when she'd tried to do a handstand on his deck. Children. Inseparable until they weren't. Until she'd gone away the summer before high school, and when she came back, something had shifted between them. Suddenly they were teenagers instead of children, in a high school so large that they'd only had one class together the whole four years. This naturally led to different friends, different everything. She dated boys from the soccer team and went to midnight movie premieres and once attended a party across state lines in Portland. Then she went away to college, and he didn't, but by that point they were so distant from each other he was just a wry memory to her. There and then not. Hers and then not.

At prom, she had run into him outside the hotel and they'd hugged with that why-not agreeableness that came with the end of senior year. She'd smiled up at him, handsome and navy-eyed under the stars, her long green dress sweeping the sidewalk. It had felt like a reprieve to see him smile back at her that night, to talk for just a few minutes, to say each other's names. She hadn't even realized until then, the guilt she felt about how she'd let him go.

I put you away, she thought, looking at him now. *Like a toy I'd outgrown.* Outside, snowflakes stuck to the window in jagged circles.

"Catherine Ellers," he said. "Catherine Luana Ellers."

She rolled her eyes. "I'd hoped you had forgotten that part."

"Never."

"Well, it's not my fault my parents honeymooned in Hawaii. It means *happy,* anyway."

"Yeah, but you never seemed too happy about it."

"Whereas Durand is such a charming middle name."

"It means enduring, *Luana.*"

"Also stubborn, *Durand.*"

They were both speaking softly, aware of her parents asleep upstairs, and there was something communal and conspiratorial in how they grinned at each other. She realized in that moment that he had no idea what had happened to her. There was a rushing feeling of relief in that; she didn't have to pretend. He was the first person she'd talked to in days who had no idea what she'd been through, or that she'd been through something at all. To Henry, she was just a girl in her kitchen two nights before Christmas Eve, wrapping presents while it snowed outside.

So, when he asked her how she was, she walked to the kitchen table and finished taping the snowman wrapping paper around her father's book.

"Shitty," she said.

"Language," he said, bending down to cover Molly's ears.

Catherine's lips twitched. "How old is she now?"

"Nine."

"No way." As soon as Catherine looked at Molly, the dog padded over to her, panting happily. Catherine stroked her fur slowly, frowning. "Time flies. Kind of late for a walk, isn't it?"

Henry grinned. "You, uh, don't really have a choice when it comes to a dog. And it wasn't like my parents would take her. Not that I mind," he added.

She knew he didn't mind. Molly had been his idea, she remembered. He'd begged and begged his parents for a dog and they had finally relented under the agreement that Henry would take care of it entirely. Unlike most children, he had lived up to his word. Even now, nine years later, Molly still looked up at him in silent devotion.

"You've always been good to her," Catherine said with a smile, then the smile fell a little. Henry Brisbois was in her kitchen. It was the strangest thing. She felt a pang of guilt looking at him, the same feeling she'd had talking to him at prom. She glanced at the staircase, then back at the door. "Well, I don't want to keep you—"

"Right." He picked up Molly's leash from the floor, and she trotted back to him, panting happily. "Thanks for the break from the cold."

"No problem," she said as Henry made for the door.

"And, uh, sorry you're feeling shitty."

She jerked her head toward Molly. "Careful."

"Oh, she doesn't care. She's got a horrible mouth herself. Mostly because she's a dog."

Catherine gave him a look she knew was too long. This kept happening to her lately, a thousand-yard stare she couldn't quite shake, as though her eyes were taking longer to see things. Henry didn't look away.

"Sorry." She cleared her throat and looked back at the presents. "I just realized I forgot the jars."

"Jars."

"Cookie jars," she said unhelpfully, then added, motioning with her hands, "You know, layers of everything. Flour and sugar and stuff. I was going to make some for my parents. Different kinds of cookies."

"Cookie jars," Henry said again.

"They're good gifts."

"Yeah, but so are actual cookies."

She walked to a nearby cabinet. "I was going to do chocolate chip, and then this cranberry one and then a third, maybe peanut butter, but I don't know if that'll work in a jar."

Henry came up behind her, looking into the cabinet as well. "And you're using your parents' ingredients for their own gifts?"

"Flour, brown sugar—shut up, Henry—powdered sugar, baking soda," she mused, pushing aside various jars and bags. "Yeah, everything's here except baking powder and white sugar. And chocolate chips."

"They have brown sugar but not white sugar?" Henry asked, surprised.

"When I'm at school I think my parents live off expired eggs and white bread. Actually, some of this stuff might be expired too. Can flour go bad?" she said, carefully turning over the bag to search for a date.

"Maybe you should come home more often," Henry suggested. "Or get them one of those pet-feeder things off Amazon."

Catherine turned from the cabinet to look at Henry, flour bag still in hand. "Molly's sick, isn't she?"

"Nothing gets past you, Catherine." He shifted where he stood. "She's got time, we think. She can still go on walks."

Catherine tried not to look at the dog. "She's all skinny. She was always fat before. And on her neck, I felt stitches."

"Labs, you know, they tend to get—"

"Cancer." A short silence. Catherine swallowed, hard. "I had a shit time at college."

Henry didn't say anything for a moment; then he glanced back at the cabinet behind her. "Those pet-feeder things on Amazon are really expensive, and they don't do those cookie jar things you want to make. I'm pretty sure Safeway has sugar, though."

"Safeway?"

He frowned, then seemed to understand. "Oh, you weren't here. Yeah, the Albertsons is totally gone. There's a Safeway now. It's massive."

"Will they even be open?"

Henry glanced at the oven clock. "Now? No, they close at ten. But you could try tomorrow."

"They're open this close to Christmas?"

"Probably be riots if they weren't. I'm going tomorrow too, actually. Have to pick up some last-minute things for my mom. Bread crumbs or something. We can go together if you want."

She considered this for a moment, not quite believing the invitation but feeling strangely comforted by it all the same. She glanced down at Molly, who met her eyes and began to wag her tail. Catherine smiled. "Can I buy her, like, a steak or something, while we're there?"

———

Henry said he'd come back in the morning, around nine. Once he left, Molly in tow, Catherine finished wrapping the two presents and then placed them carefully under the tree in the living room. The tree was slender but beautiful, with silver and gold ribbons, and ornaments that caught the light on the edge of their circumference. The tree's lights suddenly reminded her of Henry's backyard. Fourteen years old, the tail end of a summer party: distant, adult chatter; a kernel of corn wedged in her back teeth; the stinging haze of smoke from the grill whenever she walked by. The grass had been damp under her bare feet, the backyard glowing from the string of pastel garden lights draped across the deck. Henry's face had been very close to hers, a weird mirror image. But then he'd kissed her, and it felt so normal, so natural, like he'd kissed her before, more than once, a hundred times in fact, and would kiss her again. But he never had the chance.

She'd left the very next day: six weeks at summer camp. By

the time she'd come back, things had changed somehow. She looked at Henry and it was as though she couldn't remember all the different pieces of him, not even the kiss. Like the kiss hadn't happened, or it had happened a million years ago, or it had happened to another girl entirely.

So, maybe they hadn't just drifted apart. At least, not in equal amounts, if she was being honest with herself. Whatever their ending had been exactly, she had started it. She had pushed him away for no reason and hurt him and never given him an explanation. Because there wasn't a good one, was there? She put a hand to her chest. It was happening again, that pressure out of nowhere, like someone was crushing her lungs into her back, her spine. Through her tears, the lights of the Christmas tree wavered, gold and glimmering.

It was almost Christmas. Tomorrow she would go to the store to get white sugar. She would pour it in layers with flour and chocolate and wrap the whole jar in a ribbon and put it under the tree.

And there was that word again: *tree*. Trees everywhere. Inside and outside, draped in lights and snow and sniffed at by kind, dying dogs.

I don't want to die.

She thought it to herself like a mantra.

I don't want to die. I don't want to die.

And by the time Henry knocked on her front door the next morning, Molly waiting in his parked car with a happy expectancy, she told herself it was almost true.

CHAPTER THREE

Henry was right; the Safeway was massive. A guy in an apron yawned behind a sushi display as they passed to browse the deli section. Molly sniffed the air eagerly. Catherine watched her for a moment, then glanced around, wondering if someone would say something. But it was early, and she saw no one besides the Starbucks girl, now stacking coffee lids with a morose air.

"I'll say she's a service dog," Henry said to her unasked question. "Not that I think they'll care, to be honest."

"But she doesn't have a harness."

"Doesn't need one. Federal law," he added at her expression.

"You're kidding." She put down the overpriced block of Muenster cheese she'd been examining.

"I'm not. I work at a library. Anyone brings in an animal, you can only ask them two questions: Is it a service or therapy animal, and what service or therapy does it provide?"

"But what if they lie?" Catherine asked, casting a glance at Molly, who was eyeing the discarded cheese with abject disappointment.

"Then they lie."

Catherine frowned at this, then said, "I didn't know you worked at a library."

"At Falls College. Yes, I do go to college, Cath."

"I never said—"

"You didn't have to."

She broke off. "Falls College isn't bad."

"People call it Fails College."

She said nothing.

Toward the end of her senior year of high school, the yearbook staff put together a list of the graduating students and what colleges they'd chosen. It was common knowledge that a lot of people going to the local community college would put "undecided" instead. She distinctly remembered calling it Fails College a few times with her girlfriends. Now it gave her a sick, swooping feeling in her stomach, like a sudden nausea.

Henry was watching her and Molly was whining at the cheese and the guy in the apron was stacking black containers, and without warning her head was full of the sound of a cup falling to a dorm room floor, rolling away with a grinding sound.

She didn't know who gave her that cup of water. She'd stumbled out too quickly, still half drunk, too stupid to look at the room number as she ducked down the hall, head bowed, stumbling into someone who asked if she was okay—and she was so not okay that she got halfway across campus before she remembered her dress was on backward, the tag still scratching thinly at her throat, and her arms and legs bare.

But she knew how the cup sounded when it fell, how his breath smelled like beer and toothpaste when he told her to go, remembered with perfect clarity the weight of her dress as she wrenched it off under the water.

"Catherine?"

She turned her head, the hard lights of the grocery store coming slowly back into focus. She realized she'd gone quiet again. "Falls College," she said after a moment, brain working frantically to recall the conversation.

"Yes, I like to call it that, too. Instead of Fails College."

"Which is mean," she said, getting her feet under her now. They were walking again.

Henry shrugged. "But sort of true. I mean, I get it. It's not a four-year school."

"Yeah, well. Do you like it at least?"

Another shrug. "It's something. A *stepping-stone,* my parents call it."

Catherine felt a ghost of a grin on her face and clung to it. Normalcy. Parental vocabulary, as though they'd all read the same handbook. "What did you get them for Christmas?" she asked as they turned down the baking aisle and she scanned the shelves, bare in spots from the pre-Christmas rush. It looked like the pumpkin puree was sold out, but there was still sugar on the bottom shelves. She picked up a bag and straightened up, realizing Henry hadn't answered her question. "Your parents," she repeated, then caught sight of his face.

He was staring past her, down the aisle, his features a mixture of surprise and . . . fear? Catherine spun around. A few yards away, by the frosting and cake mixes, was a slight girl about her own age with long blond hair, her face gray-white with shock. She was staring back at Henry, her hand still in the air, clutching something small, and then she wasn't.

Catherine watched it fall slowly, a small glass canister of what looked like Christmas sprinkles. It shattered when it hit the floor, the green and red pieces bursting like an explosion across the aisle.

Molly barked. The girl fled, her blond hair whipping around the corner. One larger piece of glass spun slowly in Catherine's direction, coming to rest a foot from her. It winked in the overhead lights, jagged and lethal.

She stepped back. Henry did too, pulling Molly away just as a clerk came up behind them. He didn't seem much older than they were, but his face was lined with exhaustion. When he saw the mess of glass shards and sprinkles, he swore, then glanced down at Molly.

"Service animal," Catherine said promptly.

"She didn't spill them," Henry added.

The clerk muttered something about a broom and stalked off. Henry and Catherine exchanged a look.

"Who was that?" Catherine asked.

"No clue. What do you still need?"

"Henry, you can't, the glass—"

But he was handing her Molly's leash. "Here, hold her." He

took the basket from Catherine's arm and began walking carefully down the aisle. "You got the sugar, right? What else?"

Catherine took hold of Molly with a sigh, calling out the items. By the time the clerk was back with an entire wheeled assortment of cleaning materials, Henry had gotten everything on her list except the actual jars. They hurried away from the clerk, grabbed the few things on Henry's list from the next aisle over, then found the jars in a fancier section opposite the self-service tills of specialty nuts and candy. The shelves here were filled with things like mini-cheesecake tins for twenty dollars and gleaming Le Creuset pots for ten times that amount. There weren't that many jars, though, and the ones large enough to hold all the necessary ingredients were seven dollars each.

"Shit," she muttered, glancing at the price tags.

"What?"

"I only brought a twenty," she said. "This'll put me over."

"Don't you have a card?"

She shook her head. "I . . . lost it. At college." He raised his eyebrows, and she amended, "Sort of. My license, too. Don't tell my parents."

"How'd you drive back home without a license?"

"Slowly."

She'd tried driving the morning after it happened, but her hands wouldn't stop shaking. Fine. Students had to be out of the dorms by ten a.m. tomorrow, the twenty-first. And she needed that extra day. She FaceTimed her mom to say that she was staying to help with an after-finals campus cleanup, and after a long conversation, her mother finally acquiesced. Amber gave Catherine a bleary-eyed look of surprise at this news, but she, like most of the dorm, was gone by that afternoon. Catherine spent that day entirely inside, staring at nothing, flinching every time her phone chirped with another one of her mother's text messages. She did not sleep, and as soon as the sun rose, she left.

Her hands weren't shaking anymore. Instead they were braced and rigid around the wheel as her eyes darted across the roads, her whole body alert and anxious. Just over ninety minutes of tension, cursing herself for leaving the dorms without her coat. It was probably still in that guy's room, her driver's license and debit card in the pocket along with her school ID. All she'd needed for a night out. No sense bringing a purse. But she'd needed the ID to get into the over-eighteen bars that didn't card once you were inside. And she'd always brought her debit card since that one time in October when everyone wanted to split a pizza at three in the morning and she'd used up all her cash on beer.

I have to cancel it, she thought now. *God. He could have bought, like, an Xbox or something by now. My parents will kill me. And I need a new license. How do you even get another one? The DMV. Perfect. Just perfect.*

"Catherine?"

Henry was motioning to the self-checkout. The other lines were still closed this early. "Chill out. I've got the difference."

She started to say thank you, but he just shook his head. "Forget it. It's Christmas. We'll just add your stuff to mine."

She nodded and watched him scan each item. Molly was doing the same, her eyes bright with interest at the beeping machine. "Who puts sprinkles in glass?" Catherine mused as he put the sugar in a separate bag; it already had a small hole in one corner, a fine stream that arced to the floor. Molly licked at the grains eagerly.

Henry grimaced. "Same people who sell those Le Creuset things for two hundred bucks each. Here, where's your cash?"

She handed him her twenty.

"Thanks."

"So the girl," she said, watching Henry feed her bill through the machine, then pull the difference from his own wallet. "Back there."

A sigh. "She's my ex." The change jangled and the machine spat out the short receipt.

"I thought you said you didn't know her."

"I *wish* I didn't know her. Does that count?"

"No."

He had the grace to look abashed for a second. "Okay, fair. It didn't end well. Which was weird, considering it wasn't that serious to begin with."

"Looked pretty serious."

"More to her, I think."

Catherine, looking at Henry, could picture that quite clearly.

"Heartbreaker," she said.

They walked outside, the cold stinging. The light snow had shifted into rain, a cold pattering she could feel on her scalp.

People thought it rained constantly in Washington but that wasn't exactly true; the bulk of the rainfall came in the coldest months, between October and March, which had always struck Catherine as kind of unfair: cold and wet at the same time. And irritating—the rain never quite heavy enough to be a storm, just a constant drizzle, like a dripping faucet no one had managed to fix.

Catherine ducked her head as they walked to Henry's car. "So this was recent," she said. "The breakup."

"Recent enough to make me feel bad about it," he admitted, letting Molly into the backseat and climbing into the driver's seat. "I know it wasn't my fault, but still . . ." His voice trailed. She gave him an expectant look as she fastened her seat belt but said nothing.

"It was . . ."

"You don't have to tell me," she said at once.

"No—it's—"

But then there was a dog bark, slightly muffled, coming from a nearby car, and Molly threw herself against one of the back windows, barking madly in response.

"Ah, Christ," Henry groaned. "Molly, *no*. Bad! Here." He reached into his jacket pocket and took out what looked like a very small Tupperware, but after a moment Catherine realized it was a single-serving peanut butter snack, like one a kid might have in a packed lunch. She watched as Henry peeled off the top and half threw it into the backseat. Molly dived for it, completely diverted.

"Sorry," Henry said, turning back to her. "Only thing that really gets her going these days. Other dogs. Sometimes squirrels."

"So . . . peanut butter."

"Works as good as anything." His smile faded. "We didn't work. Her and me, I mean. She wasn't—wasn't the most stable girl I'd ever met, let's just say. I don't think I've ever met a stranger person." A pause. "Save you, obviously."

"Says the boy with random things of peanut butter in his coat."

So unexpected, how easy this felt, talking to him. Like a language she'd forgotten her fluency in. It reminded her of the years when it had been almost exclusively them, when conversations with Henry had been as natural as any other sound in her world: the slapping hands of schoolyard rhymes or the chiming bells of the ice cream truck.

"What made her so strange?"

He shrugged. "Things," he said, and when she continued to look at him, added, "What made college so shitty?"

"Things." She stared out the window. They were older now, and some words were harder to say. "I saw this Christmas post the other day. It was about the Grinch. It said, *Let's remember that the Grinch didn't hate Christmas. He hated people, which is fair.*"

Henry gave a snort of laughter.

She turned to him. "Do you ever do that?"

"What?"

"Hate people."

It was his turn to look surprised; then he seemed to consider the question. "Sometimes," he said. "Maybe."

She looked back at the windshield. "So do I."

He drummed his fingers on the wheel. "I met her at Falls when I was working at the library. Thought she was cool, normal. Fun. But she wasn't any of those things, and by the time I realized that, it was too late. She lied to people. About something . . . something really personal. She, like, got off on it. Embarrassing me—" He broke off, shook his head. "Forget it."

She looked at him—his flushed cheeks, his fingers tense on the wheel—and felt a surge of sympathy. "Thank you," she said. "For helping. With the jars, and everything."

He smiled briefly at her before starting the car. "Well, all credit should really go to Molly. She's a service dog, you know."

Catherine laughed and reached back to scratch Molly's ears, so careful to brush gently around her stitches she didn't notice a single tree on the trip back to her house.

CHAPTER FOUR

Her mother padded downstairs no less than ten minutes after she got home, but Catherine shooed her back upstairs with a muttered, "Christmas presents. Give me ten." It took a little longer than that, but she finished the jars and called up the stairs that it was fine to come into the kitchen.

"Well, isn't that a relief," her mother said wryly, walking right to the coffee. "Your father will be down in a minute. Did you want breakfast—?"

But Catherine was already halfway up the stairs, and a moment later she was back in bed, her door shut. She shut her eyes too. It was amazing, she thought distantly, how quickly she could go back to that night. Like it was always there and always would be, just waiting for her to step back into it.

After the encounter in the dorm bathroom, Cordelia's hands wet from Catherine's soaking dress, the RA had stared at Catherine and refused to look away. Catherine had stared blankly back, taking in Cordelia's tall, wide form. It made her think of Buffy. *In that show, the character of Cordelia had been gorgeous and mean.*

"Do you want to tell me what's going on?" Cordelia asked her.

Actually, now that she thought about it, there had been an episode

about a snake demon thing that was supposed to be a metaphor for assault. There had even been a date-rape drug in it. Not that she had been
drugged. At least, she probably hadn't been. She remembered throwing
back drinks, her chin up, throat exposed as though for a vampire. Pa-
thetically vulnerable. A girl gone before the opening credits.

"Did something happen to you?" Cordelia's large hands came off the
dress. Catherine, following the pointing fingers, put her own hand to the
bruise at her throat.

"It's nothing."

But Cordelia called campus police all the same.

They had looked at Catherine dubiously when they'd arrived, as
though she'd brought a dog into the deli section of a grocery store. Disbelief and pity and a vague impatience. Two of them: one man with a
mustache and snapping gum, and a woman with her hair tied back so
hard Catherine could see the taut skin of her scalp. She seemed like the
kind of woman who never drank, or wore dresses, or went to parties.
The four of them sat in the large study room down the hall from the bathroom, Catherine now dressed in sweats like Cordelia, her hair running a
damp line down her back. She found herself staring at the window over
their heads, the darkness pressed like a palm against the glass.

"If you make this claim, we have to follow through. Take you to the
hospital. File a report. You okay with that?"

Her answer came without thought. An instinct like breath. A girl
facing a wide yawning pit of unknown blackness and they were asking
her if she wanted to dive into it and drown.

"No. I mean, yes. I'm okay. Fine. Nothing . . . I don't have a claim."

"You sure?"

She'd never been so sure. She'd nodded her head like a bobble doll, wanting to sleep more than she ever had in her life, adrenaline rushing from her like poison from a wound, crashing so hard that if she didn't lie down she'd fall right off the chair. The two officers had stood up. She did too, trying not to sway. She said something else, maybe a thank-you, maybe an apology, she wasn't sure. Cordelia had been out in the hall, waiting. She told Catherine to take care of herself or she'd have to write something. A report.

But I don't have a claim.

———

Catherine finally went downstairs just before noon, unable to stand the silence of her room any longer. Her parents were in the kitchen, sitting at the table where she'd wrapped their presents earlier and talking in low voices. When her mother saw her, she jumped up from her chair, hurrying to the coffeepot, asking Catherine if she wanted any. Catherine nodded and watched her pour the dark, steaming liquid into a mug left for her on the counter. A picture of a to-go coffee waving a wand and wearing round black glasses. ESPRESSO PATRONUM. She'd gotten the mug last summer when they went to Harry Potter World in California.

She took the mug from her mom with a smile. "Thanks." She grabbed the hazelnut creamer from the fridge. "Dum da da dum da da *dum.*"

Her mom stared at her.

"Harry Potter." Catherine set down the creamer, her cheeks hot. "Remember?"

"Oh, yes." Her mother nodded too fast, and Catherine felt a pang of fear at the look in her eyes. *Don't say anything,* she silently begged. *Please don't. And don't ask me how I am or if I want to talk about it.*

It was her fault, of course, that her mother knew anything at all. *Everything* that night had been her fault.

After the campus police and Cordelia had left, she'd gone back to her room. Amber had been twisted asleep under the covers, and Catherine watched her breathe, counting every exhale, until she reached one hundred.

When she was sure the hallway was empty of RAs and officers, she closed the door to her room behind her. She slid down it. Cold and shivery and faintly feverish. Her body disjointed, pieces that didn't fit together anymore. The fear less now, a wave of despair in its place, coming toward her. She needed something to hold on to. It was like a premonition, the sight of her being swept away and under and gone.

"Mom?" She'd pressed the phone to her ear, tears burning in her eyes, down her face so fast they fell past the bruise on her neck. "Mom?"

Telling her. Stupidly, telling her, with breathy sobs and words that broke in the middle, sentences that trailed off only to start again in a different place. She never said the word, though, just that she had passed out and woken up somewhere different. Nothing more than that could make it past her teeth. But panic did, and tears. Too loud. She was worried someone would open a door, ask her what was wrong.

Her mom wanted to come get her right away. And somehow her mother's anxiety had soothed Catherine's own. She spent nearly a half hour convincing her mother she'd be safe making the drive herself—a precursor to the phone call the next day about the after-finals campus cleanup. Talking calmly until her mother was calm. Until Catherine, too, felt somewhat better, as she edited her words to I drank too much, passed out, it was stupid and I panicked. Sorry to worry you.

I don't think anything even happened.

Forget it.

But her mother hadn't forgotten it.

She knew that now, that she could not undo the damage she had caused in calling her mother that night. It was in every line of her mother's face. She could almost hear the words her mother wanted to say, and felt she was keeping them at bay by sheer force of will.

"You know," her mother said, and Catherine's heart dropped into her stomach. "Maybe we could go back. To the Potter . . . Place."

Catherine let out a breath of relief. "Harry Potter World."

"Would you like that?"

"Sure." She tried to feel some level of excitement, like a doctor waiting for a monitor to stop flatlining. "That'd be great."

"What do you think, Richard?" her mother asked her father. "Another vacation?"

"Of course. Food was excellent there, I remember. The, uh, fish and chips." He looked up from his iPad briefly and smiled at Catherine, then went back to the screen.

"I wish you wouldn't do that," her mother said.

"Do what?"

"That." She waved a hand at him. "That thing."

"I'm working."

"It's your holiday break."

"And of course, teachers only work nine to three on weekdays and not one second during the holidays."

"Richard, could you not do that?"

"Grade my students' papers? Susan—"

The doorbell rang.

"I'll get it," Catherine said at once. Maybe it would be Henry and Molly again, which wouldn't be the worst thing in the world.

But it wasn't them.

A young girl stood on the stoop, her dark hair under a white hat, her skin clear, eyes large and brown. She was holding a basket, and with her red coat against a backdrop of trees, she looked like she'd stepped out of a fairy tale.

"Amy?" Catherine said.

"Cathyyyyy!" The girl beamed up at her, stretching out her name like she always did. She'd left a blue bike lying on the walk. "I didn't know you'd be here!"

Catherine scooped the girl into a hug, trying to pull her tight while not spilling coffee on her hair. She smelled like cinnamon.

Amy Porter lived two doors down and was at least twelve years old by now. Catherine had spent three summers watching her, from the day school got out in late May to the first day back in August. Both of her parents worked so Catherine spent nine to five-thirty with Amy, who never raced around like the other hyper neighborhood children. Amy spent her time reading or lying on her back at the pool or yawning on the couch, wrapped in a blanket as they scoured the Apple TV for something they both wanted to watch.

Amy gently pulled herself away from Catherine now but grinned up at her. "Way to dump coffee on me."

"Please, you're fine."

"Hardly." Another grin. "I made Christmas bread. Pumpkin."

Catherine took it with her free hand. A heavy brown-orange weight covered neatly in clear wrapping and tied with silver ribbon. It smelled exactly like Amy did.

"How many did you make this year?"

"Three dozen, but that includes the mini ones too, and it's like three of those to make one big one. You're super lucky I gave you all a big one, 'cause the mini ones are really small."

"Amy," Catherine's mother said, coming up to the door. "I was wondering when you'd drop by. You know you don't have to do this *every* Christmas, though I won't deny it's a treat. Where's your mother?"

"Safeway."

Catherine suddenly realized where all the pumpkin puree must have gone. "I think they're out of pumpkin," she told Amy.

Her mother looked curiously at her.

Amy shrugged. "That's fine. She needs stuffing stuff anyway. What's even *in* stuffing?"

"Stuff," Catherine said.

Easy Amy-banter felt like a sweater shrugged on, reminding her of Amy's baking habit and her addiction to British cooking shows—both of them speaking in ridiculously exaggerated accents, trying to make savarin with Chantilly cream at three in the afternoon in August, Catherine silently debating with herself if three ounces of orange liqueur was enough to intoxicate an eleven-year-old and Amy saying, as though reading her mind, that she wouldn't tell her mom and that they'd forgotten all about the bottle anyway, it had been in the house since New Year's.

Catherine wasn't entirely sure when Amy had started her Christmas bread tradition. Maybe two years ago? She went door-to-door on Christmas Eve, leaving the bread on doorsteps or in mailboxes, only ringing the bell of people she knew, but people figured it out. Some waited for her at the windows to thank her. Amy would blush on the porches, but she was proud all the same. And she also delivered her treats to the library, the police station, and the firehouse, not only on Christmas; she tried to do something for most events or holidays, even church functions, if she could manage it.

Catherine's mother invited Amy into the kitchen and they all sat at the table, Amy tugging at her dark hair under her hat, twirling it in a distinctly teenager motion. Catherine's mother shot a look at her dad, and he set down his iPad in a resigned manner. Amy glanced at the screen, then at Catherine.

"Did I show you I have a website?"

"No."

"Can I—?" Amy asked Catherine's father, who nodded at once and then stood up, murmuring something about a paper he'd left upstairs. Catherine's mother watched him go with tight lips before following him up the stairs.

"It's not much," Amy admitted, swiping madly at the screen, "but I thought I should start something more official, if I want this thing to work out."

"Impressive," Catherine said as Amy logged into Instagram, pulling up her page: artsy baking photos, all flour dustings and eggshells. She clicked on a link below her name, and a new page popped up: The Bread You Knead: Best in West Falls, Washington.

"The title's not *done*," Amy said. "I wanted to do something called Amy's Baking Company or something, but then there's that crazy lady from *Kitchen Nightmares* and I didn't want people to get us mixed up. Plus, I was doing bread puns, see? Too cheesy?"

Stop loafing around and try a free sample! This was next to an option to try a free mini-loaf of any flavor; six choices were listed.

"Yeah," Amy explained. "So, they can order a mini one and if they like it they can order more. I'm charging only five dollars for each loaf, which honestly is nothing, but I think once I get a following I'll up it, hopefully double it by the summer."

"This," Catherine told her, "is amazing."

Amy beamed, cheeks almost as red as her coat. "I knew you'd get it. You always got me. My friends at school don't. They say, *Amy, I can get bread at the store in ten seconds and you can't make PB&J on, like, lemon bread, and you'll get fat from all the baking,* yada yada." She threw back her hair. "Whatever, though, right? People like my bread."

"People *love* your bread," Catherine corrected as she reached out and took off Amy's hat, smoothing her hair. Looking after Amy for three summers had made Catherine feel like something between a mother and a sister; the fierce protectiveness had surprised her in its intensity. She remembered one day last summer, looking for fuzzy caterpillars in the front yard, both of them bent double, intent and squinting, until a sudden chill erupted up Catherine's arms, down her spine, twisting her around to see a man at her back.

He was older than her, maybe late twenties, with a grimy beard and oddly yellow eyes. Filthy.

"Girl," he'd said, looking past Catherine to Amy, who was still poking at the grass with a thin stick.

"Amy," Catherine said, her voice raised, backing up and grabbing her without even having to turn around. "Go inside. Lock the door."

"Girl," the man said again. "Pretty girl, aren't you?"

"Cathy—"

"Now!"

Amy raced up the brick front steps. Catherine heard the door close. Her eyes darted around: no one was outside. But it was the middle of the day. Bright and shining. If she screamed, there were a dozen people who would hear from inside their homes. They'd come. They'd help.

But what if Amy heard her scream? What if Amy came back outside?

Then I won't scream, she thought. *I won't make a sound.*

"Leave," she told the man, her voice low. "Now."

He glared at her for a long moment—one that stretched itself across the circumference of the earth until it came full circle—then he spat at the grass by her feet and stalked away, muttering under his breath.

She watched him until he'd reached the street before racing up the steps after Amy, a cry in her throat, his spit on the edge of her sandals, her pink-painted toenails. When she got inside and slammed the dead bolt home, Amy was waiting for her.

Catherine turned back to Amy now, shutting her eyes hard for a moment to block out that memory. She pointed to the screen, scanning the flavor options and trying to smile. "So, that nutmeg-eggnog bread was amazing last year. Can I order some?"

Amy's eyes widened. "Really? You'd pay?" Then she seemed to think for a minute. "You can have them at three dollars each. Discount, 'cause you're cool and baked a ton with me while I was learning."

"Sounds like a plan." Catherine smiled, teasing. "So, does this mean you're not still learning?"

"What?"

"You said I get a discount, because—"

"Oh yeah. No, I'm still learning things. But I know a ton already. Like, do you know that people have found evidence that bread is over thirty thousand years old? Yeah, starch residue on rocks they, like, carbon-dated or something. And OMG, I heard this really funny joke." She sat up a little straighter in her chair. "Okay, so a lot of people think Jesus was all skinny or whatever, but isn't that amazing since he could make bread appear out of nowhere whenever he wanted? What? Why do you look so weird?"

Catherine blinked and looked away from her, to the iPad. "Never grow up," she told Amy firmly. "Stay twelve forever."

"Too late . . . I'll be thirteen in March."

"Jesus."

"Bam! Garlic knots!" Amy said, waving her arms for emphasis. "Ah, this comedian does it better. Hold on, I'll bring up the video." She opened a new tab and pulled up Jim Gaffigan's page on YouTube and they watched the video together, Amy's head on Catherine's shoulder, shaking with laughter. It might have been last summer, or the one before that. Like that night at college had never happened, and the only thing to be scared of had walked away and she'd been able to bolt a door against it.

CHAPTER FIVE

In the days after Amy's visit, Catherine picked at the pumpkin bread and scrolled through her phone endlessly. Hania, her best friend from high school, had texted her to meet up after Christmas, and Catherine stared at the message, wondering what to say. Catherine's roommate, Amber, had been in touch too, saying Cordelia had been saying weird things before she left, had anything happened? Catherine replied she was fine, no worries, but didn't respond to the texts Amber sent afterward. But it wasn't strange, was it, not to respond to every single message? It was the holidays; people were busy.

During Christmas Eve dinner, as Catherine sat with her parents at the table, listening to her father's short, cursory prayer, she had a sudden, vivid image of herself at nine, in that navy checkered skirt she had to wear to church—back when they'd actually attended regularly. Her father across from her at the table, both of them eating after-church donuts taken from the reception hall at First Faith.

They opened presents Christmas morning, then ate turkey and mashed potatoes and rolls in the late afternoon, exactly one uncle, aunt, and cousin joining them from Castle Rock.

Catherine ate her food without tasting it and nodded at everything said to her while only hearing every third word. She was aware of her mother's gaze on her, and her father's, too, a flickering awareness, as though she were an elderly relative with low blood pressure and osteoporosis who might lose consciousness at any moment and break in half on the hardwood. It made her miss talking to Amy, to Henry, their expressions uncomplicated and unaware.

When her extended family left, she was exhausted but too conscious of her mother's worried look to refuse her offer to break open one of the cookie jars for a late dessert. She upended the jar, the undone ribbon cutting a trail through the flour, and mixed in eggs and oil, preheated the oven, laid her head on her mother's shoulder as they stood in front of the warming door. It made her think of Amy.

"What can I do?" her mother asked.

Catherine closed her eyes. The kitchen smelled like sugar and pine. Every Christmas, the tree was real. Every January second, they left it on the street to be dragged away damp.

Her legs had been wet, sticky. Blood on her inner thighs, trickling down her right one to her ankle. A pain that cut through her in staccato bursts made her want to scream. Bending down in the shower back in the dorms, scrubbing the red off her skin, like erasing a river, using a pad—so normal, it's normal—her hands shaking on the plastic wrapping, a rustling sound like an animal in the leaves.

———

What can I do? her mother had asked.

She wanted someone to go into her brain. Cut out the memories—these little fragments that sliced her open.

I don't want to remember. I can't do it. If I know more, if I see it, I'll—

A girl in a tree, upside down. What if that was what happened? What if that was where she belonged?

Why had she gone to that party? *Why* had she gotten so drunk? *Why* hadn't she asked Amber to take her back to the dorms? Then this would just be Christmas. Her life would just be her life. None of this would have happened. She would be fine. *Fine.*

What can I do?

And it came to her. An answer. Not a perfect solution, no, but she knew she couldn't walk those paths and pass the dorms and take showers down the hall knowing what she had washed down the drain that night.

"I don't want to go back," she told her mom as the oven counted down. "In January. I don't want to go back."

———

Her mom pushed and prodded and begged for more details but Catherine just shook her head. It had been a bad night. She was fine, just still shaken up, mostly by what *could* have happened. No, she just hadn't liked it there as much as she thought she would. Lots of people transferred. Well, she could go anywhere, really. Just wanted a change. Maybe a community college, then transfer. That's what Henry was doing. Henry Brisbois, remember him? He liked it at Falls. No, it didn't have to be Falls. Anywhere. Just not back.

Am I crazy? she texted Henry that night. They'd been texting off and on. Talking to him was easier, somehow, than talking to the friends she couldn't face. He asked her how the cookie jars went. She asked him about Molly. They talked about Amy. (Henry had gotten the coveted eggnog bread this year.) Then she asked him about Falls and he asked her why.

> Bc West Washington U sucked. Falls is way cheaper

> Might convince parents to let me transfer

That bad?

> Worse

> Do you have to live at home at Falls?

No

Lots do, but there are dorms. I think there's a lottery for them though.

You serious?

> Maybe

Pretty sure that's the opposite of serious.

She stifled a laugh and sat up straighter against her pillows. Feeling suddenly very awake despite it being nearly midnight, she powered up her laptop and signed into her college account. She'd have to figure out the transfer process if she really wanted her parents to take it seriously. She'd come down in the morning with everything neat and organized, prepared to answer all their questions.

She had two emails in her school account. She clicked on those first, noticing one was from her roommate, Amber. Subject line: U ALIVE?

> Hey Cat. You're totally MIA on text. Everything okay? I heard rumors right when I was leaving, idiot Cordelia mostly. WORST RA EVER. Just wanted to make sure you're good/chill/know I'm here for whatever. And yes, that was a screw you to Prof. Kang's parallel structure. 89.7 is NOT a B+. I swear I'll come back and sue once I'm a real lawyer. Anyway, call me, text me, whatevs. Merry xmas too. Best roomie ever! PS: can we please go to the gym more spring semester?? I need cardio and kale and you. <3333

Catherine made a strange sound, something between a laugh and a sigh. She could almost hear her roommate's voice in her head, slightly raspy from cigarettes, Amber lying on the floor with her legs kicked up on the bottom bunk, holding her phone a foot from her face, squinting at a picture some random hookup had sent her. "Is that it? Is that supposed to turn me on?" She held it out to Catherine, who snorted and twisted away. Borrowing eyeliner and sharing dresses. Trying to do the drunk test, walking in a line they made with overlapping Post-it notes in the hallway, clutching each other and laughing. Complaining about finals being so many points and how group projects were literally the worst.

"I think they're secretly a test," Amber had told her over fries one night. "Like to see if you can resist committing murder, even when it's justified."

"What do you get if you pass?" Catherine asked.

"Not arrested."

"Lame."

"Totally. I think if I murder one of them, it might be worth it."

Catherine scoured her takeout box for the saltier fries at the bottom. "Well, I'm not helping you bury the body or whatever."

"Oh, come on. It was going to be that Felicia girl who literally told me she was going to do nothing because her ferret died last month and she still wasn't over it."

Catherine paused, fry in the air. "Okay. Maybe her."

"Thank you. God." Amber play-kicked her with one bare foot. "The things you have to do for a decent accomplice-after-the-fact."

Now, in her bedroom, Catherine's fingers hovered over her laptop, but she wasn't sure what to say. She was fine? Yeah, Cordelia was terrible? Hey, you need to find a new roommate?

She clicked out of the email. She'd figure it out later, along with what she was going to say to Hania.

The only other message was from her British literature professor. Subject line: Final Essay Submission.

Shit, Catherine thought, her heart skipping. Her final essay for Brit lit had been nothing short of brutal. An analysis of a collection of poetry or any of the full-length pieces they'd studied that semester. No fewer than ten pages. She'd chosen the poems, mostly because five poems were still way shorter than a full book, none of which she'd actually read cover to cover. She remembered a high school teacher telling the class senior year that they couldn't expect to use SparkNotes in college and still pass. Well, Catherine had been using them with some regularity for the two classes she needed to fulfill her English credits, and she had a B in both of them, so there. But she'd actually *read* the poems for this essay. Looked up analysis of them in the college library, too. She'd *tried* to do well on it. She thought she had, but maybe a ten-page essay on two-hundred-year-old poetry had been beyond her.

Hastily, she clicked on the email, thinking that if her professor was telling her that her failure of an essay had dragged her down to a D, that would be the last straw on a camel basically knee-deep in the sand at this point.

Dear Catherine,

I am writing to inform you of your near-perfect score on your Blake essay for my class. I do not usually email students personally, but since these essays are not returned in person and you merely see the results of your efforts on the online grade reports, I wanted to tell you that this essay really stood out from your peers. I could see the effort you had put into your study of Blake (no easy poet, either, with all the nuances in his work).

I strongly suggest you submit this piece (I have scanned my notes in the attached document—minor revisions, mostly grammatical) to the college's English Literature Conference, which will occur in May. Deadlines, I believe, are in late February, giving you plenty of time to polish this piece and send it in for consideration. I think your chances are quite good, and the three top papers shared at the conference receive a monetary prize, I might add.

I hope you have a very restful holiday season, and again, well done!

Yours sincerely,
Professor Emily Graham

Catherine stared at the screen for several moments and then reread the message before opening the attachment. Her essay downloaded onto her computer, and she scrolled through it, noting the penciled comments in the margins, the two paragraphs at the end praising her, the oversized A+ on the cover page. Ninety-seven percent. She didn't think she'd gotten a ninety-seven in *anything* before, in high school or college.

I can't go back.

But I want to.

Why the hell do I want to?

Amber and essays and the leaves falling on the quad, late-night fries and groggy early-morning coffees and the library smelling of dust and oil and ink.

She'd lied to her mom. She had liked West Washington University. Loved it, in fact. She remembered hearing about some girl in her biology lecture who had transferred out in October and being baffled, wondering what had happened to make her leave.

But could she actually go back in just a few weeks? Lug her duffel bag into her room and walk to class and study in the library at three in the morning, stifling a yawn because it was the quiet floor and people would kill you for breathing loudly?

But he didn't kill me.

What had happened to her, exactly? Would more come back to her? Could she handle it? What if it all came back, maybe in the middle of some freshman seminar and she stood up and screamed and had to run out of the lecture hall with two hundred people staring at the crazy girl who was her? What if she couldn't handle it?

But what if she could? What if this thing that had happened

to her . . . hadn't? What if her mind was making up nightmares? What if she was blowing this whole thing out of proportion? She'd had too much to drink, passed out, woke up—

blood shower bruises

and she'd been scared, which was normal. Totally normal. So she'd freaked a little and made a big deal and—

Mom Mom pick up Mom

thought something bad had happened. But maybe she was just putting details in to fill the blackness, to make sense of everything. Like when she was seven and somehow convinced herself a monster lived in the downstairs coat closet. She'd made up this whole story about how it hid behind all the stuff they shoved in there and sometimes ate their shoes, which was why she'd lost the left red sneaker of her favorite pair. But of course it had all been in her head, trying to explain away the missing shoe and the creaks the house made at night. She created something that made sense to her, that scared her, yes, but not as much as not knowing.

She grabbed her cell phone off the nightstand. If she had to be alone with her thoughts another second, she was going to lose it.

Amber picked up on the third ring. "Thank God," she said. "Where the hell have you been?"

"Amber?" Catherine asked, relieved. "You're awake?"

"No." Amber's eye roll was almost audible. "This is the Ghost of Christmas Past or whatever. Little Timmy died and I'm here to make you feel really bad about it."

"Tiny Tim."

"Oh, fuck off. Where have you even been?"

"I—" Catherine swallowed. "Do you remember the party last week? At Sigma . . . whatever?"

"I thought it was Delta. Wait, did something really happen?"

"I don't know."

"Shit. You said you were going to walk back. I . . . I said I'd come with you but you sort of waved me off and then I was talking to someone. . . . Shit. Cordelia mentioned something as I was leaving, but then she shut up about it and told me to go away. I kept asking, too, and she just told me that nothing happened and then my Uber was there. . . . *Did* something happen?" Amber asked again.

"I don't know," Catherine repeated.

"Well, what the hell do you know?" Amber, impatient, the opposite of ditzy, hating small talk and tact.

"I woke up," Catherine said, her eyes closed. She could see the laptop's glow against the back of her eyes, hear the rain against the roof as though it were trying to break through and reach her. "There was a guy—"

"Where?"

"The dorms."

"Which one? Ours?"

"No. I don't know which one. Not ours. I . . . I went outside. I didn't . . . Maybe East Johnson, or the one next to it, I forget the name, you know they're kind of grouped together—"

"Myers," Amber said. "The one next to Johnson is Myers."

"Okay."

"Okay? The fuck, Catherine? Are you hurt? Who was the guy? What—"

"I don't know!" It burst out of her, and with it, tears. "I don't know, Amber, okay? I keep remembering stuff, but then I think I'm remembering it wrong. And I couldn't see the guy, it was dark, but there was—I mean, maybe it was my period, but it hurt so I showered and fuck, you're not supposed to shower but then Cordelia was there and she called campus police and it was this huge mess and I didn't want it to be so I just said it was nothing and maybe it was—I don't fucking know—and now I just want to transfer out because when I think of going back my whole body just freaks out and I can't do it, Amber, I can't—"

"Catherine."

Her name made her suck in a breath, wipe her face. "Sorry."

"Don't apologize." A pause. Catherine could almost hear Amber thinking on the other end. She wondered where Amber was, if she was in her room. Was it raining where she was, hours to the east, in Ellensburg?

"I'm guessing that whole after-finals campus cleanup wasn't actually a thing then."

"It was," Catherine said. "But not for me. I just . . . I couldn't drive. I just couldn't."

"Do you think you were raped?"

The word sliced into her ear, burrowed in her brain like it would never leave. Like she'd forever hear it in Amber's cadence, in that exact sentence.

"Maybe."

Pretty sure that's the opposite of serious.

Amber blew out a breath. "Okay," she said. "Here's what I'm going to tell you, and you can ignore me and do whatever, okay? You have two choices here: report it or move on. Because if you stay in the middle you are going to lose your mind, okay? I say report it. It will suck majorly and maybe nothing will happen to the guy and people will hate you anyway, but at least you get to say what happened. What you remember. Or you do nothing—because I can't make you report it, no one can, not even fucking Cordelia who I hate as much as anyone—and move on. Or try to. Convince yourself it was something different, something else. Or that it was one night of your life and it doesn't define you and your life is made of hours and days of other, good things and you're not going to let some asshole take away the things that come next."

Amber's words were a torrent washing over her, and her skin grew cold and goose-bumped in the ensuing silence.

"Amber," she said slowly, "did—"

"Eight minutes. Two years ago. If I live to be eighty, that's forty-two million, forty-eight thousand minutes. I tried to figure out the fraction, like what percentage that eight minutes was out of all my minutes, and the calculator literally gave me an error message." A pause. "It wasn't rape. I was at a gas station that got held up. I wanted to buy a Vitaminwater, trying to figure out what flavor, just standing there and debating between orange-mango and mixed berry like an idiot. I still think about it, seeing what was happening in the reflection of the door first, sort of fogged and blurry, but still clear enough to know what was happening. Have you ever had a gun pointed at you?"

"No."

"It's like . . ." An exhale of breath. "Like the person holding it has already killed you, even without pulling the trigger. Like the dying's already started. Everything sort of narrows and falls away and there's just you and this thing that can kill you and you think *no* as if that would help and you realize how fucking helpless you are. That's what I remember most about it. The helplessness. Like I could literally not do one thing to change my fate. Thankfully, the guy just wanted money, and the cops came, like, a minute after he left. They tracked him down. But that's how I know it was only eight minutes, from the time he entered the store to the time he left. I think the actual holdup was, like, three."

"Three," Catherine repeated.

"Yeah."

She pressed the phone to her ear, hard. It was slick with tears. "Thank you," she said.

"Yeah," Amber said again. "I don't tell that story a lot. It's just . . . I don't know. I think I get what it's like. Sort of. I mean, it's not the same, I know that. But I know how it feels when something huge and terrible happens and you can't process it because it doesn't even seem real, even though it was real and it was the absolute worst thing in the world. Like the world was one thing before and something totally different afterward. And nothing feels safe or even okay anymore. So I get it, how big a deal it is for you to tell me what happened." A pause. "Or maybe I'm way out of line and you think I'm a total asshole and—"

"No," Catherine said. "No, you're not. Because it is like that, like the world isn't . . . isn't . . ." She struggled for a moment, then went on. "It's weird. Like, I want to know more but I don't. I think I won't be able to handle it if I know more, but at the same time it sucks not knowing."

"What do you want to do? Don't think. Tell me."

"I want for it not to have happened."

"Nothing behind door number one. Would you care to try door number two?"

Despite herself, Catherine almost smiled. "I want to see you. I want for things to go back to normal."

"Then don't leave."

CHAPTER SIX

> Ugh, ignore me. Being dramatic. Not transferring.

> ?

> I'm going to go back in Jan. Just freaked out. Being weird. Srry

> Okay . . .

> It's bc you think it's Fails College, isn't it?

> Haha no

Catherine put down her phone on the bathroom counter and towel-dried her hair. She'd been up until three in the morning thinking it over and had made her decision. Now it was eleven and she was clean and smelled like lavender soap. She'd washed and moisturized her face, tried to cover the bruise on her neck—purple before, now green and yellow—with makeup, brushed her teeth even though she wanted coffee. But that was fine. She'd wait.

Baby steps, she told herself, running a comb through her

tangles and forcing herself not to wince. *Like texting. Like showering. Like not wanting to die.*

She was going to go downstairs and tell her mom she'd made a mistake. She didn't want to transfer. She'd say whatever she had to in order to undo the worry she'd caused. She'd show her mom the email from her professor. She'd tell her dad about the conference, and he'd be proud and relieved and they could just pretend this whole fiasco hadn't happened. It was her fault, really, that her parents were freaked out: calling her mom in tears right after, telling her she was so messed up she couldn't even go back to school; her dad staring into the night, not able to even look her in the eye. She wanted to go back to before, to normalcy and peace and parents she hadn't terrified out of their wits.

"Idiot," she told her reflection, tugging hard at her tangles. "Idiot."

She was going to blow-dry her hair and then bundle up in a warm coat. She was going to walk outside for at least ten minutes and breathe in the smell of the trees she was not trapped inside. She'd force herself to act like it was a week before, and no, she couldn't make it not have happened, but she could make what had happened an error-message percentage of her life that didn't completely decimate the rest of it.

You don't get to win, she told the featureless shadow in her mind, a rage rising up, undoing her despair. *I won't let you.*

—

She spent the day almost exactly as intended. It took nearly an hour on the living room couch with her parents to convince them she was fine, the Christmas tree sitting in the corner, its checkered skirt wrinkled, all the presents gone. She plucked at a throw pillow thread as she spoke, keeping her voice low and thoughtful but kind of vague, as though the idea of transferring had been a whim, and discarded just as quickly. Her father had been pleased about the conference, but her mother kept frowning, as though seeing right through her. Catherine stared back, innocently determined.

I'm fine. FINE.

She went for a walk, her hair fully dry now, her stomach still warm from coffee. It was raining, lightly, but she told herself it didn't matter. She listened to music on her phone, the earbuds almost vibrating from the volume. But she found herself skipping songs, each one not quite right, too sad or too upbeat, and was every song in existence about love or breakups? All love-lust or aching sadness, like someone had died. She stabbed at the screen of her phone, trying to find something that fit, trying to ignore how cold she was getting, how stupid she felt.

She hadn't been a virgin. Maybe that was a good thing, better. Less traumatic. She'd been with two guys before, one of them a boyfriend in her senior year of high school. Josh Tyler, a striker on the soccer team. She'd teased him about having two first names. Sweet, but absentminded—he'd crashed his bike into a car not once but twice because he "forgot" about stop signs. But when they kissed, he tasted like mint gum, his breath cold air against her lips, her tongue. She marveled at how he could make her whole body warm. One day second semester, they skipped school and went to his house. His bedroom. She tried to relax, but the room was too bright and quiet and she was hyperaware of the sound of their breathing. No condom, just birth control she'd been on since fourteen when her cramps were so bad she couldn't walk upright. She thought about that when he pushed himself into her, and then shook her head, trying to feel something other than strange and slightly scared. It was amazing how turned on she got during everything else they'd done, how much she'd wanted more, but now that she had more she found she could have gone without it. He'd finished with a shudder while she'd looked over his shoulder to see a wet spot on the corner of his ceiling. *He should look into that,* she thought. *Fix it with something.*

The next time, an hour later, had been just as bad, but the third time, the following weekend, in his car in a darkened parking lot, had been much better. Maybe it was the risk of it, or the lack of light. Something. She'd never known her body to be so fickle.

He went to school in California. She'd looked him up online a couple of times. It hadn't been a bad breakup, or a real breakup at all. Just a four-month relationship that had fizzled as the weather warmed and life moved on without him.

Then there had been another guy, Daniel, who she'd met at a Halloween party in October. Some random house on Progress Street. She had to find his last name on Instagram: Howard.

What was with the two first names? They'd both been drunk, fumbling and laughing in an upstairs bedroom, tasting like cold, bad beer, and twice someone banged on the locked door, trying to get in, and they'd shaken with laughter, Daniel whispering, "Quiet, they might hear us," and she'd yelled, "Occupied!" in a defiantly loud voice, like it was a bathroom stall or something. Fun. Stupid. They'd gone to her dorm after, Amber tactfully sidling out with barely a word, pillow in hand. He'd messaged her a few days later, asking her if she wanted to grab a drink sometime, but she and Amber had made a pact about no real boyfriends until at least second semester, so she'd said thanks but no thanks. That next week she'd found a single red flower (not a rose) outside their dorm room one morning (no note) and Amber had teased her about stalkers (dodged a bullet). But Catherine secretly thought it had been . . . sort of sweet.

She stopped walking three streets down from her house. It was biting cold, but she kept every muscle still, wanting to feel the ice-air like a punishment. What was wrong with her? She was like the worst stereotype of every college freshman who had ever existed. Blond with big boobs and tight yoga pants. She liked mixed drinks and oversugared coffee and had never gone a week without Starbucks or Panera. She didn't think she'd ever read a classic novel. She liked flowers and reality shows and skinny jeans and turned down dating because she wanted to have fun and get wasted and chill out and—

You deserved it. Whatever happened to you that night. You deserved it.

"Shut up," she muttered under her breath.

You were so easy that night, it was almost unfair. He probably looked at you and thought, pathetic—

"Shut up!"

"Catherine?"

She spun around.

Henry was standing before her with Molly, who was looking at her anxiously.

"Sorry," Catherine said. "You just . . . surprised me."

"Yeah, I got that."

Flustered, she took her earbuds out and pocketed them.

"Wanted some fresh air," she said at his silence. She didn't have to meet his eyes to know he looked curious, even worried. "Forgot how cold it was. You should get her a coat." She nodded at Molly.

"We did, last winter. She hated it, though. Also, it's too big now, since she got sick."

Catherine thought she might burst into tears at any moment, or scream, or hit something. It was like her brain was too big for her skull, everything under her skin about to burst through, and she'd splatter against the ground, black and putrid and festering, but at least she'd be free.

"Hey, about Falls, it's totally fine. I didn't actually think you'd—"

"You know what, Henry? I really don't care what you think."

She brushed past him and within a few minutes was back at her house, stripping off her coat and sweater, kicking her boots

into the closet that used to house a monster. She half ran upstairs to the shower, shutting out her mother's call, her father's
frown. She felt bad about snapping at Henry, who she knew was
only trying to help. But it didn't matter. Nothing was going to
help.

She made the water so hot she swore she could hear it hissing. It burned against her closed eyelids and ran down her body,
down her bruises, washing away her talk with Amber and her
parents and her walk—all her early-morning good intentions.

I can't do it, she realized with a sort of awe. *I actually can't get
through this.*

—

That night, just as Catherine was downing her sleeping pills and
sitting up rigid in bed, one leg twitching in the darkness, Amy
Porter was turning a valentine-red piece of construction paper
over and over in her hands.

She was in her bathroom, waiting until her parents were totally, absolutely asleep, and she didn't think she'd have to wait
much longer. She looked at herself in the mirror. *Pretty,* she
thought, in an objective sort of way, because she was an objective sort of girl. Baking was a science, after all, and she tended to
judge things in numbers, in careful increments. Pretty meant big
eyes and straight teeth, smooth skin. Not like Nancy in her language arts class, who already had acne; Amy felt bad every time
she looked at her. But still, studying her reflection, she thought

she looked like a child, which she most certainly wasn't. She felt a little sick and put a hand to her stomach: nervous, fluttery, lurching.

> *Your bread is amazing*
> *Pumpkin-perfect*
> *I dream of your eyes*
> *Forgive the note*
> *Can I see you in person?*

She'd found it folded neatly in half and tied to the seat of her bike that very afternoon. Her friend Hannah Walsh had invited her over to see her new puppy, and since Amy's parents were being *super* lame and lazy, they wouldn't even drive her. "Hannah is three streets away, get some fresh air," her mother said.

So she took her bike, bundling up and cursing her parents; biking was only fun when she was delivering bread. She remembered a comedian she'd heard—a different one from Jim Gaffigan but she was blanking on the name—saying that anything you did outside in winter was just cold exercise. She snorted to herself as she turned the corner onto Hannah's street.

The puppy was small and impossibly white, like a T-shirt that had never been worn. Hannah was so excited she was practically crying, dragging Amy to see the puppy's bed and toys and water bowl, and it was fun but kind of tiring. Plus, it started to make Amy sort of sad—she'd *never* had a pet, not even a stupid fish—and then that made her feel kind of bad for being sad. Eventually she told Hannah she had to get back.

"My mom told me I had to be home in an hour," she fibbed.

Hannah groaned and clutched the puppy, which wiggled and yelped in her arms. "You *always* do *everything* your parents tell you to. Come on, *staaaaay.*"

"That's not true."

"Zahara thinks it's true."

Amy frowned at Hannah. Zahara wore shoes with thick heels that clacked when she walked and was always running out of pencils before tests. "What did she say?"

"It was kind of mean. . . ."

"*Hannah—*"

"She thinks you're no fun anymore and that your bread business thing is just to make other people look bad because you're always trying to be the best at everything," Hannah said in a rush.

"*What?*"

Hannah nodded. "I told her she was wrong, but she kept calling you Perfect Amy Porter. . . ." Hannah clutched the puppy to her harder and talked into its fur. "What do you think, you cute little puppy-wuppy . . . ? Is Zahara mean or—"

Hannah babbled at the dog like it was a baby and Amy left the house grumpy, only smiling when Hannah's older brother, Matt, ruffled her hair and told her that her bread was awesome.

She'd gone outside, breathing in the chill and thinking

about what Hannah had said. Perfect Amy Porter. The idea left a bad taste in her mouth, like cheap vanilla extract. She did have fun, whatever Zahara said. And the bread business wasn't about making people feel bad, what a stupid thing to say. She was so busy imagining ways to spill confectioners' sugar all over Zahara's stupid head without getting into trouble that it took her a few moments to notice something was tied to the seat of her bike: a note.

She'd read it slowly, heat coming to her face with every word, like she'd just opened an oven. She looked up at Hannah's house and then back at the note.

No signature, and the handwriting wasn't familiar, but the writer had closed the note with a place to meet that very night:

Lookout Point. Bring the note, poem's not done yet ☺

And below that, a time.

She knew Lookout Point, the clifftop where you could see for miles, always lit up at night for couples and tourists or people just passing through. That was during summer, though. People almost never went in winter because of the cold, and if they did go at all, they didn't stay long. But it was probably the most romantic spot in West Falls. It wasn't hard to guess what was going to happen.

If her parents caught her, they'd ground her forever.

But—

Perfect Amy Porter. It repeated in her head like a beeping oven timer. She *was* a pretty good kid. Good grades. Nice. Teachers liked her. Her parents were proud of her bread business, bragged about her to relatives over Christmas. Maybe she'd earned a little fun. She was probably the only girl in her grade who hadn't even *kissed* a boy. She'd be thirteen soon. It was getting ridiculous. Her friend Claire had made out with a boy named Jason Esposito at a horse camp last summer and came back covered in bug bites and swooning. She'd die when Amy told her about this. Amy could almost feel Claire hitting her on the shoulder. *You did not! He did not! Tell me* everything. Then she wouldn't be Perfect Amy Porter anymore.

Now Amy checked the clock, did the math. The clifftop was a ten-minute walk, and she'd have to walk because her bike was in the garage and opening that door would definitely wake her parents. She told herself if it was raining hard, she wouldn't go—she wasn't totally reckless—but thankfully the night was almost clear, with just a faint drizzle falling. She zipped up her coat to her chin, shoved the note into her pocket, and took a full thirty seconds to close the front door with white-mittened hands. It was freezing outside, so she walked fast, her stomach rising up to her throat. She swallowed. *Nerves. Relax. At least you won't get bug bites.* Rain dotted her hat, caught on her eyelashes. She blinked to clear them, and they fell onto her cheeks, like tears.

She came up the narrow road lined with trees, feeling almost warm by the time she reached the end. An opening in the trees revealed a wide clearing a hundred or so yards across, shaped like a half circle, the cliff's edge the circumference. It was completely deserted. A single lamppost illuminated the guard-rail that curved like a smile at the edge. She walked across the clearing toward it, blinking at the yellow glow for a moment before looking past it, to the long drop.

"Amy."

She spun around, facing the clearing again, and the road leading to the clifftop. Someone was approaching out of the darkness.

"Hey," she said as he came toward her. She tried to make her voice calm, but it shook slightly. "I got your note?" She said it like a question, but then he nodded at her and asked if she had brought it, and when she handed the note to him, her logical brain started to whirl, adjusting to this new development.

He had a scarf tied around the lower half of his face to block the cold, but she could see his eyes, a half inch of hair fringed under his hat. He wasn't who she'd been expecting—or was he? The glow of the lamppost shot his eyes white, lit his hair to amber, and it was hard to tell what colors he was made of. She blinked, squinted, trying to place him, faces shifting in her memory, one after another. "You know everyone in this town," her mother had told her once. "You've *fed* everyone in this town."

The scarf and the light were throwing her off. She could tell he was older, and the more she looked at him, the more familiar he seemed. Like she had sold him bread from behind a folding table. Or handed one to him on a front porch.

"You tell anyone you were coming?" he asked.

She shook her head. Her breath steamed in front of her in quick bursts. *I'm a dragon,* she suddenly wanted to say. *See?*

He stepped toward her. She took a step back. He chuckled, a low soothing sound that she'd heard before. That she recognized. Unlike his voice, his laugh was almost exactly the same through the scarf.

She knew who he was.

As he moved forward, she stayed where she was and watched him, tilting her head upward a little, because he was taller than her. There was a bad taste in the back of her throat and she felt her fingers sticking together inside her mittens. Half his face was wrapped in thick wool and his eyes gleamed down at her and she suddenly felt as though she'd walked out into a busy street and there wasn't time to step back; a car was coming too fast, almost like it *had* to hit her. But why? Everyone else she knew had kissed someone. It wasn't a big deal, so why—

Because I don't want to. I thought I did, but I don't. This isn't what I thought it would be like and I changed my mind. Can I do that? Here in the cold and you walked in the rain and so did I but can I say no? Even now?

He was a foot from her. He pulled the scarf down to his neck and, with his other hand, reached out to brush her hair from her face.

No.

She started to say it, actually. Sucked in a breath to tell him so, but then she felt his hand on her skin, the back of her neck, and every tiny hair there shot up, rigid, erasing the words inside her like a cloth on a whiteboard. She was still, silent, pliant and pleading, and nothing had even happened yet but she knew it would. Something shifted inside her. Everything was different. Her blood was rushing from her hands to her heart and her stomach was fighting to crawl out her throat and she wanted to scream—but that was stupid. Nothing was wrong. He was just going to kiss her and leave, but behind her was a clifftop and she was a statue in the night, waiting for him to smash her to pieces and throw her off the edge, into blackness and infinity.

CHAPTER SEVEN

Catherine awoke on the twenty-seventh to the sound of shouting. She sat bolt upright in bed, a slick layer of sweat on her skin and her comforter tangled around her ankles. She yanked it high to her chest just as someone flung her bedroom door wide and, by the sound of it, nail-scratched at the wall until the light flicked on.

Amy's mother was standing there, her eyes wet and terrified. Catherine's mother stood right behind her, saying something soft that Catherine couldn't make out. She felt a sudden chill dry the sweat on her skin.

"No," Catherine said finally, in a strange, calm voice, the question coming at her like a gun she'd finally gotten into focus. "I haven't seen Amy since before Christmas Eve."

Amy's mother was talking again, shrieking, and Catherine's mother—and now her father, appearing bleary-eyed and worried in the doorway—tried to calm her, and all the while, a realization came to Catherine, like a slow swallow of poison her body had tasted before.

The clock on her nightstand read 7:06 in the morning.

—

He did not throw her over the cliff. Whoever killed Amy Porter left her several feet from the edge in the glow of the lamplight, as though wanting her to be found. Her hat was askew, but her mittens were still on; he'd put back the one that had come off in the struggle. The rest of her clothes were on except her coat, which had been taken off and then thrown over her like a blanket, a bloodred splash across her body.

A man walking his dog found her at 8:19 that morning. The dog was a golden retriever named Shiloh, who, unlike the unfortunate Molly, was young and in good health. His owner, however, clutched his chest at the sight. Not a heart attack, but one of panic that brought him to his knees all the same. Shiloh, torn, hovered between owner and Amy, keening with anxiety, his paws scratching at the rain-soaked grass.

At 8:21, the man—a retired postal service worker with bad knees and an affinity for gardening in the warmer months—managed to dial the police, who arrived within nine minutes. Thirty-six minutes after that, the lead detective on the case knocked on the door of Amy Porter's house. They'd gotten the report of a missing child an hour before, and it was a small town, West Falls, Washington; everyone knew the girl with the red coat, the bread, and brown, brown eyes.

———

Catherine and her mother stood with their arms wrapped around their middles, shoulders hunched against the cold on the front porch. They could just see the commotion outside the

Porters' house. One police car turning to two, then three. Officers marching: suits and uniforms and vests.

"It might be nothing," her mother said, shivering a little and wrapping her shawl more securely around her shoulders. "They'll find her. She's, what, twelve now? You snuck out more than once at twelve."

"Amy didn't sneak out."

Her mother eyed her curiously. "How do you know?"

It was Catherine's turn to shiver. Just past nine in the morning, and already the day was edged in ice. It wasn't raining yet, but that mist was back, drifting like a fog, everything seen through a damp haze of gray that chilled the air. It blurred the scene at Amy's house, tinged it dark and faded like a days-old bruise.

"Amy hated the cold. This." Catherine jerked her head at the sky. "She wouldn't have just gone out. Not unless someone made her."

"Catherine," her mother began gently. "We don't know anything yet. Hold off. At least until we hear from your father."

Catherine said nothing to that. Her father had led Amy's mother back home earlier that morning, keeping a slight distance between them like she was a feral cat. He was still at the Porters' now. Close friends with Amy's father, Catherine's dad had him speak to his senior classes at least once a year. "So many of my AP students want to become lawyers," Catherine's father told her once. "Evan's very knowledgeable with his practice, and they like getting a feel for the profession."

But Catherine imagined that most of her dad's students probably wanted to be criminal lawyers, like on *Law & Order*, badgering serial killers stupid enough to take the stand and getting insanely rich doing it; they were more than likely bored to death by Mr. Porter's lectures on finance law. Amy herself had complained about it enough: "I swear to God, if he tries to teach me about *indemnity* one more time, I'm going to die."

Catherine felt herself shake again and tightened her arms around herself.

"We don't know," Catherine's mother said again. "We don't—"

But then Catherine saw someone leave the house: a familiar figure, moving slowly.

"Dad," she said.

Finally, he reached them. He didn't have to speak at all; his face told her everything she needed to know. Everything she had already known since that morning.

Distantly, Catherine could hear the screaming. The walls of Amy's house were muffling the noise, absorbing it, but she could make it out all the same. In Catherine's mind the pain of that sound overflowed. Ran down the walls like paint.

They stood in the cold, all three of them staring down the street, and then her mother seemed to gather herself—gather them—and ushered them all inside. She put on coffee and boiled water for tea and took out orange juice as Catherine sank into a chair at the kitchen table and her father stood rigid against the cupboards. No one said anything, even as Catherine's mother bustled around, setting out too many glasses, every coffee creamer they had in the fridge.

"Mom," Catherine said finally. Her teeth were chattering, though the kitchen was warm.

Her mother's face was red, her neck blotchy, her hands twitching. She was taking out the sugar.

"Mom," she said again.

A burst of sound from outside: a yell, then more shouting. Catherine spun around and, through the window, saw a flurry of confused movement outside: a blur of shapes, something streaking low to the ground, trailing . . . a rope?

Then her mother dropped the sugar canister: large, with painted flowers, it shattered on the hardwood with the force of a small and concentrated bomb. Catherine leapt off her chair as the porcelain exploded across the small kitchen. Pink pieces shot into the air and fell, skidding across the hardwood. One hit Catherine's leg and bounced off her sweats; another flew past her left eye and she felt a pain at her cheekbone like a thin line of fire.

Her father reached for her, then pulled back. Her mother sank to the floor, trying to get the pieces. Her father said, "No, Susan, your hands," and something in Catherine shivered loose from the whole and she ran from them, nearly slipping on the remnants of the canister before bolting out the door.

There was more activity outside Amy's house now; she could hear raised voices, see more movement than before. Then she noticed the large brown dog amid the crowd of police officers, and, to her utter disbelief—*Henry*. He was looking shamefaced, and even from this distance she could tell he was apologizing to the officers before tugging Molly back up the road. A moment later, Catherine realized what must have happened: a slim German shepherd was standing at attention by its handler. As she watched, the dog walked behind its handler's legs, eyes fixed on Molly, then back again to the other side.

"Henry," Catherine called as he made to cross over to the median. Then she lowered her hand: *What was she doing?* Just yesterday, after her walk, she'd sent him a long text message apologizing for snapping at him, saying she wasn't in a good place right now and just needed to be alone. It sounded stupid even as she typed it out, and it made her wonder where the words even came from, these weird phrases she used to make sure everyone around her didn't worry, didn't get upset. But she'd used them all the same to tell him to leave her alone.

So no, she didn't really understand why she was calling out to him now, watching him turn and see her, then walk back up the street, Molly in tow. All she knew was that she didn't want to go back inside and face her parents. And that shivering had started again.

"Hey," he said when he reached her. "Do you know what— Hey, what happened to you?"

She blinked.

"You're bleeding," he said, pointing.

Dimly, she touched her cheek. Felt the blood like grit under her fingers. "Sugar," she said, by way of explanation, then asked, "What did you do?"

"Not me." He grimaced down at Molly, whose sides were heaving. "Other dogs, I told you. She jerked the leash right out of my hand before I could even try for the peanut butter." Frowning, he turned to look back down the street. "Do you know what's going on down there? Some kind of drug bust or something?"

She opened her mouth, but the shivering got worse, making her teeth snap back together, her arms cross at her waist. She bent double, feeling like she was going to throw up. Through blurring eyes she saw Molly move closer to her, put her face right up to Catherine's. Catherine clutched at the fur on Molly's back, hands tight, sure she must be hurting the dog, but Molly didn't move. Catherine didn't know how long she stood there, trying to make herself loosen her grip on Molly's fur, but she had this feeling she was tipping over the edge of something terrifying and all she wanted was to grab something, fist it in her hands, and scream. But the sound wouldn't come. Her teeth were bared, and there was a low keening whine coming from her throat. She knew Henry must be wondering what the hell was going on.

She heard her front door open behind her. Catherine released Molly and stood straight, wiping her face of tears and blood at the same time. When she turned, her father was standing on the porch.

"I got your mother upstairs," he said. "She's—she's lying down."

Catherine wiped her nose with the sleeve of her sweatshirt. "Okay," she said, though she knew her mother would be unlikely to stay there.

Her father hitched a sigh and put his hands on his hips. His face was angled toward Amy's house. "They found her at Lookout Point. That's what . . . they said. What the police told them." He ran a hand down his face. "I'm going back inside. Make some calls. See what—what we can do. Catherine—"

He looked at her. Something sparked between them and she felt a burst of goose bumps down her shoulders before he turned and went back into the house.

"What," Henry said slowly, and she turned just as slowly back to face him, "the hell is going on?"

Catherine stared at Amy's house.

If I go there, she thought, *if I walk in, I'll find Amy in the kitchen. The oven light on because she always had to watch. The counter spilling with spices. Thin lines of flour in the hardwood.*

If I go there . . . she'll be there. I know it.

She began walking, had actually made it four or five steps before Henry suddenly appeared in front of her, blocking her way.

"Let me through," she said.

He shook his head.

"Let me through," she said again.

"Catherine—"

"I told you to leave me alone."

Henry frowned at her. "Okay. I can do that. But I'd suggest *not* pissing off those cops any more than Molly just did.

Jesus fucking Christ." He ran a hand through his hair and then glanced at Amy's house before turning back to Catherine. "What is going on?"

"Amy," Catherine choked out. "She's dead."

Henry looked at her like she was crazy; then he seemed to see something in her face, and his own features fell.

"You're serious? She's dead?"

Catherine swallowed. Nodded.

Henry shook his head. "But I thought . . . the dog. Drugs."

Catherine had the bizarre urge to laugh. "Who here sells *drugs*?"

Henry seemed to consider this for a moment. "James Pechman sells Adderall," he said finally. "But actually, I don't know if dogs can smell prescription pills."

Catherine couldn't summon up the energy for a response. Thankfully, Henry didn't seem to expect one.

He walked around her, sat on her porch steps, and blinked up at the sky, as though trying to see something on the air. The mist was wetter now. She could feel it on her skin, see it darkening the edges of Henry's hair.

"Do you know how?" he asked.

Slowly, she shook her head.

"We have her bread on our kitchen table," Henry said. "I made French toast with it before I took Molly out."

Catherine joined him on the steps. Molly sat between them, warm and yawning.

"I got pumpkin," Catherine said. She twisted her hands in

her lap, rolled a ring around her right finger: a Christmas gift from her parents, gold and sapphire. When she and Amy baked, they never wore rings. "You got eggnog, right?"

He nodded, and Catherine suddenly felt very, very tired. A wave of exhaustion so complete she didn't even feel cold anymore. Her hands stilled in her lap.

"Can I put Molly inside?" Henry asked her. "Just for a little while. The other dog, you know . . ."

"Yeah, sure."

Once he'd closed the front door with a few murmured words, he sat back down, and she said, her voice drowsy and quiet, "I'm sorry. About yesterday."

But Henry shook his head. "That's not . . . not even on my radar right now. Are you—are you okay?" Then he closed his eyes, as though embarrassed. "Forget it. Stupid question."

Her eyes found Amy's house again, Amy's yard, and she felt something tighten behind her eyes, something come into focus, that brief tiredness ebbing from her. Even the mist seemed to clear slightly; she could see the grass more clearly, remember when it was warmer. No mist. Just sun.

She'd never thought it could happen in the sun.

"I know who it was," she said. She could tell Henry was watching her strangely but she didn't care. "There was this guy. I don't know who. It was last summer. I was with Amy in the front yard and . . ." She blinked, that hard weight on her chest again, but she forced herself to keep talking. "He came up to us. Amy didn't see him. I didn't either, at first."

A car was driving up the road, on the other side of the median that divided their wide street. The pressure on her chest intensified as she remembered Amy suggesting they could try the median next as she poked the front yard grass with a stick, then wondering aloud if the rain had sent the caterpillars underground there, too. "Or maybe they have their own weather service like people do, and can prepare ahead of time. With little caterpillar umbrellas or something. What?" she'd added, in response to Catherine's dubious stare. "It could happen."

"A guy?" Henry asked her now. "What guy?"

"If you're asking me for a name—"

"Well, what did he look like?"

"Homeless," she said frankly. The car she'd been watching was now rounding the median, turning in the direction of the other vehicles grouped near the Porters' house. "Older. Twenties. Maybe even thirties. Dark hair, but it was so dirty it might not have—"

The car—a gray Honda sedan—stopped at her house, right on the curb in front of the walk. She and Henry stared.

A guy got out of the driver's seat and walked around the front of his car to her yard. He'd put the hazards on, and the headlights flashed red in the direction of Amy's house.

"Catherine Ellers?" he said. He looked roughly her age, but he had a quiet, uncertain voice, which, coupled with his milky skin, thin build, and violet under-eye shadows, made it seem as though he was sick, and not just with a cold.

Henry stood up. "And you are?" He glanced down at Catherine, who hadn't moved from the step, as though hoping she might answer. But she couldn't; she'd never seen this person before in her life.

She opened her mouth to say something along those lines, maybe even ask the guy a question, but then she noticed he was carrying a coat under one arm. It was black and plain and if not for a slightly ruffled hem might have been his.

But it wasn't. It was hers. The coat she'd left in the dorms that night, and—she saw with a sense of complete unreality—he was holding it out to her on her front walk, as though trying to give it back.

PART TWO

THE CRIES OF THE HARPY

Terror made me cruel.

—EMILY BRONTË, *WUTHERING HEIGHTS*

CHAPTER EIGHT

"Catherine Ellers?"

He was still standing there, not even ten feet away on the walk, holding out her coat, the damp haze misting the fabric. His face was a show of confusion, of uncertainty. She heard him say her name again.

Henry shot her another glance and then stepped directly in front of her, one arm outstretched. "Who are you?" he demanded. "What do you want?"

Catherine stood up. Over Henry's shoulder, she could see the boy still holding out the coat. He looked like a ghost, like something the winter mist had borne along.

Was it you?

Was it you?

"My name's Andrew," the boy said, glancing between them. When his eyes met Catherine's again, she felt her heart jump into her throat. "Andrew Worthington. Do you—do you not remember?"

blacksleep wake up water go hallway run bare legs blood shower no claim Mom Mom pick up pick up please

"Remember."

She said it aloud, her voice almost lost in the low wind. Henry turned to her but before he could say anything she stepped down from the porch and walked forward, until she was closer to this person—this Andrew—than to Henry. She looked him slowly up and down, as though he were something to study, to make sense of, and then it fell into place in her head like a gate slamming down, and she struck out, hard, with one bare hand.

He jerked back but it wasn't enough, his reflexes too slow, and her closed fist hit him along one cheekbone, sending a shock of pain up her hand and arm to her shoulder even as he twisted and fell onto the frosted grass.

"Catherine!" Henry grabbed her by the arms, trying to pull her back, but she was a match that had been begging to be lit for a week and she fought, spitting like a cat, yelling words that were more pain than language, raw as the winter, so bitter and hoarse they seemed to claw their way up her throat.

"*Catherine!* Shut up, stop it, the police are *right there*. Stop!"

She did, panting, glancing down the street, but she was lucky: only one person was outside Amy's house now, and by the looks of it, he was on a cell phone. The few neighbors who had trickled onto their front porches to watch the scene unfolding at the Porters' house seemed to glance over, but Henry waved at them, an *it's fine* reassurance, and they turned away, probably unsure exactly what they'd seen through the fog.

She looked back at the boy called Andrew, who by now was pushing himself up onto the grass, holding his cut cheek, and noticed her own knuckles were red, a smear of blood across her small ring. She wiped it off, a lurch of disgust in her throat, and snatched up her coat, which the boy had let fall. She scoured the pockets and pulled out her driver's license, her debit card, her school ID.

"What did you buy?" she said.

"What?" He was holding his cheek, slightly slumped. His car behind him still flared its hazards in a leisurely sort of way.

"What did you buy?" Catherine said again. "With my card? Video games? Beer?"

The boy took his hand from his cheek and examined it before applying pressure to the cut again. "No. I didn't *touch* your card. What is this? Why did you attack me? And who are you?" He directed this last question to Henry, who smiled and crossed his arms.

"Just a friendly spectator," Henry replied. "Catherine's usually pretty friendly too. Doesn't seem too fond of you, though."

"He raped me," Catherine said.

She didn't mean to say it, actually couldn't *believe* she'd said it, but the truth was there: in the sound of the words, in Henry whirling around to stare at her, in the hairs that stood up along the backs of her arms.

"You raped me," she said. She was looking at the boy, this thin, sickly boy with a cut on his cheek she'd given him, and wondered what he would say in response. But then, a moment later, she was kicking herself for even wondering.

"I didn't rape you!"

She flung the coat back at him, and then for good measure, her license and debit card and school ID. The coat fell in a heap to the stone walkway, and the cards clattered with a sound that reminded her of the grinding roll of that stupid plastic cup—

"So what was it?" she shot at him. "What would you call it? Me leaving without my coat and my dress on fucking backward and blood all down my l-legs—" She broke off and wiped her face, furious at herself for losing control, for shaking so hard where she stood that Henry had to steady her like an invalid.

But he was already protesting. Andrew. His name wouldn't fit inside her head even as he sputtered in protest.

"I didn't rape you! You really don't remember? You ran into me. In the hallway. Right? You were freaked out, I could tell something was wrong. You—There was blood, it got on the floor. . . ." He trailed off, then seemed to gather himself. "I saw what room you came out of. I went to knock. . . . I don't know, it just seemed . . . Anyway, I saw a coat on the floor when the door opened. I figured it was yours and grabbed it, but then you'd . . . you'd gone." He rubbed his cut cheek. It wasn't that bad, actually, barely bleeding, but the skin around it was red. "I went outside, but I didn't see you. You must have run or something. So I looked in the pockets. Your driver's license, it had your address on it—"

"Jesus," Henry muttered. "You didn't think, maybe a Snap-chat message? Or, I don't know, FedEx? It's just a *coat*."

"It wasn't," Andrew said, "just a coat." He looked back at Catherine. "I did find you online. I sent you a message a few days ago, but you didn't respond."

"I haven't . . ." Catherine swallowed. "I haven't been on it. Not since . . ." She looked him up and down again, trying to remember: that bump-brush in the hallway, but she hadn't looked up, even when she heard someone ask if she was okay. And yes, she had raced across campus. In fact, she'd run as fast as possible until she'd slammed into the entrance of her own dorm, one palm flat against the window—which was when she realized her student ID was in her coat. No way to swipe in. So stupid. So many times over. Freezing on the steps of the dorm, pacing and jumping and crying until a girl saw her through the glass and when she got inside she'd let out a gasp that was more a cry than anything else. She wondered if that girl had asked her if she was okay too.

"I swear," Andrew said. "I just saw . . . I saw you, and it . . . clearly something had gone down. So I got your coat and—"

"And he gave it to you?" Henry interrupted, his voice pa-tently disbelieving. "This guy? Just gave it to you? *Oh man, the girl I raped left her coat? Why didn't you* say *so? Here, don't want her to be cold!*"

"It wasn't like that."

"Yeah? Then what was it like?"

Andrew looked from Henry, who was glowering, to Catherine,

who was doing that thousand-yard stare again. "Listen. I'm sorry. Maybe I shouldn't have come. But I live about an hour from here, so I thought, after Christmas, might as well . . . just to check, you know . . ." His voice trailed off again. Slowly, he bent and picked up the coat, the cards. He held them out, like it was a few minutes ago and he'd just pulled up. "For what it's worth, I'm sorry. About what happened."

She took them from him. Questions burned at the back of her throat, but she saw the cut on his cheek when he stepped back from her, and the red of his skin there took the words away. She thought she might never speak again.

Andrew shoved his hands in his pockets and then glanced back toward his car. "I think I'll head out."

She still said nothing, but he didn't seem to expect her to. He gave her a kind of nod and then began walking to his car.

"You should drive out the way you came," Henry called to his retreating back, with the air of someone getting the last word. "You won't get through the other way."

Andrew half turned. "What?"

"Never mind." Henry gave a swift wave of one hand. "Go ahead. Drive right through the crime scene, see what happens."

"Crime scene?" Andrew looked down the street, his face full of some stark realization. "That's not the murdered girl's house, is it? The one they found at the clifftop?"

CHAPTER NINE

After a moment's silence, Henry walked up to Andrew and said something Catherine couldn't hear. Andrew seemed to say something in response and then shook his head. Henry shoved his hands in his pockets, looking unnerved. Then he walked back to Catherine.

"Henry," Catherine said when he reached her. "What—?"

Henry shot her a look as, behind them, Andrew climbed into his car. "He said *murdered*. No one else said that's what happened. How does *he* know?"

"Maybe he doesn't know for sure. Maybe it's just what he heard."

"He looked pretty sure, though, didn't he?"

Catherine shook her head, her voice just as quiet. "It's—it's an unexpected death. I bet a lot of people—also, what's he doing?" she asked, glancing at Andrew's car again.

"I told him to stop being weird and turn off his hazards." Then he added, very quickly, "He said he got into town yesterday. Last night, in fact."

She looked at him incredulously as Andrew's hazards clicked off. Clearly, Henry had wanted a moment to talk to her alone.

To share this information, as though it meant anything at all. "Henry, you can't possibly . . ."

"I just want to talk to him."

"God," she muttered, setting down the coat and tucking the cards into her pocket.

"You don't have to talk to him."

Her eyebrows shot up, a defensiveness she regretted almost at once, but it couldn't be helped. "Why wouldn't I talk to him?"

"Because you just cut his face open." Henry ran a hand through his hair, looking uncomfortable. Andrew was walking back to them. Henry held up a hand, all pretense forgotten, and Andrew stopped where he was on the walk, looking awkward. "Listen, I don't know what happened—" he continued.

"That's right. You *don't* know what happened."

"You're saying that like—like it's my *fault* for not knowing or something."

"No," she snapped, trying to keep her voice low. "I'm saying you don't know because it didn't happen to you. It happened to me. This is my problem, Henry, not yours."

"Then what's Amy? Is that not my problem too? Or does this only get to affect you?"

She jerked back, stung. For a moment they stared at each other, something feral between them, like when they were kids and would wrestle, kicking and hitting, bringing bruises to the surface of each other's skin.

Then it was gone.

"I'm sorry," she said, just as Henry said, "Sorry, Cath—"

They grinned briefly at each other. Slowly, Henry reached out a hand and brushed her cheek. She stilled under his touch, very aware of Andrew watching them.

"Sugar," he said, pulling back. "You going to explain that?"

"I'm fine."

He said nothing to that, but turned and motioned for Andrew to come forward. He did so, the hazards off on his car but his cheeks flushed, as though they'd absorbed the warning color.

———

His explanation was rushed and halting at the same time. Clearly intimidated by Henry and uncomfortable around her in general, Andrew spoke in words that ran over themselves and braked like the progression of a car accident.

"My uncle's a cop. That's how I know about her. Well, actually he's not my uncle. His wife is my mom's best friend, so I've called them my aunt and uncle basically since I could talk. Bob and Minda. They live by the rec center. I stayed the night at their place and this morning I woke up to Bob running around, apologizing for waking me and then to Minda for stepping on the cat. Anyway, he was saying that some girl had been killed and did I remember coming to the station last Christmas and a girl dropped by with some bread? Well, that was her and she'd been strangled and he probably wouldn't see me before I left so have a safe trip back—"

"She was strangled?" Catherine said. She put her own hand to her throat, feeling the angles of it, feeling sick.

"That's what he said. And then got mad at himself for saying it because he wasn't supposed to . . . but yeah."

"And you knew her?" Henry asked.

Andrew looked a little exasperated now. "You want to be a cop too? Yes, I met her last Christmas when she came to the station to give everyone bread, but that was it. I didn't hurt her, and I didn't—didn't rape anyone." He ran a hand over his cut. It had stopped bleeding. "I shouldn't have said anything. Forget it. And don't say anything, okay, because I don't want my uncle to get in trouble either."

"We won't." Catherine stepped toward him. "But please. *I* knew her. I knew her really well but I don't know what happened. Please," she said again. "I have to know what happened to her."

Andrew stared at her. She realized that past the dark shadows, the thin skin, and the cut on his cheek, he wasn't as alarming-looking as she'd previously thought. He had a sort of fragility to him that reminded her of Amy.

"You can't repeat any of this, okay? Even I'm not supposed to know about it."

They nodded at once, and Andrew looked resigned.

"She was out there awhile, they think. Some guy walking his dog found her right at the edge of the clifftop. That's what's giving everyone such a weird vibe, according to Bob. Because whoever did it could have just, like, tossed her over. Right before Bob left he said something like *Son of a bitch wanted her to be found.*"

"But why?" Henry asked. "That makes no sense."

"It doesn't have to," Catherine said. She was remembering that afternoon: broad daylight in a wide front yard. "Some psychos don't care about being obvious. Some of them just come right over and—" She wiped her face. "Can I talk to your uncle, or whoever he is? Because I think I know who might have done it. Is he at Amy's house now? Can I see him?"

Andrew looked uncomfortable at that. "He's not lead on the force or anything. He does other stuff, usually. Like, people stealing DVDs from the library to pawn. That's why it was such a big deal when he got called in this morning. It's, like, all hands on deck. I can try, though. See what he says."

"Thanks."

The front door opened and Catherine's mother appeared on the porch. She started to say something but then saw Andrew and looked confused.

"Mom?" Catherine prompted.

Her mother shook her head as though to clear it. "The dog. Henry, she's got something in her mouth and there's broken—"

"I'm on it," Henry said, moving toward the front door, but Catherine stayed where she was, arms crossed. Henry looked at her expectantly, his expression the twin of her mother's.

"Be there in a second," she said with an encouraging nod to both of them. "Seriously. Just a minute."

She heard her father say something from farther inside the house and her mother, with great reluctance and a final look at

Andrew, went back inside. Henry followed her but left the door half open.

"Thank you," Catherine said again, once Henry was out of earshot.

Andrew shrugged. "It's not a lot. I'm sorry you knew her." A pause. "Actually, that's a weird thing to say. I meant—"

"No, it's okay." She shook her head. "Thank you, for finding me. Giving me my things back. There was all this stuff I was going to have to do. DMV, you know."

"Yeah." He was looking at her as though he wanted to say something more, maybe apologize again, but she put a hand up. She was very aware of how hard the cold asphalt felt under her boots, how it seemed to press back against her weight.

"Don't," she said. "Don't tell me. I—I know you probably know who did it. If you live on his hall, saw his room. But I can't know. Not—not yet."

He looked surprised, even a little alarmed, and she wanted to say more but didn't know how. How could she explain to this near-stranger that she was on the edge of a cliff too? That she hadn't felt like herself since it happened, that she hadn't felt real, like a real actual person, and instead was like a ghost haunting this place she used to know? A long-ago familiarity replaced with strangeness in the slow dying of dogs and hovering mothers and newly distant fathers and nightmare-laced sleep and a girl she loved like a daughter-sister killed in the night, and she hadn't been there.

She thought about how it had felt when she'd seen Andrew and the coat and how her mind had put that together wrong. How she'd gone mad and struck out and drawn blood, so certain, so *goddamn sure*. But she'd been wrong. And maybe what Andrew was going to say wouldn't be wrong. He probably had it right; he'd gotten her coat, after all. But that wasn't what she was worried about. It wasn't about right or wrong anymore. It was about alive and not. Functioning and not. In a tree or not. Already she was regretting asking Andrew to tell her what he knew about Amy—*strangled*—images swinging down at her like ropes with strands of brown hair on them—

"Sure," Andrew said, though he didn't look very sure. "Uh, whatever you want." He shoved his hands into his pockets. "Do you still want me to talk to Bob?"

She nodded, then, with a quick look behind her, held out a hand. "Give me your phone." He did so, and she typed in her number. "Let me know what he says."

He took his phone back and looked at her number as though unable to believe it. "I'll do that," he said. "Yeah."

"That way you don't have to drive all the way over here like a stalker. That was a joke," she added, but he grinned.

"Nah, I know it's weird. All of it." He paused. "You know, you could probably just go to the station yourself, or the cops at the house. I bet they'd take any leads at this point."

But she shook her head. She had no name, and barely a face in her memory. It wasn't a lot to go on, she knew, and this was

Amy. If Andrew's uncle or whoever it was could help in the least, she wasn't going to turn that opportunity away by looking stupid in front of someone else.

"Let me know," she said as she turned to walk to the front door, but Andrew called to her, and she looked back at him.

"I think your brother hates me," he said.

She laughed without thinking, and it was nice, she thought, that her body could still do that. "He's not my brother," she said. "But I think you got the other part right."

CHAPTER TEN

"We're going to the church," Catherine's mother told her as soon as Catherine walked inside the house; Catherine thought she'd probably spent all of a minute lying down. Henry was leaning against the counter, watching her parents shrug on their jackets, a strange, inscrutable look on his face. Molly was at his feet, looking guilty, her muzzle dusted with sugar. The broken pieces of the sugar canister had been cleaned up, and a mini-dustpan and broom sat on the counter.

"First Faith?" Catherine said, surprised. They hadn't gone to church—besides the occasional Christmas or Easter service, and even those holiday visits had pretty much fallen by the wayside—since she was maybe ten.

"John Pechman is organizing the neighborhood," her mother explained. "To support the Porters. Obviously as the pastor he wants to help, though I don't know how . . . Anyway, everyone's meeting at the church to see what we can do, make food, give donations . . ." She trailed off again. Her coat was misbuttoned, the collar too high on one side. Catherine watched her dad put a hand on her mother's shoulder.

"It's going to be okay," her dad said.

"No," she said. "Not for Jennifer. Not without her daughter—"

She went to Catherine then, wrapping her arms around her tightly. "Are you okay?" she asked into Catherine's hair. "Who was that, outside?"

"No one." Catherine pulled away as gently as she could, then looked down at herself, at her sweats and boots. "I'll meet you there," she said.

"Oh, but we can wait," her mother said at once. "Of course—"

"No," Catherine said. "You go. I'm a mess. I need to shower and change and—"

I need a moment. Alone.

Catherine watched her shift, uncertain, then glance around the room, giving a little start when her eyes landed on Henry, as though she'd just remembered he was there.

"Henry!" she said. "Your parents—will they be at the church as well?"

Henry spoke without hesitation. "They'll be there."

"Your mother's always so good at that," Catherine's mother said distractedly. "Your whole family, really. Church functions, never missed . . ." She looked back at Catherine's father, who gestured to the door, but she still frowned. "Are you sure?" she asked Catherine.

"I'm sure," Catherine said. "I'll be there. I just need . . ."

Time.

Or rather, to undo it. Undo all of it. Everything. Yesterday. This entire last week.

"Let's go, Susan," her father said. "Henry has to be getting back home to his parents now."

Henry took the cue, leading Molly to the door so he would be out of the house before Catherine's parents. "See you later," he said.

Catherine watched him go, feeling oddly regretful, an unease that intensified even more when her parents closed the door behind them and she heard the dead bolt grind home.

⸺

For the first time in she didn't even know how long, Catherine got ready to go to church. She showered, put on a dress, tights, and makeup, and looked in her bathroom mirror, trying to pull herself together. It was pointless.

Amy

Amy

Amy

The name repeated in her head like a nail being driven down by a hammer, deeper and deeper with each blow. By the time she arrived at the church, her eyes were red, her teeth clicking, and it took all her resolve just to navigate the already-busy parking lot without hitting anyone. It was different from how she remembered it—the parking lot. They must have expanded it, because there was a large square section off to the side, the asphalt slightly darker, newer. The church itself, however, looked the same: brown and gray with a sharply slanted roof and a tall cross stretching into the blue sky. She could see it, even through the gently falling rain, the mist that still hung on the air, and she had to admit there was something kind of comforting about it.

It made her wonder, not for the first time, why they'd stopped going to First Faith.

Sure, her family wasn't that devout. And her mother was hardly a morning person after her long nursing shifts that sometimes fell on weekends, while her father craved sleep after a long workweek. But still. So much of the neighborhood attended, well, religiously. She didn't even know of any other major churches in the area, though there was a synagogue on the edge of West Falls that did host a decent kosher food truck event every September. But First Faith was kind of everywhere. It wasn't necessarily the religion aspect, she didn't think, but the community part: bake sales and outdoor concerts in the summer, so many things secular and open.

She had begun to make her way to the tall church doors, topped with stained glass, when she realized that the dozen or so people in the parking lot were all heading to the attached reception hall on the left-hand side. After a moment, Catherine followed them. Her feet were freezing on the asphalt in her black ballet flats and when she entered the reception hall with a group of low-murmuring women, she exhaled at the sudden warmth.

It was a wide, square room with tables along one wall and stacks of chairs people took down and arranged into small clusters. There was coffee in the corner, small paper cups people held as they spoke. Everyone was gathered in groups, either standing or sitting in the chairs they'd angled into almost-circles: little cliques that made Catherine's sense of awkwardness spike.

"Excuse me, dear," said a voice behind her, and Catherine jumped.

She was still standing in front of the door.

"Sorry," she said, moving to the side, her shoulder nearly hitting the large bulletin board on the wall. It was hung above a narrow table covered with even narrower brochures. As a group of people passed her, her eyes flicked over the different-colored papers, hardly even reading them—until one in particular caught her eye.

COMMUNITY SOUP KITCHEN
2nd and 4th Thursday of each month
6:30 p.m.
West Falls Food Bank
Acceptable donations permitted,
see John Pechman for details.
Whoever has a bountiful eye will be blessed, for he
shares his bread with the poor.
—Proverbs 22:9

What did he look like? Henry had asked her.

"Homeless," she breathed now, her fingers hovering millimeters from the pale blue brochure.

Was that what had happened? Had the man seen Amy at the soup kitchen? But . . . had Amy even volunteered at the soup kitchen? It seemed like something she would do—*acceptable donations permitted*—but it struck Catherine that she didn't know if Amy had ever been to the West Falls Food Bank. She thought she knew so much about Amy, but there were holes. Of course there were holes, she told herself sternly. No one could know everything about another person.

But she's mine.

She was mine.

Her fingers touched the paper, her ring gleaming under the lights. Was she right, or was she wrong again, like she had been with Andrew? She thought of all the bread Amy must have baked over the past few years, delivering to God knew how many houses, selling it to countless people in town. Giving it away for free, maybe, to those with the greatest need.

Well, she thought, half hysterical, *at least I can narrow it down to people who eat.*

"Catherine."

She whirled to see her mother's face a foot from hers. She looked marginally more composed than she had at the house.

Catherine tried to smile, unbuttoning her coat. "Just looking," she said, nodding at the bulletin board, the flyers. "They— they do a lot here."

Her mother reached out and squeezed her hand. "I'm so, so sorry, Catherine. I don't know if I—if I said that, back at the house. You two were so close."

Catherine said nothing, just felt her eyes burn and saw her mother's face waver in front of her.

"Come on," her mother said gently, now taking her arm and

leading her from the entryway to the wider part of the hall. "Your father's been cornered by Dave Lester—do you remember him?"

"No," Catherine said truthfully as they walked across the room. It glowed from the sun through the windows, casting wide rhombus patches of light onto the carpet.

"He used to go antiquing with your father. Sold him a knife from the Civil War—supposedly—and then a whiskey bottle that smelled so bad I made him keep it in the garage. No, maybe you don't remember. Well, your father's always had doubts about their authenticity. Not that he'd ever admit it to Dave, but still, we should probably . . ."

Her mother was babbling, which she often did when she was nervous, and when they found her father and Dave—a stout man with a graying mustache—the former was looking increasingly put out.

"No, I don't think I'm interested," her father was saying firmly. "Not now, anyway, with what's going on . . ." He spotted them and his face seemed to relax with relief. "Dave, you remember my wife, Susan, and my daughter."

Catherine smiled weakly. Dave snapped his fingers at her.

"You used to watch little Amy, didn't you? Came to the museum a few times, if I remember. I used to work there. Retired last year, thank the good Lord."

They'd gone twice that first summer, Amy's mother suggesting they do something "productive" now and again. Catherine and Amy had walked through the small history museum, bored and quiet, for an hour and only went again later in the summer so they could tell Amy's mother they had done so. Catherine bought Amy a too-large ice cream cone after, leading to a stern morning text message about Amy being sick.

"Worth it," Amy had told her later. "Cookie dough add-ins are always worth it."

"Yes," Catherine said now, her chest tight. She struggled to focus on Dave's face. "A few times."

Dave nodded, turned back to her dad, seemed to read his expression correctly, and, with a last smile, wandered off.

"That bottle," her father said as soon as Dave was out of ear-shot, "wasn't genuine amber."

"Richard—" her mother began.

"And don't even get me started on that knife."

"Didn't you take it to be appraised?"

"It's still undersized."

"Don't do this now, Richard. It's not the time—Oh, hello, John. And James, isn't it?"

Catherine spun around.

A tall man in his fifties was standing just behind her. He had a slight paunch and a thick head of black hair. His eyes were hazel and serene behind wire-rimmed glasses, his jaw freshly shaved. Next to him stood a boy about her age, who could not have looked more different with his wrinkled shirt, an almost-scowl playing around his mouth.

John Pechman chuckled. "All we need is Matthew and Mark,

but the twins are with Kathleen. She's around here somewhere. Never did manage to get a Luke."

Catherine shared James's grimace. When he looked at her, he gave a jerky nod.

"Hey," he said.

"Hey."

"Ah, yes," Pechman said, his eyes now on her. "You know James, don't you? Went to school together? James is a senior now. Are you at college?" When she nodded, he beamed. "How fast the time goes, doesn't it? I still remember you in Sunday school. You know, I saw you all across the room and I just had to come over. I thought to myself, I haven't seen the Ellerses in far too long. But you know, I think that's what happens with tragedy"—at this, his voice lowered—"with loss. It brings people together. We need to gather, to mourn communally."

"Are Evan and Jennifer . . . ?" Her mother trailed off, and Pechman shook his head.

"No, I believe they're still with the police. I wouldn't . . . wouldn't expect them to come to something like this. It would be overwhelming, I think. But it's for them all the same." He gestured to the tables lined against the far wall, the people grouped around them. "We have sign-ups. Meals for the next two months. Donations. There will be a memorial, of course. A funeral. Our goal here is essentially to ensure that Evan and Jennifer do not have to do more than is absolutely necessary during this difficult time. Whatever we can do for them, it will be done."

Despite everything, Catherine found herself a little moved by this. John Pechman had always been over-the-top, a little too charismatic—although, she thought, what successful pastor wasn't?—but within hours of Amy's death he had gathered and organized dozens of people for the sole purpose of helping Amy's devastated parents. All she had done was hit a stranger and wonder about a soup kitchen flyer.

"Did Amy help out a lot here?" Catherine asked. "I know she did bake sales."

"Oh, yes. She did so much for us. She was a delight, I have to say. An absolute delight."

"Like with the soup kitchen?" she asked, unable to help herself. "Things like that?"

Pechman nodded. "If there was any event she could make food for, she did so without question. I was disappointed she didn't manage to make it to the church this year for her Christmas bread, but I think she may have stretched herself a bit too thin. Did you hear she was trying to sell online?"

"Yes," Catherine said.

"So industrious. I know a great many people were interested. What an amazing girl. A loss, a loss for the whole community . . ." He trailed off, then smiled at them, a more genuine smile than before. "I just want to say . . . Please don't feel any pressure. I know it's a lot to think about, the—the aftermath of something like this. It's enough that you're here, showing support. I—we—just wanted to say, welcome."

James wiped his nose with the sleeve of his shirt. He had

narrow shoulders and red-blond hair. She remembered he'd been nice in high school, if a little awkward. He dated Stephanie Spencer last year. Catherine remembered Stephanie—JV cheerleader, her brunette ponytail always insanely thick and shiny—complaining about him in third-period calculus after they'd broken up.

His eyes were tinged red, and she realized he smelled—not bad, exactly—but sort of raw, as though he'd just been out for a run.

"You see Henry?" he asked her.

Catherine started. "Um, I think he's supposed to be here. Somewhere."

James nodded, looked her up and down through bleary eyes, then said, "Cool. Tell him I'm looking for him?" He walked away and John Pechman sighed.

"Please forgive my son. He's . . . at a difficult age, as my wife and I say. Though I don't think nine-year-old twins are much easier. Never a dull day at the Pechman house, I can tell you that." He shot her father a rueful look. "Children challenge us in many ways, don't they?"

Her father smiled back, but his eyes were grave. "They do. But I'd take that over the alternative."

"Yes," Pechman said, nodding again. "Absolutely. Anyway . . . as I said . . . welcome back."

He walked away, after his son, and Catherine's mother tutted.

"What?" Catherine said, casting her a look.

"Oh, I just . . ."

"Your mother never liked him," her father said flatly.

"That's not true."

Her father looked almost amused at her prim indignation; Catherine saw his eyes soften.

"It's not true," her mother said again. "John was just always . . ."

"What?" Catherine said.

"Nothing."

"Let's just say your mother was happy when you finished Sunday school," her father said.

"Well, that's not a crime," her mother insisted. "And anyway, we're not the only ones who've left, you know," she added, her voice lowering. "It wasn't just me, or us, or however you want to put it."

"If you're talking about Ken—"

"Ken?" Catherine echoed blankly. She searched through her memories. "Ken . . . Itoh? The deacon?"

"Pastor," her father corrected. "He became a pastor."

"Well, he still is, from what I heard," her mother said. "Just not here."

Catherine looked between them. "I don't—"

But her mother waved a hand. "It's not important. I don't even know all the details. Just gossip, really. And now's not the time for it. We're here for Amy. Richard, should we look at the tables? See what we can help with?"

Her father gave a noise of assent and they walked off, perhaps expecting Catherine to follow, but she didn't. Her mind was spinning, full of soup kitchens and half-heard gossip and

Amy. She felt like she was falling again, or about to, that strange need to hold on to something coming back to her as her fingers clenched, looking for something to grab, some edge of purchase.

Then she spotted him.

Henry was standing by a table in the corner, taking out a spool of cups from thin plastic and stacking them by the coffee-maker. Within seconds she found herself walking toward him with a surge of relief so strong her fingers uncurled from her palms, as though casting a die.

CHAPTER ELEVEN

"James Pechman is looking for you," she said when she approached.

Henry turned to her, crumpled the remaining plastic in one hand, and tossed it in a trash can underneath the table. "I'll bet he is," he said ruefully. "Coffee?" He gestured to the newly stacked cups.

She nodded. He poured them each a small amount and Catherine grabbed a handful of creamers from the bowl on the table and began slowly turning her coffee as white as her skin. Henry watched her, appalled.

"That's not even coffee anymore," he said.

"Well, how do you drink yours?" she asked, taking a sip.

He held out his own cup so she could see. "Black. Because I'm an adult."

She almost snorted, then drank some of hers. "So . . . how do you know James?"

Henry looked unabashed. "I buy from him *one* time during finals last May and the kid won't leave me alone."

She raised her eyebrows.

"Okay, maybe again a few months ago. Oh, don't look so superior," he said, though his voice was low. "We're . . . friends.

I guess. He asked me over to his house yesterday. We played video games and hung out. He wanted to sell to me again. I said no." He shrugged. "It's not like I wanted to make it a thing. You take those things too much and you can't sleep and your mouth gets so dry you can't swallow. No thanks."

Catherine scanned the room. James was nowhere to be found, but more people were still arriving, faces she vaguely recognized but couldn't name as they came in from the cold.

Where was Amy now? Surely she wasn't still there, outside? What happened to a body after—?

She slammed her mind shut. Cut off the words before pictures could form.

There were people milling around them, trying to get to the coffee. Henry jerked his head and she followed him a few paces away, where they leaned against the wall, coffees in hand, watching the room. Catherine saw her parents on the other side, looking at some papers on one of the tables.

"I can't remember the last time they went to church on a—" But she didn't know what day of the week it was.

"Friday," Henry supplied. "It's Friday."

Catherine closed her eyes. Just days ago, she and Amy had been watching YouTube videos together, so close she could see the faint flour marks on her red coat, dusting the cuffs.

"They're going to make casseroles," she said faintly. "Everyone in the neighborhood is going to bake something or other and none of it will be as good as what Amy could make." She glanced at him. "Where are your parents?"

"Probably with Pechman. Writing him a check, more likely than not. God, they're predictable." He looked around the room, slightly annoyed, and Catherine followed his gaze, spotting Mr. and Mrs. Brisbois standing by one of the far tables, indeed talking to John Pechman. Catherine took in Henry's parents: well dressed and tall and stiff, as though made entirely of corners, like well-crafted origami—though maybe that was too mean of her. At least about Henry's dad.

But Mrs. Brisbois had always kind of hated her.

Henry took a sip of his coffee. "Can I ask you something?"

She turned to him.

"What did you say to that Andrew kid? After I left?"

She felt a smile flick across her face and welcomed it. "He doesn't think you like him very much."

"I don't *know* him. I just think he's . . ."

"What?"

"Weird," Henry said. "I think he's weird."

"Define *weird.*"

"*Weird* is saying he saw you that night," Henry said without hesitation. "*Weird* is how he just got into town last night, when Amy . . . then he just happens to know exactly how she died?" And when she didn't budge, he continued, "Come on, Catherine. One of those things, okay, I might buy, but *all* of them?"

"I think you're reaching."

"And I think you're—" But he stopped himself.

"What?" she demanded. She was very aware of the press of

people around them, the biting scent of coffee, and she suddenly wondered if her shower had been enough, or if she still smelled a little bit of night sweats, those nightmares her body remembered more than her mind. "You think I'm what?"

"Confused," he said. "Or too trusting. I can't decide."

"Oh, fuck you, Henry," she said, but her voice was quiet, taking the sting from her words. "I cut his face open, remember? I hardly call that trusting. Not to mention I was wrong. I'm not about to accuse him of—"

"How do you know you were wrong?"

She blinked, taken aback. To buy herself time, she drank some of her coffee, feeling him watching her closely. But, she realized, he wasn't actually that close to her. Not physically close. There were several feet between them, as though he was trying to keep his distance, and she was oddly grateful for it. At the same time, she didn't like that he was treating her differently now that he knew. It was so strange, not even knowing what she wanted. Even if someone asked her point-blank how she'd like to be treated, she'd be unable to provide even the start of an answer.

"How do you know you were wrong?" Henry repeated, his voice a little firmer, his eyes intent. "You said so yourself. You don't remember."

"I—" She broke off. "It . . ." Her face was getting hot, a flush rising to curl around her throat. *Strangled.* "It wasn't him."

"But how do you know?"

"Because I know!" she shot back at him, and some people getting coffee turned. She lowered her voice. "I was wrong, okay? I won't be wrong again. It wasn't him."

Henry gave her a long look. "Fine," he said. "Fine, if that's what you want to go with."

"What is that supposed to mean?"

"Forget it."

"No, tell me."

"Catherine—"

"Tell me."

"No!" he shot back at her. "You don't get to boss me around. We're not kids anymore."

She didn't turn to see if anyone was watching them this time. She was focused only on him, all her indignation seeping away from her like water down a drain.

Because if she was being honest with herself, there had been a time, shortly before their falling—out? away? apart?—when the scales had shifted between them when she was not much older than Amy. Henry no longer racing ahead of her, always faster, braver, able to climb higher on trees that scraped her palms raw, Catherine thudding onto the grass with a groan, glaring up at him as he swung ostentatiously above her, teasing. No. Fourteen had been . . . dresses. She'd started shaving her legs, wearing makeup, lip gloss so sticky it clung to errant strands of blond hair she straightened until it shone. She started to catch him watching her, his blue eyes dazed, and she'd realized, one day, one moment, like a light clicking on, that he had fallen for her.

An August sun shower. A pale yellow dress, her skin fair, cheeks pink. She'd been in the front porch rocking chair, drinking white grape juice and watching the rain. Henry sat on the porch step, watching as she tucked her legs underneath her and tried not to look at him.

It's like a movie, she'd thought. *We are a picture that isn't real.*

That had been the afternoon before the night he kissed her in the backyard, the garden lights violet, green, and gold. She'd reached down and found his hand, squeezed it so hard he'd let her go, breathless, dizzy, and, strangest of all, wanting him to do it again.

But of course, she hadn't let that happen.

"I'm sorry," she said now. Her voice was quiet. Outside the wide windows, the mist had finally given way to rain. She could hear it like a heart, like his heart. "I'm really sorry, Henry."

"Forget it." He took another sip of coffee, not looking at her, but she saw the tension in his face. It made her want to cry all over again, and she wondered if something had broken inside her, something vital she hadn't even been aware of until now.

But then, had she ever been that strong a person? Or—forget strong—even just a *substantial* person? Wasn't she flighty and vague a lot of the time? And she didn't always make the best decisions. She'd been stuck-up in high school and then reckless in college.

But that didn't mean she couldn't change. She was going to do something tangible and real and she wouldn't let history repeat itself.

"I want your help," she told him, her gaze focusing on the entryway of the reception hall: the narrow table with the narrow flyers, a pale blue one that seemed to glow the color of her eyes. "We can do it together."

"Do what?" Henry asked.

"I want to find the guy. The one I told you about. I want to tell Andrew's uncle about him. I want to know his name." She looked at Henry, a little wary of his reaction, but when he took in her face, he looked relieved, as though he, too, had sensed the shift in her, a kind of resurrection behind her eyes.

"Okay," he said. "Where should we start?"

CHAPTER TWELVE

They spent the late-afternoon hours scrolling through the sex offender database, Catherine's fingers hovering over the keyboard and her mouth turned down in disgust as she read. Henry sat next to her at the table. They'd gone to the Panera by the Westfield shopping center. Henry got a sandwich with cheese that dried on the bread like white glue and she slathered a chocolate muffin in butter and felt sick.

They gave up after a little over two hours. No face was right. None matched what was in her memory. Henry suggested they try again tomorrow. She agreed, but once at home she couldn't help thinking back to their spat at the church, that bitterness just under the surface. Her fault, she knew. A mistake over four years old now.

After that summertime backyard kiss, she'd left to go to her house, confused and overwhelmed, but in a good way. She hadn't even made it down the street before she heard her name and turned.

Mrs. Brisbois had called out to her from the front porch.

"Catherine Ellers," she said as Catherine walked up to her. "And what were you doing with my son just now?"

Shame, white-hot at her throat and face. Mrs. Brisbois's mouth twisted.

"You follow my son like a shadow, girl. I don't like it one bit. I'm going to have a talk with your mother, see if we can't distance the two of you from each other."

"I'm leaving," Catherine said stupidly, a little desperate. "So you don't need to do that."

"Leaving?" Mrs. Brisbois was so thin she made Catherine think of Halloween skeletons. "Leaving where?"

"Here. For camp."

"When?"

"Tomorrow." Maybe that was why Henry had kissed her, she thought. A goodbye kiss.

The camp was near Olympia. Six weeks, during which her nerves and homesickness slowly morphed into something approaching joy. She'd always loved being outside. She scraped down thin sticks for art projects and wrestled with the straps of orange life jackets and laughed over sparking fires with girls who liked her as though by default. Catherine met a boy there with black hair and freckles on his tan skin. She couldn't stop looking at him during mealtimes, and he grinned back at her, flushing at the ears. They kissed in the middle of a nature scavenger hunt, looking for *a leaf that has been chewed by an insect*. It had been different from the kiss with Henry, quick and shy and damp from the heat. They'd hugged hard that last day of camp, and he gave her a handwritten letter on yellow paper. When she got home she put it in her jewelry box with the letters her other camp friends had written her. Catherine returned home feeling like someone new, older even. And, just like that, Henry didn't fit into her life the way he used to.

She remembered that first day back, how he ran to her door as soon as he realized she was home. She'd looked at him across the threshold and felt a pang of loss she couldn't explain to herself. Maybe Henry's mom had been right. Maybe she and Henry had been too close. Had she been his shadow? She didn't want to be anyone's shadow. Henry suddenly seemed so far from her, even though he was just feet away. Talking to him felt different, the words jagged, something large and awkward between them she couldn't shift and didn't really want to. Something had changed; his name didn't quite beat in her like blood the way it used to.

I put you away.

She shook her head, hard, forcing herself back to the present, to winter and Amy and the task at hand. She showered again, ate dinner, and waited for sleep. It came, finally, but in nightmare-intervals: flashes of Amy in a cold room, stripped, with a tray of scalpels waiting next to her.

She woke at nine in the morning to a text from Andrew.

His uncle was interested in meeting with her. Could she come to the police station?

She did, Henry in tow, with Molly left behind because, in Henry's words, "I'm not trying that therapy dog thing with actual police officers." Andrew met them in the lobby, standing by a potbellied man around her father's age. As she and Henry approached them, Catherine felt like she was sleepwalking through a bad dream, like any minute the roof would cave in, or the cars just outside would turn into giant white spiders and rush the front doors.

She told herself to get it together. She told herself the world was real.

They reached Andrew and his uncle.

"Robert Harper," the man said, giving her a brisk handshake, then Henry. "But people call me Bob."

"Bob Harper?" Henry echoed as his hand fell back to his side.

The name rang something in Catherine's memory.

Bob laughed. He had white-pink skin, as though mildly sunburned. "Yes, like the weight loss trainer. *Biggest Loser.* I get it all the time." He slapped his stomach. "I like to mess with people, tell them I saw the error of my ways with all that health crap. Some even buy it." He turned to Catherine, his tone changing at once. "Andrew tells me you knew Amy Porter."

"Y-yes," she said. "I used to babysit—nanny. During the summers."

He nodded at that. "Come with me."

He led them through the lobby and down a few hallways with distinctly lower ceilings. The more they walked, the less impressive the already humble building became: green checked tiles like the high school, and a faint smell of dust, as though the place only went through the most cursory of cleanings. Eventually he led them to a larger room, with desks stationed at intervals and uniformed police officers milling about with a few in plain clothes, coffees in hand. There was the sound of typing, of chatter, a general aura of activity. Nearby, a man took a mechanical bite of an English muffin as he pored over a stack of papers; he didn't seem to notice that an unopened bag of granola had fallen to the floor at his feet.

"Over here," Bob directed them, or rather just her and Henry; Andrew seemed to know his way around.

"I used to come here a lot when I was younger," he explained as they squeezed their way past a group gathered at one of the desks. "Wanted to be a cop. Thought it was the coolest thing."

"And now?" Henry asked.

"Not so much."

Catherine said nothing, even as they reached Bob's desk— close to a thick metal column that went right to the ceiling—and he began to rummage in the drawers. They hovered awkwardly, then, with various items in hand—paper, pen, phone—he led them down a side hallway into another room: it was small, with green walls and two chairs on opposite sides of a metal table.

"You boys can wait out here," Bob said good-naturedly.

"But—" Henry and Catherine said at once.

"Come on," Andrew said to Henry, sounding resigned. "There's coffee and stuff in this room down the hall."

Henry gave Catherine an uncertain look, but she tried to smile as he walked away with Andrew. She hadn't realized she would be doing this alone.

"I hate this room," Bob said, closing the door behind them. "Always makes people nervous and never the right ones. Don't worry. It's just so we have some privacy." He sat down heavily in one chair, and Catherine took the other. She wondered now if she'd been right in even coming here, in thinking she'd have anything useful to add to all the activity she'd just seen. What if she got in the way? What if she wasted his time?

"We record all these," Bob said, "just to let you know." He waved a hand vaguely toward the ceiling. "Completely standard. But I wanted to mention it."

"Sure," Catherine said, her heart thudding.

"So you used to watch Amy Porter during the summers?" Bob asked her, now picking up his pen.

She nodded, swallowing against a sudden lump in her throat. "Summer of 2017 to last summer—2019," she said, trying to sound like she knew what she was talking about. "Started when Amy was ten."

"What was that like?"

"What?"

"What was your typical routine? What did Amy like to do? Not like to do? You spend time with any other kids or adults or was it just the two of you? What places did you two frequent? Things like that."

"We baked a lot," Catherine said slowly. "Amy . . . liked to bake. We watched movies. TV. We didn't really hang out with other people that much. Well, Hannah Walsh, sometimes—a kid, Amy's best friend," she added before Bob could ask. "But usually it was just . . . kind of the two of us." She sat up a little straighter. "Amy didn't really like going outside that often unless she was delivering her bread. I wanted to mention that. She was a very indoors person if the weather wasn't perfect. If given the choice, I don't think she would have gone out the other night. Not on her own with it that cold. I just—I don't think that's what happened."

Bob nodded. Catherine could tell he was taking in her flushed cheeks, her bright eyes.

"You say you have a, ah, person of interest? Maybe someone paying too much attention to Amy—"

"Yes," she said at once. She was feeling jumpy. She wanted to stand up but forced her palms under her legs. She began to tell Bob about last summer, the front yard and the sudden arrival of—

"Well, I don't know who *he* was," she admitted as Bob wrote quick, illegible notes. "Henry and I spent hours yesterday looking up names, sex offenders, and I couldn't find him. No one who looked exactly like him, anyway. But he was . . . There was something *wrong* about him. About how he looked at her." She broke off as images flashed into her mind, the room spinning away to make space for them. How small Amy was compared to a full-grown male, that obscene proportion, the horror of it all. The fear.

She sucked in a breath. Her arms and neck were covered in goose bumps. She made herself continue: "Amy did a lot with First Faith, and I think she might have met him at the soup kitchen while she was volunteering. This man—he looked like he might be homeless. I wonder if she—if he saw her there and . . ."

"Amy volunteered at the soup kitchen?" Bob asked, jotting down a few more lines, his eyes still on her.

"I don't know for sure," Catherine admitted. "But I think so. I can maybe check—"

"Leave that to us. You okay to work with a sketch artist?"

Catherine stared at him.

"A sketch artist," Bob repeated, picking up his things and getting up. Slightly startled, Catherine followed him from the room. "We have a good one," he continued, leading her back to his desk. "Assuming she's in today, but I think—Sandra?" He addressed a person at the desk next to him, a large, well-dressed woman with almost-violet lipstick. "Takira in today?"

Just then, she saw Henry and Andrew appear around the corner, paper cups of coffee in hand. She waved to them, and they began to weave their way toward her through the desks and people.

"Everyone's in today, Bob," the woman replied wearily, barely glancing up from her computer screen. Her brown-gold skin made Bob look, in contrast, like a blotchy snowman. "Try asking Grant."

Bob rolled his eyes, sat down in his chair, and called, *"Grant!"*

The woman winced and shot Bob a glare. "You are an infant," she said.

"Couldn't do it without you, Sandra," Bob said cheerfully.

"What are you up to now, Bob?" a resigned but amused voice said, just as Henry and Andrew reached her.

Catherine turned to see a bald man with a stack of papers in a folder under one arm. It was the one who had been eating the English muffin. Bob grinned up at him, hands behind his head.

"Sandra said Takira was with you."

"I did not," Sandra replied, eyes still on her computer. "I said—"

The man called Grant rolled his eyes. "She's here. You got a witness?" He scanned the three of them, as though sizing them up, then his eyes stopped on Henry and his gaze hardened. "You kids see anything?"

"They're mine, Grant," Bob said with exaggerated disapproval. "Go do your own work."

Grant was still looking at Henry. "You see anything?" he asked again.

"Not me," Henry said with a nod toward her. "Catherine."

"Huh." Grant seemed skeptical at that, even suspicious. "Well, I sure hope it's something useful. I'll tell Takira you're looking for her."

He strode away.

Catherine turned to Henry, eyebrows raised. His cheeks were flushed as he watched Grant disappear into a side office.

"You done?" he asked her.

She shook her head. "No, I have to do a sketch—work with a sketch artist, I mean. You know that guy?" she added quietly, though she could tell Bob was listening.

"Sort of."

She raised her eyebrows a little higher.

"I know his daughter," Henry admitted, his voice just as quiet. "Went out with her a couple of days ago."

Bob snorted. Henry gave him an indignant look.

"We went on *one* date. That guy—her dad—*came to the restaurant*. Like he was checking up on us. Kind of killed the mood. I drove her home after that."

Bob chuckled but Andrew was looking at Henry impatiently, his fingers drumming against his jeans. Before anyone else could say anything, a black woman with impossibly lean arms was at the desk.

"So," she said briskly. "Who here has a face in their mind?"

Stupidly, Catherine half raised one hand. Like she was in class or something.

The woman gave her a steely smile. "Well, then. Let's give it a name, shall we?"

———

The two boys sat alone at Bob's desk; he had been called away on some errand or other and Catherine was still with the sketch artist, who had led her down a side hall to a separate office, just as Bob had. Henry was sprawled in a chair dragged from a vacant desk nearby, and Andrew sat in Bob's chair, spinning it in circles. He watched the room blur around him, trying to convince himself that he was calm, that Catherine would be done with the sketch artist soon, that Henry was not about to kill him.

He couldn't shake the feeling that Henry *really* didn't like him, though seeing himself from Henry's perspective, he kind of understood: him coming to Catherine's house, the connection to her . . . attack (his mind skipped around the word *rape* like a crack in a sidewalk). Still, Andrew didn't like how Henry looked at him, with frank suspicion, almost as if he were daring Andrew to comment on it.

Not that Andrew would. He wasn't big on confrontation. It

had taken all his courage to even come to Catherine's house to return her cards and coat, and he had been checking Snapchat and Instagram and even Facebook on his phone as he drove to her house, hoping she would respond and they could do this whole thing a different way.

"So why did the guy give you her coat back?" Henry asked him now, clearly on the same train of thought.

Andrew planted his sneakers on the dirty floor and the chair stopped spinning. Henry was leaning back in his chair as though relaxed, but Andrew could tell his body was coiled, tense.

"He didn't fight me," Andrew said. "I knocked and he opened the door. I was going to ask what had happened, but then I saw the coat on the floor—"

"How'd you know it was hers?"

"It had ruffles. And it was small. I just picked it up and left. I didn't want to stick around."

"So you didn't say anything to him?"

"Not really."

"What does that mean, *not really*?"

"It means not really."

Henry nodded as though he'd just thought of something and sat up in the chair. "So, you're in her year?"

"I'm a freshman."

"What's your major?"

"Not sure yet."

"And you're close by?"

"What?"

"Where you live. You're close?"

"I guess."

"Your parents don't care you bailed at Christmas?"

"I was home for Christmas," Andrew said, not bothering to correct Henry's use of the plural, though he felt his irritation spike. "I left afterward. You want to know my address, too? My middle name?"

To his surprise, Henry let out a short laugh.

"What?" Andrew asked, his face heating up.

"Catherine and I have a thing about middle names."

Andrew paused. "Lane."

"What?"

"That's my middle name. Lane. Andrew Lane Worthington."

"Hang on." Henry dug into his jeans pocket and pulled out his phone. After a moment he let out another short laugh, eyes on his phone screen. "It literally means *road*. There's no, like, other significance to it."

"It was my mom's maiden name."

"Let me check Worthington . . ." Henry tapped his screen. *"By a river,"* he said. "I actually thought it would be something about—"

"Being worthy."

"Yeah. Guess not. Jesus, that's dull. You know what Andrew means?"

Andrew shrugged.

"Manly," Henry read from his phone. "Masculine. Strong. Warrior." He looked up at Andrew, his eyes glinting in amusement, but then it was gone and he said, "Well, my name means

I'm a stubborn ruler of a household who cuts down trees, so there you go."

Despite himself, Andrew's mouth twitched. "What does Catherine's name mean?"

"Catherine Luana Ellers . . . It's like . . . innocent, pure, and happy, and then Ellers means she lives by an alder tree."

"Huh."

"Names, right?" Henry pocketed his phone. "It's fucked up, what happened."

"Yeah."

"I would have punched the guy. I don't know why you didn't."

"Guys," Andrew said quietly.

Henry stared at him.

"Three." Andrew suddenly felt very tired. "There were three guys. That's why I didn't do anything." He ran a hand down his face. He could feel the place where Catherine had hit him like a burn. "I should have, though. I know that."

Henry's shoulders gave a flinching sort of jerk. He was still looking at Andrew, but not as though he actually saw him. Andrew could almost see his mind working, frantic. "You can't tell her," he said. "Not yet, anyway. She's barely—"

"Don't worry," Andrew said. He'd just spotted Catherine walking toward them down the hall, and a sudden, fierce unease swept over him. "I know how to keep a secret, if I need to."

CHAPTER THIRTEEN

Catherine took a seat and the sketch artist—Takira—handed the pencil drawing to Bob, who had just come back to his desk, freeing a cinnamon roll from its sticky plastic wrapping. He took a good long look at the drawing: fringed hair, thin beard, long nose, small eyes. "Eric Russell?" He said it like a question, then bit into the roll, eyes still on the sketch as he chewed.

Takira shrugged and crossed her arms. "You know that's your job. I'm just here for the art and free coffee."

Bob swallowed. "There's only the coffeepot in the side office. The Keurig's broken."

"*Still?*"

Bob gave a grunting noise and went back to examining the sketch. Takira, with one last shake of her head, smiled at Catherine and walked away.

"Does it look like someone?" Catherine asked, a little hopefully. She wasn't at all sure she'd done a good enough job with Takira. But the face on the paper was very close to the one in Catherine's memory. Would that be enough?

Bob shooed Andrew out of his chair, sat down heavily, and pulled it toward the computer, typing quickly, the cinnamon roll just next to the keyboard. Then he leaned back so they could see the screen. "What d'you think?"

The image—from some sort of database, Catherine could see a search bar and multiple tabs—was of a tired-looking man in front of a height column showing him just shy of five-nine. But she'd remembered him looming over her, at least six feet tall. Maybe that had been the fear making her think he was bigger than he was. After all, she was only five-four.

And there was something else—the man on Bob's computer looked . . . well, *better* than the man she remembered encountering. He was clean-shaven, for one, and he seemed younger somehow with no facial hair, his hair combed behind his ears. He almost looked like a college student after a night of partying, and likely closer to a senior than a freshman. Had she seen this exact picture yesterday and dismissed it? She couldn't even remember.

"Is that a recent picture?" she asked.

Bob scrolled down for a moment. "Taken two years ago."

Catherine frowned, trying to see past the extraneous details and focus on the man's features, his eyes, knowing all the while that she was taking too long to answer, that she had to say something—but what if she was wrong again? What if this wasn't the guy at all? Or what if it was, and her uncertainty was a mistake that kept him free?

"I . . . Maybe," she managed. "Yeah, it could be."

Bob shrugged. "Well, he's a sex offender. Originally from

Montana. I know him because my job a lot of the time is to respond to calls from local community centers. Rec center, library, the pool. And . . . we've had some complaints."

"He watches porn in public places," Andrew translated, downing the rest of his coffee.

Bob shot him a glare. "We *do not* provide details like that to the public."

"Right," Andrew said blandly.

"Anyway," Bob continued, "this is someone we'd be talking to regardless, since he's local with a record. But this is helpful," he added, looking at Catherine directly, "hearing that he might have had contact with the victim. How positive are you on the ID?"

I'm not.

"Seventy-five percent," she decided.

Bob gave her an appraising look and handed her a sticky note. "Jot down your contact information for me: full name, address, email, and a good phone number for you. I may call you in again, depending on how it goes with Mr. Russell here, if he's able to provide an alibi. Course we're still waiting on time of death for that, but from what I've heard the autopsy's already done, so—"

Amy scalpel cold stripped

"—once we get the report we can start narrowing down our window. You okay with maybe giving a statement? How old are you?"

"Eighteen."

Bob nodded. "That makes it easier." He took her details from her. "I appreciate you all coming in. I know this is . . ." He paused, scanning the room, his eyes settling on a small unlit Christmas tree on another officer's desk some distance away. "Right after the holiday. Jesus Christ." He took another bite of the roll.

Andrew cleared his throat and Bob looked at him.

"Who else are you looking into?" Andrew asked him. "If you can say."

"I can't," Bob replied, his easy grin back in place as he chewed.

Andrew seemed to be considering something. "I can tell Minda you keep chocolate-covered pretzels in the pantry behind the paper towels," he said.

"Pretty sure she already knows," Bob said mildly, swallowing the last of the roll before eyeing them all in turn. "Listen, I know you want to help. It's been tough, this one, and it's going to keep being tough." He looked just at Catherine. "I have your information and we'll keep this sketch on hand. But for now, go home. Be kids, for God's sake. You all eighteen?"

They nodded.

"Enjoy being kids," he said, standing up, telling them kindly but in no uncertain terms they were dismissed. "It's almost over."

———

When they reached the lobby, Catherine shrugged on her jacket. Outside the window, it was raining again and it looked freezing.

She saw the day stretch out ahead of her, completely, terrifyingly empty, just that endless sound of the winter rain pounding down against her ears. It made her want to scream.

But it also made her want to do something to fill that time.

She remembered what she'd promised herself at the church gathering. She was going to do something. Hell, she'd *already* done something. The sketch. A possible suspect. Small steps that led away from that nothing-emptiness that threatened to drown her. She just had to keep taking those steps. Keep holding her head above the surface.

She turned to Andrew. "What's your plan?"

Andrew looked taken aback. "Sorry?"

"Your plan," she said again. "Are you leaving?"

"Leaving?"

"Going home."

Andrew blinked. "I don't know. I guess so."

"Don't."

Henry shot her a look. She ignored it.

"You need to stay. At least a few more days. See if the sketch comes to anything. You're a direct line to this, the investigation, whatever you want to call it. I think you can help."

Andrew looked uncomfortable at that. "Bob has your info. He'll contact you."

"And what if he doesn't? What if the sketch isn't right or Russell's not the guy? You need to stay—in case something else comes up."

Henry was looking at her as though she'd lost her mind, but

she fixed him with a glare. "What?" she said. "What's a few more days?"

Henry shook his head and shoved his hands in his pockets, his body rigid with tension. Then it seemed to slip away from him, all at once; she watched as he cast his eyes to the ceiling and began rocking on the balls of his feet, his expression cool and contemplative. As though he were half awake, the rest of him in a dream.

"Henry?" she asked.

Because he had that look she remembered, back when they'd been inseparable: late-night sneak-outs at nine years old and ding-dong-ditch at eleven, that wicked smile when they turned fourteen. Broken rules and no regret and let's-do-it-why-not-don't-you-trust-me and she'd never been able to give him an answer, so instead she went. Every time.

"I have a suspect too," he said.

CHAPTER FOURTEEN

They sat in Henry's car in the police station parking lot, heat streaming from the vents and turning their cheeks pink. Henry and Catherine were in the front, Andrew in the back, leaning forward, looking curiously between the two of them as they argued.

"You're insane," Catherine told him. *"Insane."*

"Oh, come on," Henry retorted. "Just hear me out. All I said was the name and you're freaking out."

"I'm not freaking out. It just makes no sense."

"Why not?"

Catherine let out an irritated breath and sat back in the passenger seat. "Because John Pechman is hardly an ax murderer. He's a *pastor*."

"Yeah, and religious leaders never do anything bad. Also, she was strangled, not ax-murdered."

"Why does that matter?"

"Because strangulation is, like, intimate. Though admittedly ax-murdering probably is too. But—and, Catherine, stop me if I'm upsetting you—it's a crime of passion, or whatever they call it. The person had to know her. And Pechman knew Amy."

"Yes, but not *well.*"

"Actually, he did," Henry countered. "She was around more and more lately, baking and even advertising. She had these little business cards and everything. I know it was working out for her too, because she was always super happy when she was at the church. People just complimenting her all the time. She'd do the food for free and then if anyone wanted extra, she sold it at a discount. Luring them in. Jesus, sorry."

Catherine had taken her hand from one of the vents to wipe her eyes. "Fine," she said, a little fiercely. "I know about the church baking stuff. But still. Why would he kill her? Do you think he was . . . ?" She trailed off, unable to finish, remembering her mother's disapproving look at Pechman's back, her father's words.

Let's just say your mother was happy when you finished Sunday school.

"I don't know," Henry said. "If anything was happening . . . I mean, I never saw. But I did notice that he . . . well, he paid attention to her. I know that sounds stupid. I mean, she was there, right? But I did see him hanging around her a lot. Thanking her for everything. He even was trying to talk her into doing the Easter play next year."

"Amy wouldn't have done it," Catherine said immediately. Amy had once told her about her first and only drama production, back in elementary school: *Alice in Wonderland.* She'd thrown up all over this kid—Billy or Bobby or Brett—dressed as the White Rabbit and all that came up was this red Kool-Aid she'd had beforehand. "I looked like I'd murdered a bunny," she'd told Catherine. "Never again."

"Yeah, but he wanted her to," Henry continued. "Kept talking about how she'd get over her stage fright, he'd help her . . ." His voice trailed off. "And then Ken Itoh left."

Catherine sat up a little straighter. If anyone would know the details, it would be Henry. His family had always been more involved in First Faith than her own. If she remembered correctly, a good portion of their money—Henry's mother's inheritance from a long-dead relative in France—went to the church.

"My mom is crazy religious," Henry had confided in her years ago. "Or just crazy. I can't decide. But she gives so much money to the church it's like she personally killed Jesus herself and is trying to make up for it."

"So what did happen with Ken Itoh?" Catherine asked Henry now. "My parents were talking about it and then they wouldn't say any more. Said it was gossip."

"It is gossip," Henry said. "But it's also true."

Catherine turned to Andrew, who she realized had not said a word since they'd gotten into the car. "Your neighborhood this interesting?" she asked, chancing a smile, not wanting him to be left out.

Andrew gave her a thin smile in return, as though he knew exactly what she was trying to do. "There's this girl who lives next to us who plays her piano at night. It's super loud. My mom says she's going to complain, but she never will."

"Yeah, this was way more than that," Henry said, and to his credit, angled his body a little bit so he wasn't just facing Catherine. "Ken Itoh was like, second-in-command or whatever. They said he was going to take over First Faith whenever Pechman decided to retire. Ken was doing more sermons and there was this rumor going around that people liked his stuff more than Pechman's. Ken's younger, cooler, wears skinny jeans and has an earring. His wife's like this hot doctor and Pechman's isn't. Sorry."

Catherine waved a hand. "How does Amy come into it?"

"I'm getting to that," Henry said, and when he resumed the story, his voice was a little lower, confidential, as though he was afraid of being overheard. "A few weeks ago, Ken Itoh said at the end of his sermon that he had an announcement. He played it up a ton, stalling, I think. Like, *This has been a hard decision* and *after much prayer*. On and on. Eventually he admitted he was moving to another church. And not just that. He was moving out of town. And there wasn't a reason. Like, his wife got a new job there or, I don't know, school systems for their kids or whatever. He just said that it was a hard decision but he thought it was the right one and God was calling him somewhere else."

Andrew was frowning, looking almost disappointed. "I . . . still don't see it. A pastor left a church. This is murder we're talking about here."

"Well, give me a second," said Henry, with a touch of impatience. He seemed a little disappointed at their lack of enthusiasm. "Because I went to Ken Itoh's office after the service."

"You followed him?" Andrew asked.

"Stubborn," Catherine muttered.

"Enduring," Henry corrected her. "Anyway, he was in his office. His wife was with him. They were—well, not arguing, but they were talking loud enough that I could hear what they were saying through the door. Well, most of it. She was harder to hear, but he was pissed and not, like, yelling, but—"

"What were they saying?" Catherine cut in.

Henry took a deep breath. "She was saying something like, 'I'm not happy about this, Ken, not happy at all.' And he said, 'It's done, Danielle, I'm not talking about it anymore. I'm out. All of us are. It's done.' Then she said something about how she hadn't wanted him to tell the congregation this Sunday but wait until things had cooled down. And then that's when it got more heated and I could hear it more clearly. 'Cooled down, Danielle? Cooled down? You think something like this will just blow over?' Then she said, 'Not necessarily, but after some time, he might see'—I think she said, like, 'the error of his ways.' And then Ken kind of laughed but not like a funny laugh and said, 'I can't believe I even have to tell you this, how serious this is. How it would destroy the church. How many other churches has the same thing destroyed? And all the while John wants me to pretend it never happened.'"

"Sex abuse," Catherine said faintly, and even Andrew looked unnerved. "That whole thing, about the other churches . . ."

"Yeah," Henry said, looking much more encouraged now. "I told you I'd get there. Anyway, then Ken started saying something about how he wanted to get out before it got bad and everyone found out. Danielle asked him if he really thought it would get that far—and that's when he mentioned maybe going to a lawyer."

Catherine's heart was beating hard. "If John Pechman was . . . was abusing kids and Ken talked to a lawyer about it . . ."

But Andrew was shaking his head. "No way. You don't go to a lawyer with something like that. You go to the cops."

"But it doesn't sound like Ken knew it for a fact," Catherine said. "From what Henry overheard, it sounds like Ken strongly suspected but didn't have any way to prove it."

"Exactly," Henry said. "People like Ken, but he's only been here a few years. There's no way he could make an accusation like that without hard evidence. It would be like accusing, I don't know, Mr. Rogers of torturing animals. No one would—"

Catherine suddenly sat up, remembering something. "Amy didn't deliver bread to the church this year!"

The two boys stared at her.

"I heard Pechman say that. Said maybe she'd spread herself too thin or something—*but Amy's dad is a lawyer*. What if Ken went to him for, like, general legal advice, and he admitted he thought something shady was going on with Pechman? And that's why Amy skipped the church this year? Because her dad told her to?"

"But why wouldn't *Mr. Porter* go to the cops?" Andrew countered. "Child sex abuse? And his kid was in the church?"

"I don't think Ken would tell Mr. Porter everything he knew,"

Henry said slowly. "Maybe he just went to him to get some contacts, or he asked how to go about protecting himself legally, and Evan realized something was going on in the church. Actually, now you mention it, I haven't seen the Porters around the church as much the last few weeks."

"But Pechman is doing the funeral," Catherine pointed out. "Mr. Porter would never allow that if he thought Pechman had something to do with Amy's death."

Henry shrugged. "I doubt Mr. Porter thinks Pechman actually *did* something to Amy. There's a difference between being cautious and outright accusing someone of a crime."

Catherine thought of her parents, of their shifting discomfort, the gradual way they'd left the church. Not a hard break, nothing dramatic, but those slow backward steps you took when you didn't know for sure. And then there was that scream she'd heard from down the street. The pain in it like the raw edge of something just broken. She couldn't imagine anyone thinking logically through that kind of agony. Couldn't imagine them thinking at all.

"Maybe you could talk to them," Andrew suggested, nodding toward Catherine. "I mean, you've seen Amy's parents since it happened, right?"

"Actually, no," Catherine said, slightly uncomfortable now. "From what I've heard, they don't really want to talk to people right now. And to be honest, we've never been that close."

"But I thought you and Amy—"

"Oh, *Amy* and I were," she said, "but not so much with her

parents. They weren't mean or anything, but I had this, sort of, discretionary fund to keep Amy entertained and we kind of went over it. A lot. All the baking. And I didn't really care how much Amy baked or ate or whatever so sometimes she'd get sick and her mom would tell me off. In a nice way, but still. Like if Amy was sick the next day, I'd wake up to a text from her mom or something." Catherine shrugged. "Plus she always wanted us to get out and do stuff and Amy would just rather stay home and chill out and I thought that was fine. None of this was major stuff. I mean, we got along okay. But still, I would feel weird calling them. And I definitely wouldn't want to ask them who they think killed Amy."

"Why did Amy get sick?" Andrew asked.

"She had a weak stomach. Maybe lactose intolerance or something, we weren't sure. Points for irony. She'd always tell me this story of a chef she'd heard about who was allergic to spices and would break out in hives just using, like, black pepper. She said it could be worse."

Andrew turned back to Henry. "So that's why you think Pechman killed Amy? Because he was abusing her?"

"I think it's possible, yeah."

The car fell silent. Catherine looked past Henry, out the driver's-side window. It offered a long view of the land: the misty gray-green edges of the trees, mountains stretching into the sky, their tops white. The winter sunlight was brittle in its intensity. It shot against her eyes through the glass.

"She would have told me," she said. "I would have known."

But Henry just gave her a strange look, and she knew what he was thinking.

Did you tell her? Did you tell me? Did she know? Did I?

Her thoughts must have shown on her face because Henry spoke quickly, as though to soothe her. "It might not have been that. She might not have been a victim. Maybe she was—I don't know—a witness. Maybe she just saw something, overheard something. Something she didn't even understand at the time but Pechman knew she'd seen or heard something, and he just got more and more nervous, wondering if she'd figure it out and tell someone." Henry paused as though considering something. "And you know, it might not have even been Pechman that did it. Pechman knows everyone in town. It could have been . . . I don't know, someone else on his orders. Maybe he didn't want to get his hands dirty. Maybe they weren't supposed to even kill her, just talk to her alone, find out what she knew. And then they found out that she did know something and it got out of hand. But you said"—he turned to Andrew at this—"that Bob said she was strangled, right?"

Andrew nodded.

"Well," said Henry, with that touch of impatience again, "can you think of a better way to silence someone?"

CHAPTER FIFTEEN

That night, she dreamt of Amy.

It wasn't the first time. She'd had, on occasion, rather ludicrous dreams involving Amy and some baking mishap: They were making a cake only to open the oven and find it full of flour that poured out and turned to snow that melted all over the hardwood just as Amy's mother got home. Or she'd somehow allowed Amy to eat three gallons of Cold Stone ice cream and Amy vomited blue remnants of cotton candy flavor while Gordon Ramsay scolded them both over a recording system.

But this dream was different: She was sitting up in bed with the sheets folded neatly to her waist, covering her legs. She stared straight ahead as though waiting for something. The clock read eleven at night. She watched the red numbers, waiting for the clock to change, to read 11:01, but then there was a scratching sound and she turned only her head to the left, her palms soft and flat against the coverlet.

A tree was scraping one thin branch down the pane, reaching the bottom only to rise up again, making a thin, reedy noise that roused her from bed like an alarm. She stepped with bare feet onto the floor and walked over to the window, watching the tree move slowly up and down, almost keening now, and she reached out a hand as though to ward it off. But the moment her fingers touched the cool glass, the spindly branch froze, thickening and lightening, becoming something altogether different: an arm locked at the elbow, a small palm flat against the glass.

"Let me in!" A face hovered beyond the arm outside her window. Too white to be real, long and ghostly. More air than substance, but the voice was true. "Please, let me in!"

"No," Catherine said. She took her own hand from the window. "No, I will not!"

"Please," the voice begged. The face was ghastly, stretched, the eyes so dark they were like holes against a backdrop of skeletal branches. "Please. I lost my way in the trees but I found it! I found you! Please, *let me in*."

The hand began to scramble at the window, pulling it up. Catherine tried to wrench the window back down, a low wail coming from her throat but nothing more because she couldn't scream. Finally, the ghost managed to thrust its hand through the narrow gap it had made and grasped Catherine's wrist.

She felt as though she had been stabbed through with a knife. She cried out, twisting, but the scalpel-like fingers were clawing, drawing blood that burned its way down her skin.

"Let me go," she begged. *"Let me go!"*

"Cathy," the face behind the window said. "You have to look."

The face was solidifying somehow, becoming human. Familiar.

Blood dripped down Catherine's arm. The girl hanging in midair amid the trees began to fade back into them.

"No," Catherine breathed. "No."

"Look," a ghostly Amy told her. *"Look."*

Catherine woke up gasping, her hand at her chest, sucking in air as though she'd been drowning. She wiped her face and got out of bed, moving toward the window. The scene outside reminded her of a body: the bones of branches and land that stretched across the earth like a layer of skin. She put a hand to the window, staring at the glass very hard, wondering if she was imagining the marks on it. She shivered and pulled her nightgown around herself. When she turned to look at the clock, she saw it was just past two in the morning.

—

Andrew's sleep, though free of nightmares, was hardly restful. He spent most of the night twisting under heavy blankets in the guest bedroom of Bob and Minda's house, his window facing the overgrown front yard and mailbox, slightly tilted, from that time Minda had been late to work and backed down the driveway too quickly.

"I am a gastroenterologist," she'd told Bob with a solemn air through the car window as he rubbed his eyes. "If I'm late for a Crohn's patient in a flare, you have no idea the cleanup involved."

That had been when Andrew had stayed with them this past summer, interning at the police station, which had been a surprisingly relaxed job. Mainly Andrew delivered things—memos in manila envelopes, bad black coffee, sometimes handwritten witness statements, which would have been interesting to read if Andrew could have deciphered them. But he hadn't minded; it wasn't the worst way to spend five hours a day. He had wished at the time for more excitement, for Bob to be a higher-up officer who did more than respond to library calls and traffic accidents.

Now he wished he hadn't.

U okay?

A text from his mom flashed on his phone. Six in the morning and she was already texting him, half her words always abbreviated to letters.

How r things?

Andrew sighed and typed a response.

Fine

I'll be home for New Years.

Minda says u r helping Bob. U can stay as long as u like.

Good experience.

Andrew turned on the lamp and in the mirror he could see his reflection. Not clearly in the dim light, but enough to know he looked sick. He felt a little sick too, but that wasn't surprising. He'd been feeling sick for a week now, ever since that night in the dorm.

Looking back, it felt like a dream he remembered just enough to know it was a nightmare: seeing Catherine frozen in place, one hand at a closed door, her eyes dazed under the glare of the hallway lights, so pale she seemed translucent. Black makeup under her eyes. The tag of her dress at her throat.

He'd told himself it wasn't real. That she wasn't real. But then he went to her and she ran from him and he took one step down the hallway after her, and another. His feet were bare, the tiles cool on his skin, and wet. He stopped, lifted one foot, and looked at the underside, swiped his hand across his skin. It came away dark at the fingertips. He turned and looked back at the door she had been standing against: four or five droplets of blood against the pale tile, and a smeared half footprint that was his own.

That was when he knew it was not a dream. What had happened to her was as real as her blood on his skin, copper-smelling and slick. It made his own blood pound inside him and when he knocked on the door she'd come out of, it was with a profound and terrible guilt, as though he had been the one to make her bleed.

Andrew pressed the heels of his hands into his eyes for a long moment, then released them, blinking as the sun came up gold outside the guest room window and the trees cast long black shadows in protest.

———

When Catherine walked downstairs, her parents were waiting in the kitchen, her mother wrapping a shawl around her shoulders, her bleary-eyed father drinking coffee.

"You look nice," he said when she came down the stairs.

"Thanks." She pulled her hair from the collar of her dress and shifted her feet. It had felt strange, getting dressed to go to the Sunday-morning service. "Henry says they still have those donuts afterward."

Her mother's mouth softened. "You've been spending quite a bit of time with him."

"Who?"

"Henry."

"We're friends."

"You two," her mother said, "were never friends."

Baffled, Catherine stared at her. "We were friends for *years*."

"I wouldn't call it friendship, what you two had."

"What would you call it, then?"

Her mother shook her head. "I don't know. I don't have a word for—"

"*Shouganai*," her father said.

They both turned to look at him.

"It's Japanese," he said, his eyes focused on a point just beyond Catherine's shoulder. "It means *it cannot be helped*. I used to think that, looking at you and Henry. As though I was looking at something inevitable."

Her mother rolled her eyes and plucked his coffee mug from his hands. "This happens every time he does his Japanese unit with his students. Comes home with all these unpronounceable words that don't translate to English."

"*Yugen*," he continued, even as Catherine's mother began rinsing the mug over a loud stream of water. "The profound, mysterious sense of—"

But Catherine didn't hear the rest. The sound of the water had raised goose bumps on the back of her arms, made her swallow as she remembered that cup thrust into her hands, that one mouthful of warm tap water.

The water shut off. She blinked. "We should go," she said finally, pretending to look at the clock on the stove. "We're going to be late."

—

She spotted Henry almost as soon as she got out of the car in the church parking lot. He was standing on the steps before the large wooden doors, talking to his parents. Bracing herself, Catherine walked toward them, her parents flanking her, and when she reached Henry and his parents, he took her hand briefly, as though to steady her.

What word had her dad used? She couldn't remember it now.

Cultural appropriation, she thought sternly. *That was the word for it. He was just being dumb. Forget it.*

But still—

What did it mean, that translation? *It cannot be helped?*

She turned from Henry to his parents, who were greeting hers. Henry had gotten most of his looks from his mother, and just enough of his father's height to top out at five-nine. His mother had delicate features and a full mouth; his father was taller, with graying blond hair and dark eyes.

"Hello," Catherine said, nodding her head so low it was almost a bow.

"And to you." Henry's mother was wearing a dress of deep purple, her short blond hair cropped close around her fine-featured face. She was eyeing Catherine with a smile so insincere it seemed like an insult to her intelligence. "You look well."

"Thank you."

Henry's mother gave a deep sigh and turned to her husband. "It's quite cold, should we . . . ?" And without waiting for a response, she joined a group of people making their way through one of the tall doors.

Henry turned to Catherine. "Is Andrew coming?"

"I texted him. Maybe he's late?" She turned and looked across the parking lot.

"I don't see him," Henry said, scanning over her head. "Should we . . . ?"

She nodded and they followed their parents into the church. It looked almost exactly as Catherine remembered: everything brown and wooden, the ceiling impossibly high, stiff-looking pews and impressive stained-glass windows. The sun shone through them now, casting splashes of scarlet and gold and navy across the aisles.

"So what is the plan, exactly?" she asked in a low voice.

"We go to church," Henry said. "You try not to burst into flames—"

"And you try not to be so—I don't know—sanctimonious."

"There she is, Ms. Four-Year College."

"Shut up."

He grinned, then lowered his voice even more. "Joking aside? Basically, we just watch out for Pechman."

"Watch out for what, exactly?"

They began to file into a pew on the right-hand side, after their parents.

"Anything," he said as they took their seats. He reached for a Bible in the little built-in shelf at the back of each pew and opened it to the front to find a yellow brochure. "Today's program," he said. "Here."

She took it from him and glanced at the sermon message, which was in the middle of the front page, below the church's logo: First Faith, with a dove pictured between the words, an olive branch in its beak.

Sunday, December 29, 2019

MESSAGE
Life in Death, Faith in Christ

VERSES
1 Thessalonians 4:13–14
Brothers and sisters, we do not want
you to be uninformed

> *about those who sleep in death,*
> *so that you do not grieve like the rest*
> *of mankind, who have no hope.*
> *For we believe that Jesus died and rose again,*
> *and so we believe that God will bring with Jesus*
> *those who have fallen asleep in Him.*

John 5:28–29a

> *Do not be amazed at this, for a time is coming*
> *when all who are in their graves*
> *will hear His voice*
> *and come out.*

An image came to Catherine's mind then, of a hand at her window, Amy's voice, horribly distorted, begging to be let in.

She thrust the program back at Henry, who took it just as John Pechman came into view.

He entered from a small door set to the side, near the musicians (piano and flute and violin), and began to walk toward the podium. His eyes were alight behind wire glasses, his suit jacket dark, his shoes unshined, and Catherine took all this in with Amy's words reverberating in her head like the violin strings under the bow.

You have to look.

I am, she thought back, gripping her phone so tightly the screen flashed on, the time glowing in white numbers. *Amy, I'm looking as hard as I can.*

The trouble was, as Pechman began talking to the congregation, kind and slow and thoughtful, Catherine thought of the
cut she'd given Andrew, of a ghost talking to her behind glass,
and wondered if she could trust her suspicions at all. If they
were justified, or if they were merely the products of nightmares,
both real and imagined.

CHAPTER SIXTEEN

The donuts were better than she remembered.

Catherine held hers with a napkin as she chewed. Had she and Amy ever tried to make donuts? No, she remembered. You needed a special pan for that, and Albertsons hadn't sold them.

"So," Henry asked her. "What do you think?"

"Really good." She wiped her mouth with her free hand.

"Great," Henry said, deadpan, taking a sip of his coffee. "But I was asking about something else."

"Someone else, you mean," she said, scanning the room. It was just before noon, and the service had gotten out ten minutes ago. They were in the attached reception hall again, but this time the atmosphere was brighter, the smell of fried dough warming up the cold room. Fifty or so people milled around, some hanging up their coats in the closet by the bathrooms, which already had a short line spilling out the door marked WOMEN. Her mom was in the line, talking to Henry's mother, who was stamping one foot as though it had fallen asleep. Her father was getting coffee—eyeing the various coffee pod flavors on a spin display with some distrust—while Henry's dad was talking to a group of men by the tall windows. As Catherine watched, Pechman walked over and began talking to Henry's father. She couldn't hear what he said, but it was followed by good-natured laughter that made its way around the group.

"The sermon was okay," she said finally, turning back to Henry. "I didn't spot any red flags. Or a confession."

"Well, it was about death."

"*For a time is coming when all who are in their graves will come out,*" she said. Henry stared at her. She shook her head. "I had a nightmare last night."

He said nothing.

"A bad dream," she added.

"And you said you didn't think I was an idiot for going to Falls." But his voice held no rancor. "I know what a nightmare is. I even know its etymology."

"You do not," Catherine said, wondering vaguely if he had been hanging out with her father.

"It comes from this Latin word that means, *One who lies down with the sleeper.*" He drank more of his black coffee.

"Now you're just showing off."

"Of course I am."

She swallowed another bite of her donut. "*One who lies down with the sleeper.* That doesn't even make sense."

"It does, sort of. Like there's a monster—an evil spirit—who comes when you're sleeping and causes the nightmare."

"How?"

"I don't know."

"That's helpful."

Henry raised his eyebrows at her and she flushed and looked away.

She spotted Pechman walking across the room, toward the donuts, and she moved back, closer to the wall. Henry followed her.

"Sorry," she said shortly.

"It's fine."

"Amy was at my window," she said. "Begging me to let her in. I didn't. I left her outside. That was my nightmare."

"Jesus."

She gave a short, brittle laugh. "Isn't he the one who's supposed to awaken everyone? Sounds more like the zombie apocalypse to me."

"Actually, we don't start on the zombie apocalypse until the new year," Pechman said.

He was a foot from her, smiling down with a donut in hand. He'd used a napkin too.

"She was joking," Henry said.

Dimly, Catherine nodded. She wanted to say something but found she couldn't speak. The glare from the windows seemed far away, the room stretching and narrowing, goose bumps erupting under the coat she hadn't taken off. She remembered shoving the coat Andrew had brought her into the trash last night after the nightmare, under the bags of wrapping and ribbon and Christmas leftovers, stuffing it down and slamming the lid. Freezing in her bare feet in the garage, sobbing bitter, furious tears, her mind so full of Amy it was as though nothing else existed.

Catherine forced herself to meet John Pechman's eyes. "I actually liked it." Her voice was shaking a little but otherwise almost normal. "How it was about hope, and everything."

"Well, I'm glad that part came through at least." He was still smiling. "And I have to say, I'm glad to see you and your parents at the service this morning."

"Yes." And then, with no intention of saying it: "We're actually thinking of getting back into it. The church, I mean."

"Wonderful!" Pechman chewed his donut thoughtfully. "You know, it's been a difficult time. But I think life's challenges . . . they can do good. That's what I was trying to get at today. *Hope.* Though of course zombies shouldn't be ignored."

Henry looked awkward and drank more of his coffee.

"Can you get me some?" Catherine asked him.

"What?"

"Coffee." She pointed to his cup. "Get yourself some more and a cup for me. Tons of creamer," she added pointedly, and he walked away, a little bemused.

"So does that mean you'll be staying in town?" Pechman asked her. "I was under the impression you were at college."

"I might be staying." *I'm letting you in, Amy. Help me here.* "I was thinking about getting more involved with the church. I know Amy—knew her. She used to bake. I could help take over with that. I baked a lot. With her." Her heart was beating hard, almost painful. She felt the donut she'd eaten like lead just below it.

Pechman looked at her pityingly. "Are you involved with the funeral?"

"I . . . No. I hadn't heard . . ."

"It's Thursday the second." He pulled out a slim navy planner from inside his suit jacket pocket and flipped a few pages. "Wanted to wait until after the new year. If you're interested, you are more than welcome to assist. I know you and Amy were close. She talked about you quite a bit."

"She did?" Her voice went stupidly high, stupidly grateful.

He nodded. "I'm so sorry for your loss. What happened to Amy . . . we have all lost something, in losing her."

Catherine felt her eyes burn. "I can help," she said, desperate to cut him off.

He gave her another kind if patronizing look, then glanced back at his planner.

She took the opportunity to see if Henry was coming back, almost wanting him to. But no—Henry was still by the coffee-maker, talking to James, who clapped him on the shoulder.

"There's a meeting Wednesday to finalize some of the de-tails," Pechman said. "New Year's, so not ideal, but early enough that you'll be home for dinner. It's at three. We'll have pizza. You can bring some ideas for food for the funeral, and the recep-tion afterward, at the Porters'. I know we already have some vol-unteers bringing hors d'oeuvres—little sandwiches, things like that—but you can never have enough food, I say." He pocketed the planner. "We'll see you there, then?"

Henry was coming back, two coffees in hand. She took hers as

Pechman gave her one last smile and walked away. She watched him go, then took a large swallow of coffee, which scalded its way down her throat.

"Careful," Henry told her. "Hey, look."

She followed his gaze. Andrew had just walked into the reception hall, shaking his dark hair out of his eyes and looking self-conscious.

"Go get him," Catherine said. "I'll be right back."

And before Henry could say another word, she darted down the hall with the bathrooms, turned a corner, and disappeared.

—

The thermostat for the reception hall was exactly where it had been ten years ago. But it had been a yellowed spin-dial then, and this new one was white and square and digital. Mounted on the wall at face height around the corner from the bathrooms, it currently read sixty-seven degrees. She and Henry had once tried to lower it, her sitting on Henry's shoulders to reach—in an attempt to make it snow inside, which somehow made a kind of sense at eight—before their parents caught them and took them home, no donuts at all.

She shot a glance left and right, saw no one, and, coffee still in hand, used her free one to stab at the UP arrow until the thermostat maxed out at ninety.

Then she walked as normally as she could back to the hall.

—

Henry and Andrew were still standing by the door. Catherine grabbed at the handle to make sure it was closed firmly, then turned back around to face their curious stares.

"I have a plan," she said unhelpfully.

"Care to share?" Henry asked.

"No." She turned to Andrew. "Where were you?"

"Late. Sorry. I'm here now," he added at the look on her face. The small cut on his cheek was healing, scabbed over and small. She averted her eyes.

"Why'd you send me away when you were with Pechman?" Henry asked her.

"I wanted to talk to him."

"About what?"

"Things." She walked away and came back a moment later with two donuts. She shoved them at Andrew, who looked dead on his feet. "Eat before you pass out."

"Thanks." Andrew took the donuts and, to her surprise, ate them hungrily. "So, what are we doing?" he asked, his voice slightly muffled.

"Waiting."

"For what?"

Across the room, a large woman walked over to the closet by the bathrooms to hang up her heavy fur coat.

"That," said Catherine softly.

It took fifteen minutes for the room to warm up a little, another five before people started to notice, edging away from the windows and shrugging off their coats, but it was another ten, just as the reception was winding down and people were starting to leave, before those remaining—about half—began to wonder aloud if the room was supposed to be *quite* so warm.

Henry's mother began to complain and Henry said she and his dad could leave and he'd catch a ride with Catherine's family. But then Catherine's parents came up, asking if she was about ready to go, and thankfully Andrew chimed in, introducing himself as a friend of Catherine's from school, saying he'd give Henry and Catherine a ride back. Her mother looked quickly to her at that, but Catherine smiled reassuringly, and her mother's face relaxed a little.

The four adults left just as John Pechman pulled off his suit jacket and walked down the hall to check the thermostat.

As though she'd just heard a starting pistol, Catherine shot forward. There was a general commotion in the hall as people wondered about the temperature and others began to make their way to the front doors. No one noticed as she took the suit jacket off the chair and walked to the coat closet on the pretense of hanging it up. At the last second, she ducked into the women's bathroom, which thankfully had no line now, though one of the three stalls was occupied.

Catherine ducked into an empty stall, slammed the lock right, and grappled furiously for the planner. It was slim, with white pages and navy lines the same exact shade as the cover, each week spread over two opposite pages. John Pechman had very neat writing and a penchant for abbreviations. No names but initials, and times were always written on the left without a.m. or p.m. For this Wednesday he'd written: *3–4/5, fun. plan, order 2 lg pizzas.*

Funeral—the stall next to hers flushed and she jumped—*fun.* was funeral.

But then something else caught her eye, something added with an arrow, the handwriting just a little cramped in the margin, the arrow pointing to just above the Wednesday meeting.

12 K.I.

She shut the planner, stuffing it back into the inner pocket of the jacket. She had walked out of the stall, intending to hurry past the sink, when someone called out to her.

She froze, heart in her throat, and turned to see a young girl coming out of the other stall. It took a moment for Catherine to place her; then she realized:

Hannah Walsh.

Amy's best friend.

"Hi," Catherine said automatically. "Hannah. Hi."

Hannah looked at her glumly, then walked to the sink and began to wash her hands. "This is the worst Christmas of my life," she said. "Including that time I got an ear infection and had to get a shot in my butt because it hurt so bad."

Catherine didn't know what to say to that. She didn't have a rapport with Hannah the way she'd had with Amy. Sure, Catherine had taken Amy over to the Walshes' several times for playdates, and Hannah had been over to the Porters' house almost as much, but Catherine had never had a conversation with Hannah without Amy in the same room.

Hannah turned and grabbed a paper towel, wiping her hands dry with unnecessary vigor. She had brown hair that was lighter than Amy's. Her nose was tiny, her skin poreless and childlike. In fact, Catherine was struck by how *young* Hannah looked: short and thin, wearing a blue dress and white tights, her skin completely bare of any makeup.

Twelve years old, Catherine thought, and something wild rose up inside her. She fought it back, even as her mind whirled with a sudden rage. She thought if Amy's killer were here, in this bathroom, she could kill him—*would* kill him—and it wouldn't even be hard.

"Amy was in my dream last night," she told Hannah, trying to recover from this sudden insanity, trying to say something that might help. "I—I think about her all the time, too."

Hannah shoved the paper towels in the trash can. "I hate church. I didn't even want to come today."

"Me either," Catherine admitted.

Hannah shuffled her feet, then toed the trash can with one shiny black shoe. "I used to come here with Amy. It's no fun without her."

Catherine said nothing.

"And Matt didn't even have to come. *He's* sick, so he gets to stay home." She glared up at Catherine. "He's not even really sick."

"Oh," Catherine managed, because Hannah was looking expectant now, and angry. "Well, maybe—"

"He's *not* sick. He's just crying. I heard him. Crying like a girl. But he's not a girl. *I'm* a girl. Amy's a girl. Or was. Or is. I don't even know. It doesn't matter. But *I* want to cry. I want to cry *at home*. In my *own bed*. *Not* at church. I want *Amy back* but Amy's not *coming back* and those donuts *suck* and I *hate* this, all of this—*I hate it!*"

She struck out at the trash can. For such a small child she had a lot of force behind her kick. The tall metal trash can tipped, then fell, crashing onto the tile with a bang that rattled the mirror. A half dozen paper towels spilled out of the hole in the top, and Hannah stomped on each one before she left the bathroom.

CHAPTER SEVENTEEN

Catherine stood in the bathroom for a solid thirty seconds before something seemed to snap back into place in her mind. She bent down, righted the trash can, and picked up the spilled paper towels. Then she walked out into the hallway.

She'd taken maybe three steps from the bathroom door when she caught a sudden movement to her right and turned to see John Pechman striding toward her.

I can't.

You can. You have to.

"Oh, good." She found herself walking to meet him, her heart a drum inside her that she was sure he could hear. "Someone told me to hang this up for you. Here."

She handed the suit jacket to him and he took it, looking a little puzzled.

"Or I can still hang it up," she continued, gesturing to the coat closet between the men's and women's bathrooms.

"No, thank you, Catherine." He was sweating a little at the temples and did not put on the jacket. "Thermostat's acting up. I put it back down, turned on the AC, in fact. Should be back to normal soon."

"That's good." She smiled at him and made to walk back

down the hall, but then he continued talking and she had no choice but to turn and face him.

"Yes," he said. "Temperature was up to the max. Perhaps a child, playing games."

She said nothing, forcing her face to remain neutral.

"I believe you did something similar, years ago."

"We tried," she said. "Me and Henry."

"Mischievous, you two were." He gave her a thin smile. "Or are you still?"

She said nothing. Fear was coming like water, lapping at her ankles, bitterly cold. She tried to open her mouth to speak, but he cut her off.

"Well, I'll see you Wednesday, shall I?" He nodded at her before walking past, the suit jacket in his hands brushing her arm as he went.

———

Five minutes later, all three of them were in Andrew's car, the leather seats freezing even as Andrew turned up the heat.

"Don't do that," Henry said, twisting the knob back down. He was in the passenger seat, Catherine in the back middle. "It's just blowing cold air."

"Suit yourself," Andrew said. He turned to look back at Catherine. "Did you do something in there?"

"Yes." She was sitting on the edge of the seat, quite literally, her legs hitting the compartment between the two front seats.

"Care to elaborate?" Henry asked.

She did. She told them about talking to Pechman and upping the thermostat to steal the planner. About Wednesday: the meeting with K.I. at noon.

"And then I ran into Hannah," she finished. "And after her, Pechman. I gave him back his jacket."

"Hannah?" Andrew asked.

"Hannah Walsh," Catherine explained. "Amy's best friend. She kicked over a trash can, she was so upset about Amy."

"Strange," Andrew said.

"It's really not," Catherine said, then paused. "She told me Matt was crying."

"Who?"

"Matt. Her brother. She said he wasn't at church today because he was sick, but she knew he wasn't really sick; she'd heard him crying."

"Younger brother?"

"No, he's a teenager. Sixteen, I think."

Andrew frowned at that. "Was Matt close to Amy?"

"No," Catherine said after a moment. "I don't think so. Whenever we went over to the Walshes' house, Amy only hung out with Hannah. I barely even saw Matt."

"But that was last summer, right?"

Catherine nodded.

"So maybe something—"

But Henry cut him off.

"Can we just focus on one thing at a time here?" His eyes were on Catherine. "You said you ran into Pechman? Did he say anything to you?"

"Like what?"

"Like, about his jacket. Was he suspicious that you had it?"

She didn't answer right away. She was remembering how quickly she'd run into him after leaving the bathroom, how she couldn't be sure he hadn't seen her *leave* the bathroom with his jacket. Had he bought her story? Maybe. But the way he looked at her, spoke to her—*mischievous . . . or are you still?*—it made her wary, like an animal confronted with an unfamiliar scent.

"I don't know," she admitted. "It's hard to get a read on him."

"That's true," Henry agreed. "But . . . Catherine, this is *good*. I mean, you didn't need to do it alone, we could have helped, but still—a meeting with Ken Itoh this Wednesday. That's got to be something."

"Are you sure it's Ken Itoh?" Andrew said.

"Who else would K.I. be?" Henry said. "Odds are, it's him. Especially the arrow thing you mentioned. I wonder . . . like, if right after Ken heard about Amy, he called up Pechman and demanded a meeting. That would explain why it was added, right? Because you said otherwise everything in the planner was really organized."

Catherine nodded. "It stood out. Like it had been added after everything else."

"But where's it going to be?" Andrew asked. "Where are they going to meet? Did it say?"

Catherine shook her head. "No. But neither did the Wednesday-night meeting, and that's going to be at the church."

"But that doesn't necessarily mean he'll meet Ken at the church, does it?" Andrew said.

"No, you're right," Henry agreed. "They could meet . . ." He trailed off. "Actually, there's only a few places."

"Where?" Catherine asked.

"Pechman's house," he said, ticking off a finger. "Or Ken's. The church, obviously—"

"It won't be at Pechman's," Andrew said.

They both turned to look at him.

"What?" he said. He seemed embarrassed. "Okay, you know how I was, like, waiting in the front of the reception hall? I couldn't see you all right away, so I kind of hung out there. . . ."

"Lurking," said Catherine, with some amusement.

"Anyway," he continued, disregarding this, "there's this bulletin board by the front door and I was sort of reading it and there was this bright yellow paper that stood out. *Baby Bible Study*. Wednesdays at eleven a.m. It said something like, *between naptimes. Excessive coffee provided.* You were supposed to email Kathleen Pechman. She runs it. That's why I remembered, because that's his wife, right?"

"But what if the Bible study is at the church?" Catherine asked.

"It's not," Henry chimed in. "Bible studies are almost never at the church. It's not intimate enough or whatever. People host them at their houses. Community building, et cetera." He gave

Andrew an approving look. "Okay, nice. So if Pechman's wife is hosting a bunch of moms and babies at their house an hour before the meeting, it probably isn't going to be there."

"You said Ken Itoh's house too," Catherine reminded him.

Henry shook his head. "Actually, now that I think of it, I don't think he would let Pechman into his home. Not with his kids there."

"Plus, they're trying to move, right?" Andrew said. "So it might be full of boxes."

"Maybe." Catherine was still unsure. "But actually, this meeting could be *anywhere*. Starbucks, or they might grab lunch—"

But Henry was already frowning. "No. Not something like this. Nowhere public. Not where they could be overheard."

"Then maybe they'll drive around in a car and talk."

This time it was Andrew who looked unsure. "I . . . don't know about that. If I were going to meet with someone about something illegal or horrible or whatever, I wouldn't get in a car with them. I'd want more control than that. A way to get out, at least. No, I think it's the church."

"Why?" she asked.

"Because it's his," he said simply. "That bulletin board. I thought it was really interesting. He was all over it. Even his wife's Bible study thing, his email was listed too. His name was on every single flyer, and it's not like he can be a part of all of those things. It was more like he wanted his mark on everything that happened inside the church. Because it's his. All of it."

"I thought you didn't want to be a police officer anymore," Henry said.

"I don't. But that doesn't mean I don't notice things."

Catherine said nothing to that. She was thinking about what Andrew had just said, about the flyers. Pechman's name had been on the soup kitchen one as well. Then she remembered the way Pechman had stood behind the podium just an hour before. She'd had a public speaking class in high school. The teacher had shown them videos of different people talking—presidents and motivational speakers and also speeches gone wrong, meltdowns, and nervous tics—trying to illustrate what was good and what wasn't. What was best, and what was worst.

Pechman was best. He didn't hide behind the podium. He walked around it, in front of it, not pacing nervously, but more casual, his voice never wavering, but not shouting, either. He had a cadence that made you want to listen, even if you didn't necessarily agree with everything he was saying. His tone was measured, polite, but firm, too. It couldn't be clearer that Pechman felt at home at the church, speaking before his congregation, slightly elevated on that stage, a small mic clipped to his lapel. Even at the reception, he milled around and talked to everyone, including her. The only time she saw him flustered was when she'd messed with the temperature. He was an organized man, from church to a pocketbook planner, and as long as things were kept a certain way, he was fine.

Had Amy challenged that order in some way? Turned the

heat up around him until he'd had to find a way to turn it back down again?

Or was the perpetrator someone else? A man from the streets? A teenager just houses away?

Can we just focus on one thing at a time here?

Henry was right. Bob had the sketch of Eric Russell, and Matt Walsh's tears were proof of nothing more than sorrow. Pechman was their suspect right now. If that came to nothing, then they could look elsewhere.

"We have to get into that meeting," she said. "We have to be able to hear what they're saying. Everything. Can we listen outside . . . wherever it's going to be?" She directed this last question toward Henry, who eyed her doubtfully.

"Probably not," he admitted. "If it's in the church, it'll be in Pechman's office, guaranteed. He *loves* that office. I think he's redecorated it three times by now. Anyway, there's no window on the door. Ken's office has one, and that made it easier, but Pechman has this thick door—mahogany or whatever—and I don't think you can eavesdrop through it, especially not if you want to hear everything. Eventually they might argue and yell, but even then . . ."

"What about bugging?" Catherine suggested. "Recording devices."

"Buy *and* learn to use them in three days? And we'd have to get in anyway just to plant the stuff."

"My cousin had a friend who did stuff like that," Andrew

added. "It's expensive—we're talking hundreds, maybe thousands, for something like that, and it's not like in the movies. It's glitchy as hell unless you pay for it not to be."

Henry nodded in agreement. "Exactly. I don't think that'll be the plan."

"But you have one," she said. She was watching him closely, noticing that glint of intelligence behind his blue eyes. She'd seen it before.

"I do," he said. He was watching her just as closely as she was watching him. "But you can say no, if you want."

CHAPTER EIGHTEEN

The plan was this: Pechman's office had no closet, no alcove or wardrobe or anything relatively simple like that. But it did have a large bookcase—with cabinets.

"It's really like two connected bookcases, with these cabinet doors at the bottom," Henry explained. "But when you open them up you see the two cabinets are connected inside to form one bigger area. He stores his old seminary books in there; they're not as nice as the ones he keeps on the shelf for people to see."

"How do you know all this?" Andrew asked, and Catherine didn't need his crossed arms and tense jaw to know he was against every word now coming out of Henry's mouth. It was kind of strange. Andrew struck her as almost meek at times—someone who hovered at church entrances and put on his hazards just to park—but there was something about Henry that seemed to change that.

"Because I've been in his office."

"Why?"

"Because he's writing me a letter of recommendation," Henry said, and then, to Catherine, "No, I don't plan on staying at Falls forever. I do eventually want to go to a four-year school. So Pechman said he'd write me a recommendation and since then I've literally said yes to anything he asks." Henry gave a long-suffering sigh. "I actually put that cabinet together *and* organized the books inside it. By publication date. After this, if you all want to steal the cabinet and burn it in a field or whatever, I'm game." Then his expression became more serious, his eyes traveling up and down her body. Catherine felt her cheeks flush. "I think you could fit," he told her.

"No," Andrew said. "No way."

Henry shot him an irritated look. "Why not?"

"Because you could get her killed. But not only that, how do you even think she'll get in? I'll bet he locks his office, am I right?"

"Sometimes, yeah," Henry admitted. "But I also know where he keeps all the keys, including the master, which can open anything."

"I know what a master key does," Andrew said, and to his credit his voice was calm. "But you said the cabinet was full of old books."

"We'll take them out."

"And put them where?"

Henry waved one hand. "Anywhere. It's a big church."

"When are you going to move them?"

"Before the meeting."

"And if, during this meeting, he decides he wants one of those books?"

"I don't think that'll happen."

"But you don't know."

"No," Henry said. "I don't."

Silence filled the car. The two boys reminded her of animals placed together in a pen—tense, almost combative—but when Catherine spoke, they both moved, following the sound of her voice.

"Can you be sure," she said slowly, "that I'll fit?"

Henry blew out a breath. "You know I said he remodeled his office a bunch of times? Well, Pechman got all his stuff from this place in Seattle. High-end stuff. *Really* high-end. He kept asking people to try out his chair and stuff. *Roche Bobois.*"

Andrew raised his eyebrows. "What?"

"Roche Bobois. We could go and look at the cabinet."

"Assuming they still have it," Andrew pointed out.

"We could call," Catherine said, not quite believing what she was saying. "Before we drive two hours. Call and see if they have it there. And if they're even open on Sundays."

Andrew turned to Henry. "You said it's in his office. Why not try now?"

Henry didn't answer, but Catherine knew what he was thinking and spoke for him.

"Because it's risky. If we get caught now, that ruins our chances for Wednesday. He'd move the meeting. He'd know something was up."

Henry looked at her. "That's why I said you could say no."

But she didn't say no, and Henry called Roche Bobois and described the bookcase, then gave them a thumbs-up and disconnected. Moments later, Andrew was pulling out of the church parking lot and they were on their way to Seattle.

———

It was a quiet drive.

Catherine spent most of it looking out the window at the passing landscape: gray sky and gray roads, the industrial skeletons of bridges over Andrew's car, the steel curving over them like a rib cage. Henry and Andrew spoke cordially to each other in the front seats, talking vaguely about college, majors and classes and professors. Several times, Henry half turned to her, trying to get her to talk, but she didn't really try, and soon enough Henry pulled up Radiolab on his phone, but the most recent episode was about assisted suicide. After a few minutes of it—*digestive tract paralysis . . . feeding tube . . . Switzerland*—Andrew switched on Spotify, and a song she'd never heard before filled the car. She slowly tuned it out.

She felt as though she should be panicking, as though any moment something would snap home in her mind and she'd lean forward and say, "You know what? This is totally crazy and I'm not doing it. Turn around." But minutes and miles passed, over and over, and then they were pulling into a parking lot near Roche Bobois and she still hadn't done it.

They found the cabinet toward the back of the showroom, Henry brushing off eager salespeople as politely but firmly as possible. "Don't want anyone hovering for this," he said, and they both nodded. Catherine realized she hadn't said anything in a while and wanted to comment that it was a good thing they had come on a Sunday, especially so near to closing; there could have been a lot more than the few customers she saw now. But her throat didn't seem to be working.

The showroom was massive, with a lower ceiling than she'd expected, and a generous amount of space between the furniture. It wasn't crowded at all, and the general feeling of the room was that it was trying to promote relaxation, though the effect was tempered somewhat by the furniture itself: leather so shiny it gleamed, couches too plush for comfort, and glass lamps perched like delicate birds on spindly, polished nightstands.

The cabinet was part of a larger room set, complete with a long desk, a high-backed chair, and an ornate rug with a spiraled design of brown and gray and white. She stepped onto the rug, closer to the cabinet, one hand trailing the length of the desk, which was so smooth it felt oiled.

"That's it," Henry said. He ducked down and opened one of the cabinets. "At least this one's not filled with books. Look: empty." He opened and closed one cabinet door a few times, then glanced at her for a reaction.

"I won't fit," she said.

She was sure of it. The cabinet was gray and tall, the top two-thirds devoted to open shelves and the bottom comprised of the cabinets: two doors, each with a narrow drawer above it. The doors had black knobs and opened to show an unobstructed cabinet space, except for one thin piece of wood in the middle of the opening, where the doors met. She looked at the darkness of that space and took a step back, picturing herself crawling into it, unable to get out.

"Can I help you all with something?" A skinny man wearing a suit had appeared out of nowhere, looking determinedly pleasant.

"Not right now," Henry said, straightening from the cabinet. "Just looking."

"I can see why," the man responded at once. "Such a great piece."

"Yes," Henry said. "Thinking of a late Christmas gift for my dad, actually. Something for his office. But again, just looking for now."

The man seemed to take the hint. "Well, my name is Tim. I'll be at the front if you need me for anything at all."

"Thanks. We'll do that."

He smiled at each of them in turn and departed, making his way smoothly around the furniture; Catherine had a feeling he could have navigated the showroom blindfolded if needed.

"Okay," Henry said in an undertone. He was scanning the area around them. "Quick, it has to be now."

And when she didn't move, he took her by the arm and walked her to the cabinet. "Just try," he said.

She said nothing. She wasn't in her body. Her body only existed where he was touching her—those three inches on her forearm—and when she felt the pressure of his hands pushing her down, she dropped.

Down to the spiral-patterned carpet, arms braced under

her, crab-walking into the cabinet, feet going in first and then her upper body twisting to get around the piece of wood at the opening.

The cabinet space was slightly elevated from the floor, and she worried for a second the wood would give way under her weight, cracking in half to drop her down an inch or two, but it held. She pushed her way in deeper, scraping her ballet flats against the wood and pressing her shoulders back. Without warning, the cabinet doors shut and she snatched her hands away just in time as the world went black and small and cavelike.

"Perfect," she heard, muffled, and then light came back as the doors opened and Henry was pulling her out by one arm, dragging her upright, and she half fell into him, dazed.

"Perfect," he said again. "Breathe. You're done."

She nodded into him for a moment. Henry smelled like the store: expensive and polished, but also of cold air from outside, and a little of Molly, which should have been unpleasant but wasn't because it was a scent she knew. He pulled back a little to look at her. He asked her if she was okay. She said she was and then withdrew, trying not to look at the bookcase, trying to force a smile, but then she caught sight of Andrew's face.

He looked . . . *worried* wasn't the word for it. There was something else in his features she couldn't place, something between anxiety and fear and . . . disapproval.

Almost—but not quite—jealousy.

CHAPTER NINETEEN

She arrived back home before eight. Having told her parents the three of them were going to the mall to walk around and see a movie, she made up a very dull story about shopping and vague references to a film she was fairly sure was still playing— superheroes and an apocalypse and the world in danger.

"So, you had fun?" her mother asked her, passing her a bowl of yellow rice. Catherine spooned some onto her plate. The plate was beige, and the color of the rice seemed to bleed into it.

"Yeah," Catherine said. She turned to her dad. "Have you talked to Evan Porter?"

Her father looked a little surprised, his fork pausing half-way to his mouth, a piece of lemon chicken speared on the end. "No," he said. "No, I haven't. Not exactly. He's not up to . . . Well, anyway. I'm not sure what I would say to him, to be frank."

"Oh."

"Why do you ask?"

Catherine shrugged. "Just wondering."

He ate his piece of chicken thoughtfully, then swallowed. "Every parent's worst nightmare, what they're going through."

Catherine said nothing. Her mother, she saw out of the

corner of her eye, was staring down at her own plate as though it was a complete mystery to her.

"Do you remember when you got lost on the beach?" her father said abruptly.

"What?"

"We lost you," he said. "You were maybe four or five. First time at the beach. God, you were fast then. We thought about those child leashes a few times, remember, Susan?"

Her mother nodded, and then, as though it was a struggle, ate a bite of rice. "My mother thought it was abusive. Grandma Nelly," she added, as though Catherine needed the reminder.

"Alki Beach, just after one in the afternoon, I think it was," her father continued. "A woman near us started feeding the gulls and of course it got out of hand. People running, ducking, trying to hide their food, the birds screeching, and I suppose your mother and I were distracted—and when I turned back, you weren't there." He paused. "I kept looking at your towel. Barbie something or other, this pink-and-yellow little thing, but you weren't there and . . ."

"It was like the earth stopped," her mother finished softly. "Time and the ocean. Nothing moving at all." She shook her head. "Don't look too alarmed. Fear like that . . . it stretches things, makes it seem so much longer than it was. In reality it was only a minute. You were a few yards away. A family near us had a Great Dane and you thought it was a pony and wanted to ride it. But I remember fear. The . . . horror. I don't think I'll ever forget it, and I can't imagine it not ending, getting worse, and that's what Jennifer—" She stood up, her voice cracking. "I'm sorry, excuse me." She hurried from the kitchen, up the stairs. Catherine watched her go, her heart sinking.

"I'm sorry," she said, turning back to her dad. "I shouldn't have said anything."

"Don't apologize." He put down his fork and leaned back in his chair. He seemed to not want to look at her again. "It's hard. For everyone. What happened."

"Yes."

A beat of silence.

"That movie," he said finally. "It's on DVD now. It's not playing in the theaters."

She said nothing.

"I like Henry," he added. "And that other boy seemed fine, the little I talked to him. You dating either of them?"

"No."

"Both of them?"

She choked back a laugh. "No."

He got up from the table, taking both their plates. He walked to the sink. She almost missed the next thing he said, his face in profile, but she managed to just make it out over the sound of the running water.

"Are you okay?"

"Yes," she said.

"I don't know what happened, exactly. With what your

mother told me . . ." He still wasn't looking at her, his arms damp to the elbows under rolled-up sleeves. "But I want to know you're okay."

"I am."

"And you'd tell me if you weren't."

"Sure."

He turned to her at that. "You know, it's not true that George Washington said he could never tell a lie. His first biographer, a minister called Mason Weems, came up with that. He wanted people to think good things about Washington after Washington's death, and invented the whole story."

Catherine considered this. "So, no cherry tree?"

"Likely not." He turned off the water. "But I take away two things from that—one, no one always tells the truth, and two, sometimes people lie for good reasons." He dried his hands on a towel hanging from the dishwasher. "Whatever your reason, be careful, Catherine. You're the only one we have."

—

Henry's mother had made roasted quail with a balsamic-pomegranate glaze and he found it ridiculous. It wasn't how it tasted; it was good actually, tangy and juicy, but he found most things about his mother ridiculous. He suspected his father felt the same way, though he hid it well. Better than Henry did, anyway. Especially lately. Now that Catherine was back in town, his mother was even colder than usual, her lips thin and her eyes watchful, as though any moment Henry and Catherine might elope and run away to Europe or something and she'd have the unenviable task of altering the will.

Henry stabbed at a quail leg. His mother raised her eyebrows.

"Are you coming with us to the cabin for New Year's?" she asked, referring to their condo in the Cascade Mountains. Cold. Snow. He hated skiing.

"No," he said. "I have schoolwork."

"Between semesters?"

"There's a final project for European studies that we have until January tenth for."

A lie, but the idea of staying in the condo with his parents—watching them pull on slim layers of skiwear and afterward sip espressos in tiny expensive mugs by the electric fire—made him almost wish for his fictional schoolwork to be real.

Plus, he couldn't leave Catherine alone. Not as long as Andrew was in town.

Henry took a bite of the quail, wondering for what felt like the hundredth time what that kid was hiding.

"Does Catherine have work as well?" his mother asked.

Henry looked up at her. She had a piece of asparagus on her fork. As he watched, she chewed it slowly, then took a sip of red wine before placing the glass back on the table. It was a rustic table, with carefully distressed wood, and one side had a bench instead of chairs; Henry had never once seen anyone use the bench, let alone his mother. The entire room was an extension, added on a year ago because, as far as Henry was concerned, his mother had been bored. He imagined she must have seen the room in a magazine and copied it entirely from a single picture.

No wonder she got along so well with Pechman.

"No," he said. He took a sip of his water. He could hear Molly just behind the French doors; she wasn't allowed in this room and was whining softly in the kitchen. "I don't think so."

"You don't think so?" She cut another piece of asparagus. He could hear the knife grind across the bone china.

"No," he said again. He tipped his glass more, draining it. "I don't think so."

"And here I thought that when it came to Catherine Ellers, you knew all."

Henry reached across the table. He plucked the wine bottle from the center and poured a measure into his now-empty water glass.

His mother looked sternly at him. "You know I don't approve of that."

"It's fine, Celia," his father said. He sounded almost bored.

His mother barely spared him a glance before turning back to Henry. "Do I have to say it?"

"Say what?" Henry asked, setting the wine down.

"You know I don't like you spending time with that girl."

Henry restrained himself from rolling his eyes with great difficulty. "No," he said. "Had no idea."

His mother took back the wine and topped off her own glass. "I just don't want history repeating itself."

"Celia," his father said.

"No." She shot Henry a dark look, as though he'd been the one to protest. "Believe me, I am well aware I am the only one in this family who acknowledges what happened between you two."

"Nothing happened," Henry said.

His mother shook her head. Her neck, he noticed, was flushed, though her carefully made-up face was still composed and bone white.

"You were so upset about her. So distressed. For her to just—just *do* something like that—"

"She didn't do anything," Henry said, but his hands tightened on a slat under the table. How ridiculous, to make wood look old when it was so new, so expensive, a plate in the center of it holding stupid small birds that cost four times as much as an actual chicken.

"She sent you to the hospital," his mother said. "I don't call that nothing."

Henry did roll his eyes at that, his hands releasing the table. That incident had happened four months ago and she'd never let him forget it.

He drank some more wine, if only to infuriate her further. "It was hot. I went on a hike. Ran out of water."

"Thank God that other hiker found you—"

"I wouldn't call it God," Henry muttered. "More like peak hiking season."

"—but that was the same week she went away to college. Don't think I don't know."

"It was also," Henry said, trying to keep his voice calm, "*my last week before college*. I wanted to hike the trails one last time before I got busy with homework and exams and everything. I was stupid and forgot to refill my canteen before I left. It didn't have anything to do with Catherine. I'd barely talked to her in years by that point."

"You were so ill you had to have an IV—"

"For, like, an *hour*," Henry protested. He turned to his father. "You know. Tell her."

His father sighed. He'd long ago finished his meal, his plate clean. He always ate quickly but neatly, like an unfailingly polite victim of starvation. "Let's not go through this again, Celia. I know you've never been fond of the girl after she and Henry had that falling-out, but I don't think it's fair to blame her for that incident. It was likely distraction, not distress, that caused him to pack so irresponsibly."

"Thanks, Dad," Henry said wryly, leaning back in his chair. His eyes found his mother's again. "You know it could have been the exact opposite, and you'd still blame her? Like, instead of running out of water I could have drowned and you'd have been like, *Well, Catherine's always liked water, hasn't she?*"

His father chuckled at that, and his mother shot him a fierce glare until he coughed and subsided.

"Do *not* joke about that, Henry," she said. "And I'll thank *you*, Charles, not to encourage him." She took a steadying breath. "I'll admit, this is not about Catherine. At least, not just about her."

"What's that supposed to mean?"

"It means," she said slowly, returning to her food, "you choose poorly when it comes to girls, Henry. It's proved troublesome. After Leyna—"

Henry felt his face grow hot. "I don't want to talk about Leyna."

His mother raised her eyebrows. "How fortunate. Neither do I. She didn't give us much of a choice, though, did she? Ridiculous girl." Her voice became biting for a moment, then smothered itself back to calmness. And there was something else in her expression, something so fleeting it was gone before he could register it fully—affection?

"Mom—" he began.

But she shook her head. "You're a good boy. Trouble is, you never meet girls good enough for you. And I'm not just saying that because I'm your mother. I'm saying that because I've seen the way they treat you."

She took another sip of wine, then looked out the window that spanned almost the entire wall. "The mountains will be nice," she mused. "See some real snow. It's too green here. I'm rather sick of it. You sure you won't join us, Henry?"

"I'm good," he said, a statement so far from the truth he waited for his mother to protest again. Instead she merely finished her meal in silence, leaving black-red streaks on the white china, a single bone off to the side like something unearthed from an excavation, or a grave.

"You'll miss the funeral," he told her. "If you go on the first."

"We'll leave on the second, right after," she said, and rose from the table. "I find death ceremonies rather distressing and would rather not linger." Outside the window, Henry barely saw any snow. He hoped the mountains were green for her on Thursday. Green as emeralds, or ivy.

CHAPTER TWENTY

The next day or so passed in lurches and stops, the hours dragging but the nights arriving abruptly, so that Catherine found herself settling into bed with surprise, as though she'd expected each day to continue on indefinitely. But they didn't. The sun rose gray-yellow and set in amber to reveal the moon above the trees. Fog pressed against the windows, settled on the ground, and the air developed a strange, acidic tang from the rain mixing with car exhaust before soaking into the asphalt.

Catherine, like most in west Washington in winter, spent her days indoors, watching shows on her laptop and finally answering a few text messages from her high school friends—including Hania—who wanted to *hang out catch up how are you what are you doing for New Year's let's go out omg is college not the craziest thing ever I have to tell you—*

Shared lockers and AP classes, drowsily copying each other's homework before first period. Passing stupid notes about stupid boys and asking why MAC makeup was so expensive and would it be the worst to steal just once from Sephora when they already shopped there, like, *all* the time?

Catherine texted back vague excuses. Most, like Luiza and Julia, were understanding, but Hania was more persistent and

eventually Catherine stopped responding, a dull sadness war-
ring with her frustration. She was being unfair, she knew it.
They had promised they wouldn't grow apart after high school,
swearing it over last summer's Firefly and lemonade—Hania's
drink just the latter—their shoulders tanned under thin white
straps, their shorts dark and denim and a little too expensive for
so little fabric.

We'll never change.

Never forget.

Like some tragedy had happened or something. Even then,
toasting with a plastic cup on Hania's deck, laughing and day
drunk and feeling actually beautiful, Catherine had thought
distantly, *We don't mean it.*

Amber was better; she and Catherine messaged on and off,
though Catherine couldn't help but feel that Amber was checking up on her. She half wished she hadn't told Amber anything,
but it was too late to undo that now.

Catherine put down her phone. She was lying on her stomach on her bed, her laptop open to HBO. It was Tuesday afternoon. The last day of the year—New Year's Eve. Tonight she'd
probably stay up until midnight with her parents, feeling decid-
edly lame watching the ball drop and people kiss in the freezing
cold on the other side of the country.

Outside her bedroom window, the light was weak and fading, even though it was barely four-thirty, and the fog was back,
the cold crystallizing on the window where, just nights ago, the
Amy from her dream had made her bleed.

Catherine shut her laptop with a snap and grabbed her bag from beside her nightstand.

She had to get out. At least for a little while.

—

She went to Starbucks. Not the most creative of places, but it wasn't a grimy bedroom or a church, and there was a familiarity to it that made her think of high school again. Had it really been less than a year ago that she'd been studying for her AP exams? Applying to colleges? She remembered being so stupid-happy getting her acceptance letter, almost crushing it in her hand before sprinting around the kitchen, finally banging her hip into the granite countertop. But even then, she'd laughed as her eyes watered, a happiness so intense it was like a drug.

Catherine ordered a latte and opened her laptop. She'd work on her essay, that's what she'd do. If she *was* really going back to college in a matter of weeks, she might as well act like it. At the very least, she had to respond to her professor's email.

She read the message over, scanned her essay—minor revisions, very doable—and felt her fingertips tapping against the keys but not typing. Finally, she began:

Dear Professor Graham,

Thank you for the feedback. I really appreciate your help with this and am glad you liked the essay.

But no. *Liked* wasn't the right word. She was glad her professor had . . . found the essay to be . . . satisfactory? Good? Contest-worthy?

"Catherine?"

She looked up. A girl with brown hair just slightly darker than her skin tone met Catherine's eyes.

"Hania," Catherine said, her heart suddenly hammering in the back of her throat. But she got up and hugged her friend all the same.

"I thought you said you were sick?" Hania's lipstick was red-purple, her eyes sparkling as Catherine pulled away. She was like Amber—a little softer maybe—but still had that straightforward conversation style, with no interest in gossip or rumors or small talk. Catherine had found Hania refreshing during high school but felt a thrill of dread facing her now. Hania was like a human lie detector sometimes.

"I am," Catherine said, and was gratified to hear she did actually sound pretty bad. "But I had some work to do and wanted coffee."

Hania nodded and took a sip of her own drink, her eyes still on Catherine, who suddenly remembered the bruise at her neck and hastily pulled her hair forward.

"Bummer," Hania said. "Well, Abbey and I are going to try to get everyone together before we all have to leave again. We're thinking Six Seven, that place in Seattle. A fancy dinner, maybe next week? When does West Washington start up?"

"The twenty-first."

"Lucky. We go back the week before."

Just then Catherine's phone on the table buzzed. A text from Henry. Hania's brows shot up.

"Henry Brisbois?"

Behind them, an oven was beeping and something clattered to the floor but didn't break. The sounds were distracting and she felt uneasy, which she knew was stupid and pathetic.

Catherine picked up the phone and pressed the side. The screen went black.

"It's nothing," she told Hania.

"Uh-huh. Well, he's gorgeous. So that's not nothing." Hania gave Catherine a brief, searching look. "You do look sick."

"Love you too, Hania."

Hania flashed a grin at that. "All right then, I'll leave you to it. But respond to me, okay? And feel better." At the counter, someone called out Catherine's name and drink order. Hania raised her coffee in farewell. "See you later."

"Catherine," a barista called again as Hania left the coffee shop. Catherine got up from the table.

"Thanks," she said automatically, taking the coffee from the low counter.

"No problem," the barista said. "Be careful."

"You too—" Catherine began, already turning away.

She stopped. Looked back.

The barista was eyeing her under a green headband, her blond hair pulled back from her face.

"Sorry," Catherine said. "What did you say?"

"I said be careful out there."

Catherine stared at her.

The girl gestured out the window. The rain was picking up. "Don't want to get hurt."

"N-no," Catherine managed. She looked at the girl a little more carefully. She had a face that was like a word on the tip of the tongue. Catherine knew she'd seen her before. "Right. Thanks."

The girl gave her a thin smile, then turned, pressing something on a machine and making it roar to life.

Catherine walked away, coffee in hand, though she didn't much want it anymore. When she got back to her table, she glanced down at her laptop for a long moment before putting it back in her bag. She unplugged the charger she'd brought too, and stuffed it inside with the computer, almost wanting to cry at her previous optimism. The store was closing in an hour anyway, for the new year.

She shrugged her heavy tote over her shoulder and strode toward the door—but no sooner had she wrenched it open than she collided with someone outside. Whoever it was stumbled backward, giving a muffled grunt of pain and surprise.

"Sorry—" Catherine said. "God. *Sorry*. Are you okay?"

The person looked up.

Matt Walsh.

Catherine gaped at him. His hair and face were wet, his eyes swollen and red as though from allergies. He was wearing only a T-shirt and jeans even though it was freezing out, and she could see fresh scratches up and down both his arms to his elbows. He looked . . . terrible. Wrecked. All dull brown hair and eyes. His skin gray except along his jaw, which was flushed red with acne.

"Are you okay?" she asked him. Even though he was sixteen and at least six inches taller than her, he seemed almost vulnerable somehow, his thin shoulders hunched like a child. "Are you—?"

"What?" His voice was hoarse. Hannah must have been wrong; he even sounded sick. She remembered one summer he'd had mono and she, Hannah, and Amy had made him chicken noodle soup from scratch, boiling the bones for over an hour just to make the broth. This had been before Amy's interest in food had narrowed to baking, to bread. But Matt had said the soup tasted the same as the stuff from the can. Hannah had threatened to pour it over his head and Amy had to pull her back. But he'd eaten all of it, grudgingly admitting to Catherine in private a full month later that it was the best soup he'd ever tasted but to never let Hannah know he'd said that.

"She'd never let me live it down," he'd said. A pause. "You can tell Amy, though."

"Matt," Catherine said now. "I'm Catherine. Catherine Ellers. Do you—do you remember me? I used to watch Amy in the summers."

"What?" he said again. He looked her up and down. "Oh. Yeah. Right."

She had a sudden urge to walk away, but just then the door opened behind her and she and Matt stepped to the side. As a group passed, forcing them both under the awning, Catherine grappled with something to say.

"I saw Hannah at church the other day."

"Hannah's a fucking wreck," Matt said. He wiped his nose again. "What'd she say?"

"Say?"

"Yeah. She say anything to you?"

Catherine shook her head.

"Yeah, well," Matt muttered, turning back to the door. "Good. She never knows what she's talking about anyway."

Catherine swallowed, not knowing how to respond, but thankfully Matt turned from her without another word and went into the coffee shop. She watched the door close slowly behind him—it was on one of those timers—and by the time it shut all the way she realized she was standing half in and half out of the rain. She gave herself a shake, blinking back the rain, and nearly ran to her car.

It wasn't until she'd gotten into the driver's seat and put her coffee into the cupholder that she remembered what the barista had said to her.

Be careful out there.

Don't want to get hurt.

She pulled out of the parking lot and onto the street. The car's wipers jerked left to right as she drove through the growing storm. It was too much. She shouldn't have gone out. Hania knew she was hiding something, Matt was a wreck, she herself couldn't compose a stupid email, and some random stranger had just told her to be careful driving in the rain. She thought no advice had ever been so pointless in all her life.

Then something clicked inside her mind, just as she was watching the rain gather on the windshield before being wiped clear again. And again. And again.

The raindrops, scattering across her field of vision, reminded her of tiny rocks, like pebbles, or something even smaller—

Sprinkles.

The barista's face. Where she'd seen her before: at the grocery store, the baking aisle shelves completely empty of pumpkin puree. Molly barking at the broken glass.

Henry's ex-girlfriend.

CHAPTER TWENTY-ONE

Catherine awoke early on Wednesday morning and immediately curled her body inward, knees to her chest. She tried to control her breathing, making herself count the inhales and the exhales, forcing herself to focus on today, on the one thing she had to do: go into the cabinet.

God, it sounded strange. Ridiculous, even. But it was true. It was six in the morning now and in an hour, they'd be at the church. They'd gone over the plan endlessly the past few days, talking back and forth, repeating it, almost quizzing each other, looking for weak spots, but now it was final:

The three of them would park at the Westfield shopping center and walk up North Marsh Road to First Faith. They'd get in through the back, a door that didn't need a key, but a code. It was mostly used for volunteers and deliveries and opened to a small room with nothing in it but hooks on the walls for coats and a battered welcome mat. The purpose of this room, Henry explained, was to get people out of the cold right away so they didn't have to wait outside; if the church knew they were coming, they gave them the code ahead of time. And even if this code got passed around, it wasn't that big a deal, because all it accessed was a ten-foot-long mudroom, and on the other side was a locked door. One that needed a key, or at least someone on the other side to answer the buzzer.

Henry had "borrowed" the master key on Tuesday when he was there helping to set up for the New Year's service and unlocked that door before putting the key back. They were counting on the fact that no one would notice the unlocked door in the hours between Tuesday afternoon and Wednesday morning.

The last locked door they had to deal with was Pechman's office, which the master key *could* unlock, but they would have to be sure that (a) Pechman was not in his office, hence their very early start, and (b) the cabinet had been emptied of old seminary books.

"We can bring them down the hall," Henry suggested. "Put them in the maintenance closet. It has recycling and trash and random stuff that doesn't fit in the janitor's closet. No one goes in there unless they're . . . what do you call them? Maintenance workers. Pechman won't go in there."

They'd unlock Pechman's office, move the books, and (her heart thudded as she thought about it) lock Catherine inside the office. Henry and Andrew would even stay inside the church, just to be safe, hiding out in that same maintenance closet, just down the hall.

"So you won't be alone," Henry said. "It'll feel like it, but you won't be."

They'd already told their parents they were going to Castle Rock for the day. Mount St. Helens and pub pizza. Maybe hiking, if it warmed up enough, but they were leaving early to get breakfast on the way. A famous donut shop with a famously long line.

"They'll be open on New Year's?" her mom asked, looking surprised.

"Yes," Catherine said at once. "There's a special."

They wanted to be at the church no later than seven that morning, and in the office with the books cleared out before eight. That would leave four hours until the noon meeting, probably one or two at the most before Pechman arrived at the church. Assuming the meeting *was* in Pechman's office, or at the church at all. Catherine pictured herself waiting in that cabinet, growing increasingly panicky and desperate, while all the time the two pastors were talking in Ken Itoh's living room miles away.

But they had to try. *She* had to try. She kept thinking of the face at her window. A pale oval between the pines, the eyes dark and fixed.

You have to look.

The clock read 6:17. Inside the frame of her window, the world looked like a painting done in black and gray, the jutting elbows of mountaintops bleeding into the wide bruise of the sky.

—

They left Andrew's car in the shopping center by the Starbucks. Catherine eyed the shop, thinking of Hania, of Henry's ex, of Matt, and then of the water bottles dripping with condensation under the bakery items on display in neat rows.

She hadn't had any food or drink since the night before—almost ten hours now—because it wasn't like she'd have access to a bathroom while trapped in a cabinet. Her stomach was empty, her lips dry.

They walked through cold the sunlight couldn't touch, not talking. All three of them kept looking around, eyes darting nervously. Well, Andrew looked nervous. Henry seemed more determined, his moving eyes more curious than wary, and when they met hers, he gave her a reassuring smile.

"It'll be fine," he said.

"Yeah." She looked down at herself. She was wearing all black: slim leggings and a fitted turtleneck, her hair pulled back from her face. "I feel like we're about to rob a bank," she told him.

Henry gave a short laugh but Andrew just glanced over at her. He looked very pale in the sunlight, his skin almost translucent. She wondered, not for the first time, what he was thinking. With Henry, she almost always knew, but Andrew seemed to be made of empty spaces that could be filled with anything at all.

They were approaching the church and veered off the sidewalk, into the trees, so they could circle around to the back. Catherine looked over her shoulder, her heart speeding up. There was a panic that she was trying to ignore, and she was slightly ashamed she was already feeling so uneasy. *Get it together. Nothing's even happened yet.*

They walked quickly across the asphalt in the smaller back parking lot until they reached the door. A keypad was installed just above the handle, a familiar-looking setup with numbers 1 to 9, as well as a pound sign. Henry pressed the pound sign first, and then 53161 and then pound again.

"The five is for *J*, for John," Henry said as the keypad beeped loudly and he pulled the heavy door open. "Three-sixteen, obviously, and then one because it needed another number."

"John like the apostle," Andrew said, stepping into the small, narrow room.

"Or the pastor," Catherine said, following him.

"Fair," Henry said, closing the door behind the three of them. The room was in darkness for a moment; then he hit something on the wall and a dim light came on overhead. He walked past them to the door at the other end and Catherine held her breath, part of her wishing it wouldn't open—but then Henry turned to her and, with a grin, pulled it wide.

"Open," he said unnecessarily. "Thank God."

Catherine could see a long, darkened hallway with closed doors on either side and more hallways leading off in the distance. There was something unnerving about a building—any building, really—when it was unlit and empty, and the dark church seemed like a labyrinth made of shadows, a thing of nightmares, where monsters lived.

Abandon all hope, ye who enter here.

Thank God, Henry had said. Trust in the Resurrection, Pechman had preached. But she wasn't sure she believed in God. Not after what had happened to her, to Amy. Perhaps not even after learning about Dante's *Inferno*. That seventh circle, with the self-murderers, a woman upside down. Hell like a forest, the trees stretching endlessly. Did God think they deserved it? Was hell something you chose?

Maybe. A little.

Catherine walked past Henry, into the darkness of the church.

CHAPTER TWENTY-TWO

They used their cell phones for light. The hallways were silent and carpeted and their phones lit their path in unsteady white circles, occasionally sweeping up the walls and then back, like pendulums. Catherine felt nauseous, her empty stomach lurching.

Henry was slightly ahead of her, Andrew behind, the hallway lit with the dancing glow of their phones. They'd turned more corners than she could count. It made her think of children's fairy tales, of bread-crumb trails. She kept listening for footsteps that weren't theirs, for distant voices growing closer, but there were none.

They turned another corner. Henry stopped at a gray box sticking out from a wall, about a foot high and a foot wide. It was shut, but there was a closet nearby and he opened it, seeming to feel along the wall, and a moment later he emerged with a thin metal instrument. Not a key so much as a screwdriver, but even that wasn't entirely right. Whatever it was, Catherine held her phone light aloft and watched as Henry pushed the small object up, into a hole in the bottom of the box. There was a small *click* and the box opened. She saw several rows of keys. They glinted, turning slightly as Henry reached inside.

Henry grabbed a key on the left and, without a word, led

them farther down the hall. Andrew was looking at her. She could feel his eyes on her more than she could see them, so she turned her phone to get a better look at his face, but then he was moving, following Henry. She went after them, not wanting to be left alone in the dark.

"Here," Henry said quietly. He'd stopped by a door on the right side of the hall. She could just make out the edges of it in the darkness, and then there was a scratching sound, Henry's ragged breath, and he pushed the door open.

"Can we turn on the light?" she asked almost as soon as she stepped into the room.

"I don't know," Andrew said. He sounded uneasy.

"Oh, come on," Catherine said. *I can do this. But not in the dark. Not all of it in the dark.* "This is his office, right? We're already here. We have to move the books. How can we do that in the dark?"

"How about this?" Henry offered. He flipped a switch on the wall. A light clicked on: a lamp on Pechman's desk, toward the middle of the room, flooding the space with light. Almost immediately, Henry unzipped his thin jacket and threw it over the lampshade. The room dimmed, and Catherine took her hands from her eyes, blinking as her vision adjusted.

"Mood lighting," Henry said, and, when neither she nor Andrew looked amused, shrugged. "Well, it's something, and it's not so bright you can see it from three hallways down. Okay, here."

Catherine took a moment to look around the space. John Pechman's office was almost a perfect square, a little smaller than her family's living room. There was a dark green couch near the door, and a coatrack right next to it. The majority of the office was taken up by a large desk, which was shaped like an L and jutted into the middle of the room. It held not one but two computers, with a fat, high-backed leather chair behind it that she recognized from the office set at Roche Bobois. Another chair—this one wooden and strangely circular—was pushed up against the remaining wall space, right next to the cabinet.

Henry had gotten it right. Pechman's cabinet was the twin of the one they had seen in Seattle, and that more than anything made this whole thing real to her.

"Shit," Henry said now. "Shit shit *shit*."

"What?" she asked him, her voice high with fear. "What?"

Henry was kneeling in front of the cabinet, both doors pulled wide.

"He put in a shelf."

Catherine knelt down too. Instead of the open space of the one in Seattle, this cabinet was filled with books, like Henry had told them, but it also had a shelf going across it, about three-quarters of the way up from the bottom. The shelf, though it wasn't thick, made the space she'd have to fit into smaller by at least five inches.

"I can't," she said at once. "There's no way I can fit under it."

"You won't have to." Henry was craning his neck, squinting into the cabinet. "Here, shine your phone. Yeah, there. Okay." He pushed his arms inside, grabbing some of the books at the front—there were dozens, maybe fifty or more—and setting them on the carpet so he could look at the shelf more closely. "He's screwed it in. Here, at the sides. We'll have to take it out with the books."

Catherine sat back on her heels. "Can you do that?"

"Shouldn't be too hard," Henry said, and she tried not to look disappointed. "I bet there're tools in the maintenance closet somewhere, and we have to go there anyway to store the books. Andrew, give me a hand?"

The two boys began lifting the books out of the cabinet and taking them out in the hallway, cell phones still lighting the way. She knew she should be helping them but all she could do was sit on the nice cream carpet of Pechman's office and stare into the cabinet space.

Hours. That mean little voice again. *Hours in the dark. Alone.*

But I won't be. She flexed one arm in front of her. The one that had bled in her dream. *I'll let her in this time.*

—

Ten minutes to move the books. Another five to find a tool-box. Five more to find a screwdriver that fit the screws keeping the shelf in place. Nearly fifteen to actually get the shelf out, Henry panting and sweating, his arm contorted inside the cabinet, Andrew kneeling next to him, moving the light every so often. Catherine watched them from her spot on the carpet. She was behaving strangely, she could tell. That endless stare, that separateness that came over her like a cloak. She pressed her palms into the carpet and thought, *I'm not here. None of this is real.*

The boys were close together. She found this fascinating for some reason, their features in the faint light, the phone light darting like a moth inside the cabinet, casting shadows. Henry was all jaw, Andrew all cheekbones. Henry square and Andrew almost triangular in his thinness. Henry was tanner, his hair just a little lighter than his skin, but Andrew was like a male Snow White: black hair and black eyes. They weren't quite physical opposites but it was a close thing.

"Catherine?"

Henry had turned to her. The shelf was on the carpet, the cabinet completely empty now.

"It's almost eight-thirty. We should get out of here."

"Right." *We* meant him and Andrew. Not her. She, of course, was staying. She'd even used a nearby bathroom earlier, just in case, creeping down the dark hallway with her heart beating so hard it hurt to breathe. There was no need to leave again.

"We'll be just down the hall. You have your phone?" She nodded; she'd already turned it to silent. "And you'll be okay?"

"Of course she won't." Andrew wasn't looking at Henry but at Catherine. "Just look at her."

Andrew moved toward her. She heard his jeans scraping against the carpet. "Look, you don't have to do this."

She said nothing.

"You can leave. *We* can leave. All of us, right now. We'll put the books back and . . ." Andrew shot a look at Henry. "I think this is a bad idea," he said. "I just want to make that clear. I think it's dangerous."

Be careful out there.

Don't want to get hurt.

"Well, it's not up to you," Henry said calmly. "Is it?"

She knew what he meant. It was up to her. If she said no even now, after everything, Henry wouldn't argue. He and Andrew would screw the shelf back into place and return the books. Then they'd all leave and they wouldn't even think badly of her for it.

But then she'd be that girl again, the one running into the night without her coat. So scared she hadn't even thought to look behind her to check the number on the dorm room door. Crying under hot water as she scraped off the blood, feeling as though she were skinning herself, shedding pieces down the drain, emerging as something different altogether than who she had been before.

"I can do this," she said, and it had the taste of a lie: sickly sweet and said too fast, like stolen candy swallowed down.

Two minutes later, at 8:27 in the morning, she was alone in the blackness of the office, her back to the open cabinet doors, waiting.

CHAPTER TWENTY-THREE

Andrew was looking at Henry as though he'd like nothing better than to hit him in the face, but Henry thought he could take him.

They sat facing each other in the maintenance closet, which was much larger than a regular closet, filled with gray industrial tubing and massive square machines that hummed. Andrew was leaning against one of them and Henry sat against the wall several feet away. The concrete was cool at the back of his head.

"You look like you want to kill me," Henry said, his tone matter-of-fact.

Andrew scowled. "It's a stupid plan."

"Way to point that out *now*, when it's too late to back out."

"It's not too late."

"Fine. Then go get her. Drag her out of the office."

"You're talking about it like she *wants* to do this."

"She doesn't want to," Henry said, and he could tell his voice was losing its calm now. It was as though Catherine had been a buffer between them these last few days and now that she was gone and they were left alone, they could say what they liked. "She needs to. You never saw her and Amy together. I don't expect you to understand."

"Understand what?"

"Catherine. How much she cared about Amy. You don't know her like I do. Don't pretend you do."

"You're locking her in a room with a murderer. Possible murderer. Whatever."

"And another person," Henry pointed out. "And we're here. She's not alone." He gave Andrew a searching look. "Unless you think you can't help her."

"What's that supposed to mean?"

Henry shrugged, casual, but his muscles were rigid. "You didn't help her before."

"I *couldn't*—" Andrew broke off. "You don't know. You weren't there that night."

"But you were." Henry's eyes found the other boy's and he suddenly *wanted* Andrew to hit him—so he could hit him back. "I swear to God, if you did something to her—"

"I didn't!" Andrew protested; then he seemed to get control of himself. When he spoke again, his voice was lower. "I didn't do anything."

"And that's why you're here. Why you stayed when she asked you to. You want to do something."

Andrew shook his head, his expression pained, then looked back at Henry. "They found DNA," he said, his voice almost defiant. "Bob told me last night. So *that's* something."

Henry suddenly felt much more charitable toward the other boy. It wasn't the worst idea, he reminded himself, knowing someone so close to the investigation. It definitely gave them access to more information than they would have had otherwise.

But he still didn't trust Andrew in the slightest. At least, not when it came to Catherine.

"You know what DNA stands for?" Henry asked him.

"Deoxy . . . something or other."

"*Do Not Argue.* Because it's such strong evidence."

"They have the time of death, too. Around eleven, Bob said. So they're checking alibis. They can get warrants for DNA for anyone who doesn't have one. That Eric Russell guy for sure, to start."

"Eleven? You're sure?"

Andrew nodded. "That's what Bob said. Between nine and eleven the night of the twenty-sixth. What?"

Henry shook his head. "It's just—that's a weird time to have an alibi. Everyone's just going to say they were in bed."

"Maybe."

"Oh, come on. Everyone will say they were watching TV or sleeping. I mean, where were you between nine and eleven that night?"

Andrew gave him an incredulous look, but Henry didn't blink.

"I was driving here," Andrew said finally. "Got in at ten-thirty."

Henry flashed a grin. "See? Sucky alibis, every single one."

"And yours?" Andrew said. "Where were *you*?"

"On a date."

Andrew raised his eyebrows.

Henry wanted to laugh but resisted. "That Grant guy, at the police station? The one who kept looking like he wanted to kill me? I was out with his daughter that night. Well, him *and* his daughter, because he literally followed us to the restaurant. I actually don't know how long he was there but I noticed him just as we got dessert. I've never eaten a tiramisu so fast in my life."

And here he thought that date had been a huge mistake, Brittany neglecting to tell him her dad was a cop, but at least he had an alibi—unlike the boy sitting opposite him.

"Listen," Henry said, because Andrew was looking disgruntled. "I don't think you killed anyone. I just . . . I don't know you, okay? So it's weird."

"It is weird," Andrew admitted. He tapped his fingers on his jeans. "So you really think it's the pastor?"

Henry cast his eyes toward the closed door, in the direction of Pechman's office. He wondered what Catherine was doing as she waited. He could almost see her now, her pale eyes and hair still visible in the darkness of the office, reflecting even the smallest amount of light. She'd always been terrible at hide-and-seek in the woods, all those years ago, her eyes never quite as good as his, while he could spot her at any distance.

You can see me in the dark, she'd said, panting under his hands, her mouth curving up at him. *How is that fair, that you can see me in the dark?* She'd smelled like leaves and rain. Like his childhood. He'd wondered then if she'd felt it too, that ache that went all the way to the bone.

You choose poorly, his mother had said.

But she was wrong. Catherine had never been a mistake. Hell, she'd never been a choice at all.

"Henry?"

Andrew was still looking at him, waiting for an answer.

"Yes," Henry said at once, but in his mind, the image of Catherine disappeared.

And he saw James instead of John.

CHAPTER TWENTY-FOUR

At 10:32, she heard footsteps.

Seconds later, Catherine had pushed herself into the cabinet, her shoes scraping on the wood first, her legs coming next, shoved against her chest, her arms resisting, not wanting to leave the carpet but she made them and jerked the rest of her inside. She pulled at the cabinet doors, letting her fingers go just in time for them to shut, a vibration she felt surround her. She breathed in dust and darkness. She heard the footsteps, louder now, and closed her eyes. She should have gone in earlier but hadn't been able to make herself do it. Those open cabinet doors, the heavier darkness inside it—it reminded her of animal traps snapping shut, of drawbridges slamming down in fairy tales. Something in her refused to go inside the cabinet until she had to.

Inside the cabinet now, she reached for her phone, hands scrabbling across her leggings, the wood under her—

Dread like bile.

She'd left it on the carpet.

One second.

Two.

Her mind split in half along a red line of panic.

Move!

She pushed open the door and shot her left arm out, half expecting someone or something to grab it, but that didn't happen. Instead her hand was opened wide, starlike, fingers reaching, and she needed light but if there was light then that meant he was there and he'd see her and—

Plastic. Hard. She felt it click against her nails.

A light came on in the hallway just outside the office. She saw the line of it under the door.

She jerked her arm back—phone in hand—and had just managed to shift completely back inside the cabinet when she heard the lock turn.

She pulled the cabinet door closed, and this time the darkness was brief. No more than three seconds passed between when she closed the cabinet door and when the office light turned on. It sliced through to her: two thin gold beams at the top of the cabinet doors, one by her face, almost exactly at her eyeline, and another casting a stripe of gold on her black leggings, right at her bent knees.

For some reason the light surprised her. She was expecting complete darkness. She'd almost gotten used to it in the past couple of hours, waiting in the black, listening to the sound of her breath, her mind going flat and blank, the panic held back as though by an outstretched arm.

But the unexpected light didn't help. She still couldn't *see* anything; the gap was too thin. And the light was shining right at her face, her eyes, and she had to squint against it, almost like a spotlight. She waited for his footsteps to cross his office and stop, to turn toward her. Not even a minute in the cabinet before he found her out.

She realized she'd begun to sweat through her deodorant, through her clothes even. Would he be able to smell her? Her back was already starting to protest, the knobs of her spine against the wood. Her legs were okay for now but she wasn't sure that was going to last. And her neck was bent forward, her nose almost to her knees.

She hadn't realized this was going to hurt. That hadn't been a consideration at all.

You're fine, she told herself. *Breathe.*

Quiet. Slow. In. Out.

How was he not hearing her? But as the minutes passed, she grew a little calmer. He was moving around, shifting things, and that didn't make her nervous like she'd thought it would. He was humming and clicking his tongue and the sound made her realize that he didn't suspect anything. At some point he booted up his computer and she heard the whir of it like a faint engine. The keyboard tapping. His exhale. A swallow. Coffee? She peered through the gap but it was no use; she might as well have been blind.

God, her neck hurt.

In. Out. Quiet. Slow.

He was talking on the phone. She was gratified that she could hear him perfectly. If anything, his voice was slightly amplified in the small space.

"John Pechman." Pause. "Oh, no, I'm here. Rather later than I would have liked. Well, you know how it is. *Teenagers.*" The creak of the leather chair. Was he leaning back in it? "I know, I can't believe it either. I'm amazed James even agreed to spend Christmas with his lowly parents." A laugh. "No, he's thinking of California, actually. USC. Yes, his chances are good, I think. With everything taken care of now. Though some extra prayers wouldn't go amiss!" A pause. "Excellent. Well, thanks for letting me know. Really great." A pause. "Right. Exactly. My thanks again, Grant. Yes. Yes. Okay. Give my best to yours. Thanks. Okay. Bye."

She heard Pechman start typing again, and then another swallow. She closed her eyes. *Breathe.* But it was dusty. She wanted to cough. To sneeze. At one moment she thought she was going to and squeezed her eyes shut but it was entirely silent, her head jerking forward and hitting her knees, and even that was muffled. When her eyes opened again they were wet. Very slowly, she lifted her right hand to wipe her nose. Even that slight shift in movement sent a bolt of pain up her curled spine and she gritted her teeth.

What time was it? She checked her phone: 10:58. Just an hour, maybe even less, until the meeting. It wasn't like a pastor was going to be late. And look at the positive: At least the meeting was here. At least they'd been right.

Time. Time. Time. Minutes. Seconds. The agony of that hour between eleven and twelve. An exercise in mind over matter. At one point it sounded like Pechman had left his office and she actually considered getting out, collapsing from the cabinet and just breathing different air for a minute or two, but then she heard his footsteps again and that was when she started crying.

Quietly, of course. Silent crying. Her face burning. She should have felt the tears leak through her turtleneck, but she was so soaked in sweat at that point that she didn't.

She cast her mind away, apart. Tried to make it leave the cabinet, the way people said they left their bodies during the worst moments of their lives. Did the people in hell do that? The ones in the trees? She'd learned that they were flung randomly into the forest, and that wherever they landed was where their tree grew, with their soul trapped inside it. The randomness, the carelessness, was supposed to mirror how the self-murderers had treated their own bodies. They had cast their bodies aside, so in hell their bodies were cast aside as well, to be trapped and preyed on by harpies: bloated birds, like vultures that screamed and cried. But that wasn't all bad, apparently, because only when the trees were injured could they express their anguish or sorrow at all. Otherwise they were just trapped in their own still, silent misery.

Demon vultures and suicide victims that couldn't express pain unless they were hurt more. It was *fucked up,* as Amber would have called it. *Royally* fucked up.

But she got it now. By the time her phone clock showed noon, Catherine had been in the office nearly four hours, and in the cabinet, bent in a C shape, for ninety minutes. Her body was a yawning cavern of pain, her muscles screaming to her brain, which was lit up red, her neurons firing like the Fourth of July.

Something was coming with the pain, something she'd only had glimpses of since that night, when she'd struck out at Andrew, or threw away her coat, or bolted for yet another shower. Her body's pain lowering her defenses against the reality—not just that it had happened, but that it had happened to her.

I was raped.

By a stranger.

I can't talk about it.

I just want to be with Amy.

Bloated demons made of wings and talons were scraping along the gnarled length of her. She was splintering, about to break.

"Ah, Ken, come in."

She came back at the sound of Pechman's voice, staring into the thin gold light at her eyeline. And Catherine knew—just as she had known that summer afternoon in the front yard, when she'd told Amy to go inside without her—that it wasn't a question, whether she could do this. When it came to Amy, Catherine would do anything.

CHAPTER TWENTY-FIVE

She heard the door opening and closing. Footsteps. Pechman's chair shifting. Would Ken sit on the couch? Lower. Awkward. But then there was a dragging, scraping sound close to her and she remembered the chair next to the cabinet. She held her breath as it was moved, the sound of it against the carpet like the exhale of an animal. She pictured the two men sitting opposite each other, the jutting L of the desk between them.

She tried to remember how Ken Itoh looked: a Japanese man, tall and thin, with short black hair that was graying at the temples. His clothes were always neat and pressed but just a little too big for him. He had kind eyes and a voice, like Pechman's, that you wanted to listen to.

"Thanks for meeting me here." Pechman. "Got something here later so it works out." A pause. "For the funeral. You can imagine. Lots to do."

"Yes."

Another creak of leather. A pause that felt awkward even to her. "Oh, come on." Pechman again. "You asked for the meeting. I'm here. Talk away. I'm listening."

Ken said nothing.

"Don't be like that." Pechman sounded like he was reprimanding a child. "I agreed to meet with you. I didn't have to. I wanted to."

"Wanted to." She heard Ken's exhale. It was loud and made her strangely jealous. She thought when she got out of here she'd do everything as loudly as humanly possible. "I doubt you wanted to, John, though I am glad you consented to meet with me. My fear for this meeting—and I do think this fear is valid—"

"Fear?" There was a laugh in Pechman's voice. "There's nothing to be afraid of. Surely you're not afraid of *me*."

"No," Ken said. "I'm not."

Another pause, then he continued.

"I'm not afraid of you, John. I'm afraid that my absence is not having the intended effect. I thought, on the whole, that it would . . . change things somehow. You know why I left. You know my complaints. But from what I've heard, nothing has changed since my departure."

When Pechman spoke, his voice held a smile.

"Intended effect . . . You know, I've missed your way of speaking, Ken. There's a poetry in it—and by that, I mean it's pleasant to listen to but the meaning is often lost." A creak of leather again. Was he leaning forward? "Look, I'll be blunt here. Not because I'm trying to be harsh, but because that's just the way *I* talk. You leaving . . . I'll admit, I was surprised. It was overdramatic. I hoped you'd realize that, and of course I would have taken you back on. But for you to think your leaving would do something . . . for your little tantrum—no, let me finish here—

to change First Faith in some way is arrogant in the extreme, Ken. You did not build this church. *I did.* It was here before you and will be here after your *departure,* as you call it."

Catherine barely felt any pain now. Her whole body was tense, listening.

"You think my concerns aren't valid."

"No."

A short, biting laugh from Ken. "You're kidding."

"No."

She heard a hard shift of a chair. The round wooden one. Ken, moving it forward? "You know why I left so abruptly, John? I wasn't being *overdramatic.* It was not a *tantrum.* It was because I could no longer stay in a church—in an administrative position—with such abuses going on. And these were not small abuses, John. There are serious problems going on inside your church, as you call it—"

"Yes, this *is* my church. I call it my church because I built it nearly three decades ago when you were barely a child." Pechman's voice sounded icy. "Is it perfect? No. But you were always sensitive, Ken. Little things set you off. A perfectionism I thought distinctly un-Christian. As though you were trying to be God."

"We are all called to be Christlike."

"Do not lecture me. I went to seminary too."

Her heart vanished from her chest.

"But this isn't about theology," Ken countered. "Who has more degrees or who is more holy. It's about what is right and what is wrong. You've handled things badly, John. That's why I wanted to meet with you today. I heard of Amy Porter's death. It alarmed me, of course. But what alarmed me almost as much was that you were taking a lead role in the funeral arrangements."

"This . . . alarmed you?"

"Yes."

"That the pastor of a community was helping after the tragic death of a young girl?"

"You're not helping, John. Let's be honest here. True."

"And what is *true* to you?"

"I'm not sure yet. That's why I'm here. I want to make sure more abuses aren't occurring before my family and I move out of town. We just closed on a house. We'll be gone very soon. I need to know what I'm leaving behind. Whatever you may think, this church is important to me. I have to know if I need to take more steps, if they are required—"

"More steps? Involving Evan Porter, perhaps? I hardly think now is the time to bother him with such things."

Inside the cabinet, Catherine could feel the sweat drying under her clothes in a thin film.

"John—"

"And as First Faith has broken no laws," Pechman continued, a bite in his voice, "involving a lawyer seems a little ridiculous."

"I'd say the church has bent some laws considerably. Granted, I am not a legal expert, though Evan has provided me with some resources. I don't know if the church as a whole would be liable—"

"*Liable?*" Pechman laughed, but there was no humor in it, only a thinly concealed rage. "Liable for what?"

"For what churches are so often liable *for.*" Ken's voice was cool. "Financial fraud. The mishandling of church funds—"

"That again!"

"Yes, that again. Why do you think I scheduled this meeting? I heard about your involvement with the Porter girl's funeral. You wasted no time, gathering the congregation the day her body was found."

"And that upset you." Deadpan. Impatient.

"How much have you collected, if you don't mind me asking?"

"I do, actually."

"Why?"

"Because you are no longer affiliated with this church," Pechman said, his tone dry and businesslike. "And therefore have no right to know its financial dealings."

"I imagine you're still in the red."

"Not as much now, as we don't have to pay your salary."

"An unforeseen bonus."

"Two birds," Pechman quipped.

There was another silence, somehow denser than before. It was Ken who broke it.

"In November," he said quietly, "you spoke to me about our goals. Same as every year: in the red January through October, then in the black by Christmas. Christmas, of course, because that's the service during which we tell the congregation, *Praise God for his bounty. We have surpassed our goals for the year. God is good!*"

"He is good."

"True enough. But First Faith *didn't* meet its goals this year. You knew that and so did I. We knew in November. Over eleven thousand dollars short. There was no possible way we'd be in the black by Christmas. And still you told me to go about business as usual. We'd perform the Christmas service, we'd say the church had reached its goals. That *we* had reached those goals. You asked me, point-blank, to lie to the congregation. I refused. Not least because, from my understanding, we were not supposed to be that much in the red." A terse silence. "You have a very nice office, John."

She heard Pechman sigh. "We've discussed this at length, Ken. I'm not going to change my mind and neither are you. We are at an impasse. I don't know why you are here."

"I am also concerned," Ken said, as though Pechman hadn't spoken, "about your actions against justice."

"I've no idea what that even means."

"You interfered. You used your position to smother a police investigation."

"Frankly, I don't know what you're referring to."

Another silence.

"You know my wife," Ken said finally. "Danielle."

"Of course."

"She approached you some time ago with a sermon idea. Godly masculinity. You refused."

"I thought it a strange message, but perhaps that was just her explanation of it."

"And you would not allow me to preach on the subject either."

"I doubted it would come across any less strange in your hands."

"You know what was also strange? I've always had the feeling—Danielle, too—that you never much liked her."

"That *is* strange. We may have had our differences, Ken, but Danielle has never been a part of it."

"Is it because she works outside of the home?"

"Don't be ridiculous."

"Or is it because she's a psychiatrist?"

"Even more ridiculous. We offer counseling right here, at First Faith. I myself have counseled many of my congregation—"

"Danielle has counseled many people too. I think you know of one of them. A young girl. A teenager. She said she was attacked by a member of this church."

Catherine tried hard not to move. *Attacked.* The possibilities inside those eight letters prowled like lions across her mind.

"I don't know what you're talking about," Pechman said. "That hardly seems like a church matter."

"Yes, I agree these things should be handled by the police." A pause. "And she did go to the police."

"Well, then I'm not sure—"

"Nothing happened," Ken said flatly. "They didn't pursue the matter."

"Unfortunate. Though not uncommon with these cases, as I've heard."

"What did you say to them?" Ken asked softly. "What did you tell the police so they'd sweep it under the rug?"

"That is a ridiculous and baseless accusation," Pechman snapped.

"That's just it, though—it's not. You've gone through this before, with James. Smoothed over—no, let me finish. The girl came to Danielle after the attack. At first Danielle believed it was because the girl knew she was a psychiatrist, wanted to schedule an appointment, but the girl wanted to talk to me as well. She knew of the boy's connection here. She wanted to see if something could be done. I believe her concern was for other possible victims in the congregation, if the problem was not addressed."

"She could have come to me—"

"No," Ken said. "I don't think she felt comfortable with that option. For obvious reasons. She told me the whole story, what happened to her and how little the police had done in response. I went to the police station myself. I spoke to the officers on the case, not expecting much, knowing they could hardly tell me any details. Perhaps I merely wanted an assurance that they had done all they could, or an explanation as to why they were unable to do more. I also wanted to ask what options we had as a church in this situation, with no official restraining order.

I felt very lost, I will admit, and going to the police did not improve things. You see, there was something in their silence and apologies that told me a great deal. That's when I knew, though perhaps I had known it all along. The discomfort in their faces. The guilt. They wouldn't meet my eyes. And that's how I knew who was putting the pressure on them. Because this has happened before, when someone is valuable to you. And of course, with James—"

"*Enough.*"

A scrape of the chair. Was Pechman standing?

"This is what I'm talking about. *Sensitivity.* If First Faith were in your hands—and don't pretend that wasn't an aspiration of yours, you talked about it enough times—you'd do exactly this. Waste time with trivial matters. You have always lacked a big-picture focus, I'm sorry to say, and that is something you need in order to lead a church."

"Lead a church? *Lead* a church? *He has shown you what is good! And what does He require of you? To seek justice, to love mercy*—A girl has been attacked, John. Another *killed.*"

"And you think the church is responsible for that?" A laugh in Pechman's voice. "That *I* am responsible for that?"

"I do not think you a deviant or a murderer, John."

"Well, isn't that a relief."

"But I think you ignore things. I think you dismiss problems. I think you are content to see everything as fine to ensure that the congregation believes that as well. I think your focus is not on Christ but on the church. On making the church be exactly the way you want it to be, not how God wants it to be. That is why I'm here. I wanted one more meeting with you. I wanted to tell you all my thoughts before I left town with my family. Whatever you might think, I love this church and its people. I don't want to see it fail."

"It won't."

A pause. "I think you and I have very different views of what failure is, John. One girl has been devastated and another is dead. I want things to *change*."

"The dead can't be raised back to life, Ken."

"But is that not the very foundation of our faith? *So we do not grieve like the rest of mankind, who has no hope*?" Ken exhaled loudly. "I have hope for this church, and for you. I do not grieve, leaving it. But I worry, John, I worry."

"You shouldn't."

A dense silence. It seemed to press itself into the cabinet with her, against her skull, her brain oddly frozen inside it.

Then she heard a scrape against the carpet. Footsteps. The door opened and closed. Pechman was silent. Then, after a minute or two, he began typing on the computer. Inside the cabinet, Catherine began, very quietly, to shake.

CHAPTER TWENTY-SIX

She had a nightmare vision that the cabinet would be her coffin. It started as soon as Pechman began typing, as soon as she realized he wasn't leaving.

He couldn't stay in the office all day, could he? Surely he'd have to leave, get food, go to the bathroom? She only needed a minute. Half of one. Ten seconds. She'd be out and running—though a part of her knew her legs might not hold her.

Her fingers moved over her phone, the lock screen. She typed in the passcode, hovered over Henry's name in her call history.

Forget the books, the shelf. They could do that later, or never. Make him think it was a prank. He probably wouldn't notice for a while and anyway, who cared? He wasn't the killer, was he? Just a pastor who funneled money away from the church and into very expensive cabinets—*coffins*—and made sure crimes—*attacks*—weren't prosecuted.

She texted Henry, her hands shaking and slick, and waited.

No response. The phone was still dark.

I can't. I can't do it. Not another minute. I'll die. I'll scream.

She pictured herself covered in sweat and tears, crying as she shouldered her way out of the cabinet, causing Pechman to leap from his chair, confused at first and then furious. Her parents would be called. How would she explain? There was no story on earth that would make any kind of sense.

A knock on the door.

"Come in," Pechman said.

She heard the door open. "Sorry to bother you, sir."

"Henry? What on earth are you doing here?"

Catherine pressed her ear to the cabinet door. One movement, and it would open. But Henry was here. Henry would help, Henry would get her out. She'd never been so grateful to hear his voice.

"I'm sorry," Henry said again. "I was just out for a jog and saw a group outside the reception hall. Teenagers, I think. They had spray cans—"

"Not again," Pechman said. "We just had to repaint over the summer."

"School breaks," Henry said. She could picture his easy smile. "I guess they get restless. Anyway, I saw your car in the parking lot so I thought I'd see if you could help. Not sure they'd listen to me. Looks like there were maybe seven or eight of them."

"Well, you did the right thing." She heard the creak of leather. Was he standing? Leaving?

go go go go go go GO

Her thoughts weren't words but sounds.

Footsteps passed her. The door closed. She heard them in the hallway, then she didn't. The silence had a denseness. A safety. She could

get out get out out out OUT

stay another minute, maybe two, just to make sure. He might have left his coat, a key, and then he'd be back, opening the door and

She fell out of the cabinet.

Not a pushing exit, but a collapse to the left, her shoulder hitting the door and the top half of her body thudding onto the carpet, the bottom edge of the cabinet cutting into her ribs, her legs twisting inside, struggling to get around the divider. Her phone fell out and landed near her elbow.

She gasped and squinted, her face turning to the overhead light even as her eyes streamed with tears. Her entire body was shaking. After a moment, she used her arms to pull herself all the way free, her palms burning against the carpet, all her muscles screaming around her bones. The tops of her legs were out, then her knees, her feet. She should get up, she knew that, but she lay flat on her back, feeling every vertebra of her spine stretch and separate. She raised her arms above her head. Her hands hit the desk. She rolled onto her stomach, then slowly got to her knees, her feet. She rose up, stretching her arms over her head, her head bent back so much that tears rolled to her ears and down the nape of her neck.

She had done it. She was out.

The door opened. Andrew stood in the doorway. He took her in, his eyes moving up and down her body, stopping at her face. He looked horrified.

"I did it," she found herself saying. Her voice was so hoarse it didn't sound like hers at all. Didn't even sound human. She bent down slowly and picked up her phone. Her fingers barely worked.

"Come on," he finally said.

Her legs buckled underneath her when she tried to take a step, but Andrew reached for her at once, just like he had done in the dorms that night, and this time, she let him lead her away, hobbling instead of running, with sweat coating her skin instead of blood.

When they got to the maintenance closet, she lay down again, waiting for the feeling to come back to her legs. Andrew was talking. She tried to focus on his words, but the room had a cold floor she could feel against the thin line of skin between her leggings and shirt, right along her lower back. She lifted her shirt more and pressed her hips down, almost crying with relief, her eyes fluttering closed. She could fall asleep right here, she really could, with that whirring noise of some motor or other in the background and the dimness of the room.

Andrew was still talking, saying something about Henry. Then he was carrying things past her. Books. He was moving the books. She should help. But her body wouldn't work. She blinked at the ceiling, listening to the *chuff-whir* of that motor, going over everything she'd just heard, trying to make sense of it.

You've gone through this before, with James.

What if it was the son and not the father? Because James

was a senior, applying to colleges, and if he was even accused of something like that—

His chances are good, I think. With everything taken care of now.

Her mind raced. James instead of John. What had James done? Attacked a girl? *What* girl? Not Amy. Ken had said a teenager, and besides, the police were still investigating Amy's death.

Thanks again, Grant.

But they'd stopped investigating the attack on this other girl. Because Pechman had asked them to.

Then she remembered another voice, Henry's in the car, trying to soothe her, trying to tell her that Amy *might not have been a victim . . . maybe she just saw something, overheard something.*

Was that how Amy had come into it? Because she'd known something not about Pechman but about his son?

Not a victim, Henry had said. But a witness. A witness to an attack on a teenage girl, and the investigation was done, over before it had even started, but Amy would have changed that. Made it something other than a he-said-she-said, something that couldn't be shoved away or dismissed.

Can you think of a better way to silence someone?

Had Pechman done it? Or had James? Or had they done it together? The father and the son—*and the Holy Ghost,* she thought. It made her want to laugh and scream at the same time.

"Catherine, come on."

Andrew was trying to get her up.

"We have to go," he said.

"Henry," she said as Andrew helped her to her feet.

"He said he could give us fifteen. No idea how, but it's been about that. We have to go, now."

"Now," she echoed.

"Can you hold on to me?"

She nodded and put her left arm around Andrew's shoulder and leaned into him, her legs shaking under her. Her hand fell onto his arm below his T-shirt. His skin was cool against her burning fingers. Gingerly, as though she were a skittish horse, he slid his right arm around her waist.

"I'm sorry," she told him as he helped her out of the room and into the hallway. He kept looking around. They were walking carefully, quietly, but she could tell he wanted to move faster, that he was going slowly because of her.

"For what?"

"For hitting you the other day."

He gave a choking sort of laugh. "Don't worry about it."

She looked at his profile and could barely see the cut. Or was it on his other side? She couldn't remember.

"It was nice of you, to get my coat."

"It was nothing."

"No, it—"

"Catherine." His arm tightened around her waist for a brief moment. "Don't give me too much credit."

She frowned at him. They were past Pechman's office, turning down another hallway. No one seemed to be around. She guessed New Year's Day was a weird time to be wandering around a church—unless you had ulterior motives.

"Fine," she said, a little mutinous. "Partial credit, then."

"Is it at least pass/fail?"

She snorted and then covered her mouth with her free hand. She felt woozy, almost drunk with tiredness. "What's your major, anyway?"

"Undecided—"

"Hey, me too."

"—but I'm leaning toward journalism now."

"Why?"

A shrug. "You can catch the bad guys like cops do, but you don't have to . . ."

"Do dangerous stuff like this."

"Actually, yeah."

She laughed again and her legs shook. She hoped Andrew knew where he was going because she had no clue. "He didn't do it, by the way. Pechman. Or, at least, not just him. James did something, to someone else. And Pechman covered it up. Somehow."

Unsurprisingly, Andrew looked confused at that. "What exactly did you hear in there?"

"That his son attacked someone. And he—Pechman—went to the police and, I don't know, smoothed it over somehow. So James wouldn't get in trouble and he'd be able to go to a good college."

"Smoothed it over how?"

She hesitated—Andrew was close with Bob, after all—then said, "He was talking to the cops on the phone before Ken showed up. It was that guy from the station. Grant. Pechman was talking to him about James, how things were taken care of now. Thanking him."

Andrew's arm tensed around her again as he led her down yet another corridor. "You think Amy—"

"No. But I think she might have known about it. And I think they might have known she knew something." A pause. "James was looking for Henry at the gathering for Amy at the church. The day she died."

He stopped at that and turned to look at her head-on. "What are you saying?"

"I don't know. But maybe the cops aren't the only people here doing something shady. No offense."

Andrew blew out a breath. "Henry has an alibi."

"What?"

"An alibi. For the time of Amy's death."

"How in the world do you even know that?"

"Because we have the TOD now—sorry, time of death. Nine to eleven. Bob told me. And Henry and I were talking and . . ." His voice trailed off.

"You *asked* him for his alibi?"

"Well, he asked me for mine first."

Catherine barely succeeded in holding back a laugh. Andrew, in his irritation, suddenly looked about ten years old.

"I'm not saying *anything* like that," she told him, bemused by the idea of the two boys interrogating each other out of sheer dislike in a maintenance closet. "What I'm saying is that with

Henry knowing James—it might be useful. Henry could talk to him, at the very least."

Andrew was looking at her strangely. They were very close together, and in the dim light he looked unnaturally pale, like a creature who couldn't come out in the sun. A vampire in some Gothic novel. It made her think of high school, that one class she'd had with Henry.

Senior year. AP English literature. Gothic novels. All tall, looming houses and strange, ancient creatures. PowerPoint slides with titles like Decaying Architecture *and* An Atmosphere of Fear. *It was a miracle she'd passed the test that May. She barely remembered any details from the books—SparkNotes had been a godsend—but she could remember with perfect clarity walking in that first day to see Henry sitting at a desk in the front. His eyes meeting hers, both of them giving a strange start of recognition. She'd chosen a seat several rows away from him, a sudden heat encircling her throat and shoulders like a shawl. That whole year she'd tried to get to class right before the bell and leave right after. She'd made determined conversation with the girl next to her, who she'd thankfully run winter track with the year before.*

The memory of it made her feel sick with shame now. In the cabinet, she'd sent Henry a text saying *help me.* That was all. Two words. And barely a minute later, he'd come to her rescue. He hadn't even wasted any time messaging her back. Forget the four years they'd been apart. It was like they had never happened.

But—

A lot could happen in four years.

Henry knew James. Had bought pills from him. Had spent time at his house. James had been looking for Henry at the church the day Amy's body had been found. And she'd seen James talking to Henry again on Sunday, when she'd been talking with Pechman.

Did Henry know something?

"You really want to do that?" Andrew asked her now, still giving her that strange, almost incredulous stare. "Ask this James kid if *he* has an alibi? Or get Henry to ask him?"

She leaned heavily against the wall. "Why not?"

Andrew shook his head at her. "Because this . . . this is bothering me. Sorry, okay? But I think we've taken enough risks for today. The entire year, in fact."

Be careful out there.

"So you think we should stop?"

"I think," he said slowly, "that you can barely stand up. And there are a bunch of police officers looking into this case. And whatever you heard in there . . . I get how it sounds. But I trust them. So, yeah. I think we should stop."

She looked at Andrew. With his face so intent and focused, she could picture him as he must have looked driving to her house with her coat. She wondered what he'd thought about on the way. If he'd second-guessed himself, told himself he was being stupid and overdramatic and that what he was doing wasn't necessary so he could turn around. She was sure he must have—but he also must have felt an obligation toward her, to finish the task that had, for whatever reason, been assigned to him. She knew the feeling. She felt it, to her core, about Amy.

Because there was something about being in charge of a child that changed how you saw the world and the choices you made in it. She'd never thought about seat belts that much until Amy was in her car, or muted swear words until they watched movies together. Hadn't cared about raw eggs until baking with Amy in the sunlit kitchen, the yellow smear of egg yolk across a pink spatula. But Amy had brought out a primal vigilance in her, like a mother bird building a careful nest, or a lion crouching over its young.

Wasn't it amazing, how a child jumped to the top of your list just by being there?

"Andrew," she said. "I'm not going to stop. I'm going to ask Henry to talk to James. And if Henry won't do it, believe me— I will."

Andrew gave her an exasperated look, then glanced up and down the hallway.

"You look pissed," she said. "Do you think I'm being stupid?"

"Yes," he said. "But that's not why I'm pissed."

"Why, then?"

"Because I have no fucking clue how to get out of this place."

She couldn't help it; she laughed as she slid her arm around his shoulder again and they began to make their way down the hallway.

CHAPTER TWENTY-SEVEN

At the end of her first summer without Henry, she'd gone to the community pool with her girlfriends: breathless and dripping, white smears of cursory sunscreen on the backs of her arms, still talking about camp a little, about messages to the boy after she'd found him online, the one she'd kissed quickly during the scavenger hunt. Those messages were getting few and far between now, but that was fine. School was starting up soon. Life seemed endless and entirely hers. She'd padded over to her chair from the water and picked up her sun-warmed towel, only to see something small and white drift down to her feet. She picked it up, reading the words on it three times over before realizing what it was: the inside of a Reese's cup candy, the white paper under the orange wrapper that held the two candies in their perfect black cups.

Whatever I did, I'm sorry.

Her head shot up, scanning the pool, every dunking head, each pair of splashing feet, but Henry—and it was Henry, she knew his handwriting as well as her own—had gone. He must have seen her across the pool, perhaps turning underwater handstands with Hania and Abbey, and he'd written the note on impulse on the white paper from the candy he'd gotten from the vending machine. Slipped it into the towel he'd seen her use a million times before. And then he'd left.

Catherine thought of that note now as she faced Henry across her kitchen table, feeling wary and determined at the same time. There was so much history between them, not all of it pleasant. More her fault than his, she knew. But now she wondered if Henry was really as innocent as she had thought, or if he was hiding something from her to protect a friend. She couldn't stop thinking about James, racking her memory for anything even remotely related to him, and remembered Stephanie again, that cheerleader who had broken up with James last year. She'd been complaining about him in calculus class. What had she said? Something about how James wouldn't stop texting her. Desperate, she'd called him. Did that mean something?

Well, she had the chance to talk to Henry about James now. At least that was something. It was an hour since they'd left the church. Andrew had dropped them off, then left for Bob's house. Henry took her inside her empty house, with her mother at work and her dad out at a New Year's antiques sale. Henry waited downstairs while she showered. A long shower she had to make herself leave. Her skin was red by the time she stepped out, the mirror completely steamed over. She towel-dried her hair and pulled on some college sweats, leaving her hair to drip into the hood of the sweatshirt. When she got downstairs, Henry had made coffee, and the kitchen felt homey and pleasant and a little unreal, like it was a set for a commercial and they were only actors.

She took a mug and sat down at the kitchen table. The coffee steamed. He pushed a carton of creamer toward her. She poured it. The silence wasn't uncomfortable. It was like they were each waiting for the other to say something but it didn't matter when it happened or who spoke first.

"Thanks," she said finally. "For getting me out of there."

"No problem."

She wondered if he knew what she was thinking. As a child, he'd always sort of known. It had been the same for her, with him. But now he was a little harder to know; outwardly, he looked fine, but she could tell there was something underneath that stillness. She just wasn't sure what it was.

"Are you mad at me?" he asked her.

"No," she said.

"I thought you might be, since it was my idea."

"No," she said again.

"It was a lot, what you did."

"I kind of had to."

"Because of me?"

"Because of Amy."

"Catherine," he said, "what happened in there?"

She didn't answer at first. Instead she drank her coffee, hot and perfect, until she'd finished it all, and then she told him everything.

In order. The waiting. The phone call. The meeting. Every word she could remember, the cadence of speech. She didn't tell him what she made of it, the conclusions she'd drawn. She just waited in the silence that fell after she'd stopped talking, watching his face, trying to see behind his eyes.

"What are you thinking?" she asked him after nearly a full minute.

Henry cleared his throat. Ran a hand through his hair. "That's—it's a lot to take in."

"It is." She traced a finger along the rim of her mug. "I know you're his friend."

"What?"

"James. I know you're his friend."

"James?"

She nodded. "Do you know something?"

"About James?"

"No," she said, a little impatiently. "About our savior Jesus Christ. Have you heard the good news? Yes, Henry, about James. I know he was looking for you the day Amy's body was found and I know Pechman got the cops to cover up him attacking some girl—whatever that means—so yes, I'd like to know what you know about James. Because I think you were right when you said Amy was a witness, but I think she knew about something James did, not his dad." A pause. "I meant to say that a lot more calmly than that."

But Henry was grinning at her. "You usually do."

"Shut up." But a smile was tugging at her mouth as well. She squashed it. "So? Why was he looking for you after Amy died?"

Henry sighed and gave her a brief, searching look. "He was worried," he admitted.

"Worried about what?"

Henry sat back. He wasn't looking at her at all now. "He . . . he said something about how crazy this all was. How . . . how fast everyone got to the church. The crowd. He was upset about it."

"Upset about Amy?"

"No," Henry said slowly. "Not about Amy. Not exactly."

"But you said he was upset, worried. About what?"

"I don't know. All the attention, I guess. It wasn't exactly the most restful holiday season."

Catherine waited for more, but Henry was silent. She felt that bite of impatience again.

"What else did he say?"

"It's not . . . It's stupid. I don't think—"

"Henry."

"It was a joke. It literally just sounded like a joke."

"What was the joke?"

He waved a hand. "He was saying something about this other murder he'd read about somewhere. Massachusetts, I think. How they thought the murderer was someone in the town, so they did a volunteer thing where people offered up their DNA. He made a joke about how the first place Nazi Germany comes to in America is New England."

"Funny," she said.

"I didn't say it was a good joke."

"They do have DNA," she said. "Andrew—"

"Yeah, he told me, too."

"Do you think it's James? Do you think—?"

"Jesus, Catherine."

"What? You can accuse his dad but not him?"

"Yeah, because Pechman isn't in high school, and while Pechman's shady as hell, James—"

"Wait, you're saying James isn't shady? Are you kidding?"

"He sells pills," Henry said. "That's hardly homicide."

"Rape is pretty close."

Henry shot her a look. "That's what they said he did?"

"No," Catherine admitted. "They said attacked, but . . . I mean . . ." She broke off, suddenly wishing she could take back what she'd said.

"Is this about . . . ?"

"No."

"Look . . . If you want to talk about it, what happened—"

"I don't. This isn't some clever way of me getting justice or whatever. Making this circle back to me. This isn't about me. It's about Amy."

"Okay."

She glared at him. "I hate how you say that. *Okay.* Like you don't believe me."

"I don't believe you."

"And I don't believe you. Look how nicely that works out."

"Catherine . . ."

But she just shook her head. "Do you remember that field trip we took in fifth grade?" she asked.

"What?"

"To the zoo. Last year of elementary school. We were in the same class."

After a moment, he nodded.

"You were awful," she said. "Telling me these horrible stories about kids who snuck into the polar bear cage or fell into the wild dog exhibit and were eaten alive."

He said nothing. She continued.

"And eventually I turned to you and told you to shut up, and you apologized. And you said something . . . something like, *Fine. Sorry. I lied. Everyone's fine. No one fell into the cages. No one died.*" She felt her lips press against her teeth. "I'm fine. I didn't fall in. I didn't die."

Henry sighed and leaned toward her. "What do you want me to do, Catherine? Tie up James? Beat him up until he talks?"

"Don't be stupid."

"I'm not. But you're not telling me what you even want—"

"Find out where he was," she said. And when Henry raised his eyebrows, she added, "What? You can make Andrew give you an alibi but not James?"

"Andrew," Henry said, "has a shitty alibi."

Catherine restrained herself from throwing up her hands. "Just find out where James was that night. Nine to eleven, right?"

"You want me to get his DNA, too?" Henry asked wryly.

"Sure," she said. "Knock yourself out."

CHAPTER TWENTY-EIGHT

Henry said he'd do it.

Are you going to talk to Bob about James?

Andrew pressed the button on the side of his phone and the screen went dark, the text messages vanishing from view.

He thought he might respond to Catherine later, maybe in an hour or two, and apologize, say he hadn't seen the texts, his phone had died. Something.

He realized with a jolt that he was becoming far too good at lying.

"There you go," Minda said, putting a steaming plate of carbonara in front of him. She was off for the New Year, and when he'd walked in the door she'd taken one look at him and shoved him into a seat at the kitchen table. "You're too thin," she'd said, sounding eerily like his mom. "I'm making you something with carbs. Lots and lots of carbs."

She chatted to him as she boiled the water, made the sauce, crisped the bacon. Minda was a tall black woman, not small but not fat, either. More strong than anything, with visible muscles in her arms, and legs that could stand for hours at the hospital. She talked a lot. Andrew had always been amazed at this, how her speech never stilled even when she was doing something else. As far as he could tell, Minda paused only for breath and only when completely necessary. Then she was off again, talking about her day or a book she was reading with no need for someone to chime in or ask a question. But she wasn't self-centered; she could hold a two-sided conversation. She'd listen and ask questions. Most of the time Andrew enjoyed being around her, but now he just felt impatient and irritable.

"Where's Bob?" he asked her, lifting some of the noodles with his fork. Steam gushed out and ran up his hand.

"Oh, he'll be home by three. I'm making him come home. New Year's Day and all. I told him he's been working too hard. I said to him, 'Bob, if you don't come home and eat a proper meal you're going to get something awful from that new Panda Express'—I know when he buys it, the smell gets all over him—'and then you'll be up all night complaining about indigestion.' But he never listens, Andrew. He has a gastroenterologist for a wife but as soon as I let him out of my sight he eats the worst food in the world and then comes back and complains to me about it." She shot Andrew a dark look. "You eat up. All of it. I'll have to throw away any leftovers."

She took a seat next to him at the table. It was oval, with marks along the surface. Bob and Minda's entire house was sort of scuffed at the edges: a few paint chips, dust on the baseboards, faint stains on the carpet. Nothing awful, but far from the immaculate state Andrew's mom kept their house in. Actually, this slightly smaller, less pristine house made Andrew feel more comfortable than his own. Like he could kick off his shoes and not be glared at. Like he could leave his dishes in the sink and not hear a tsk of disapproval. His mom kept the house spotless ever since his father had moved out nearly ten years ago, as though by organizing the house, she could somehow fill the empty spaces his father had left behind. Andrew had been pleasantly surprised when he visited his older brother Rick's apartment in Castle Rock over Thanksgiving and a pit bull was sprawled on the couch near an overflowing basket of laundry.

"You need to chill out," Rick had told him, scratching the dog behind the ears absentmindedly. "Mom's too extreme. Maybe it's not all her fault, but still. I'm glad you're away at college, actually. So you can breathe."

Now Andrew took a bite of the carbonara and promptly burned his tongue. He swallowed a gulp of water. "Good," he managed, and Minda smiled.

"Bob will smell the bacon, I'm sure of it. You say I didn't give you any, okay?"

Andrew nodded and moved the pasta around on his plate. More steam billowed up. "Thanks for letting me stay here a few days."

Minda waved a hand. "Oh, we're all about children that aren't ours. That's what Bob and I say. Not childless, but child-free. Kids in small amounts are wonderful. As long as you leave in a week." She shot him a grin. "Kidding. You stay as long as you like." A thoughtful pause as she gazed at the bobtail cat sitting on the refrigerator. "Do you think we should get a dog?"

"A dog?"

"A dog." She jerked her head in the direction of the cat. "Toni will be upset, of course, but then, she's always upset. A small breed. Or maybe a Lab. I like Labs."

"Henry has a Lab," Andrew said.

"Henry?"

"This guy I know here."

Minda looked curious. "I thought you were staying in town for a girl."

"A girl?"

"Yes. Bob said you came to the station with a girl. About the case. He said she's pretty."

"No," Andrew said at once.

"She's not pretty?"

"No—that's not—I mean she's not why I'm staying in town."

"So you're staying in town for the boy?"

"No," Andrew said. Talking with Minda sometimes felt like spinning in small circles very quickly. "I'm staying in town because . . ." He sighed and put down his fork. "The girl who died," he said.

"Yes."

"I want . . . I have a theory. We do. Maybe."

"You know, a theory is an explanation of part of the natural world based on a well-established body of facts." A modest shrug. "Just sayin'."

"Fine, not a theory. An idea, then."

"What's your idea? Absent a well-established body of facts?"

"Never mind."

"Oh, don't be like that. And eat!" She gestured at him, then looked almost contrite. "Sorry. I tease too much. Bob tells me all the time. What's on your mind? What do you think, about the girl who died?"

"I . . . We . . ." Andrew thought for a moment. "I don't know. It might be nothing."

"But you have a feeling."

"Actually," he said, "yeah."

She leaned back in her chair. "Tell you what: You finish your plate, I'll spray the room to cover the smell of bacon, and when Bob gets home, we'll talk to him, okay? Don't look so nervous! It'll be fine. Worst thing you can be is wrong, right? And that's not so bad."

But that wasn't true, Andrew thought as he did his best with the pasta and Minda went to soak the dishes. The worst thing wasn't being wrong. It was being right and not doing a thing about it.

———

The night Catherine was raped, Andrew had a headache. A pounding one in his temple that made tears stream from his left eye. He pressed his palm to his head to try to stop the throbbing and popped four Advil, but it was still there. His roommate, Justin, was out at an end-of-finals party, but the thought of going anywhere with either lights or noise made Andrew feel like throwing up. He wasn't exactly prone to migraines, but he got them after looking at one thing for a long time, like the pages of a book or glowing PowerPoint review slides. Thankfully this one had held off until the end of finals, but that was cold comfort to him as he lay in his dark dorm room, panting through the pain, one palm to his forehead, desperately needing to pee.

He'd had to pee for a while now but was putting it off because the hallway lights would feel like yellow swords through his eyes. He could go in the sink, but somehow the idea that he was so weak he couldn't even make it to the bathroom was intolerable to him. It made him think of that time he'd broken his leg in two places playing soccer. Thirteen years old with a cast that came almost to his hip. How he'd needed help with almost everything and there was only his mother to help him, as Rick had just started college.

So he made himself go out into the hallway, his eyes fixed on the floor, one hand by his hairline like a visor. The light was bad, but not as bad as he'd thought. Blunt knives instead of sabers. He was pleasantly surprised he could handle it.

"Watch it."

He blinked and looked up. That hurt more, the light finding his pupils and digging into his skull. He pressed a hand to his temple again and squinted through his watering left eye. He was a few feet away from two guys who looked around his age. They were a little shorter than him, though, and one of them had shockingly blond hair, almost white. The other was tan with brown hair and was almost completely forgettable save for the beard, as though he'd participated in No-Shave November and had lost track of the date.

"Sorry," Andrew said. He began to walk again, toward the bathroom a few yards away, hand still to his head.

"He doesn't look so good," he heard one of them say before he closed the bathroom door.

Andrew sat in one of the stalls for several minutes after he peed, with his eyes closed and head bowed. The throbbing in his head was subsiding a little. He got up, washed his hands, and splashed water on his face, then blinked through wet eyelashes at his reflection. That guy had been right; he really didn't look so good.

When he came out of the bathroom, the bearded guy was still there, but the blond one had been replaced by a tall, good-looking boy Andrew vaguely recognized from his introductory honors course.

The tall boy nodded to him as he passed, and the bearded one asked, "All right?"

"Yeah," Andrew said, feeling a little bewildered. It was the strangest thing, but a sudden unease had gripped him, as though he'd walked into a room with a tiger in it and hadn't noticed it yet. He stopped and turned to look at them again.

They were leaning against the wall opposite a closed door. 417. His room was 424. He remembered his roommate complaining at the start of the year how they'd *just* missed 420 and how lucky were those bastards who'd gotten it?

As Andrew looked at the door, the bearded guy waved a hand. "Hey, you. You awake in there? What're you even looking at?"

Andrew blinked. He looked at the guys, at the door, and then back again. "Nothing," he said.

He found himself nodding and walking back down the hall, pausing when he reached his door, half turning back around. He couldn't make himself move, either to open his door or walk back down the hall. And he couldn't understand why his heart was beating so hard and why he couldn't seem to swallow. He was in a brightly lit hallway. Other people were in the hallway too. A door was closed.

Normal. A headache and a trip to the bathroom, his hair still damp from the water he'd splashed on his face. Soft clothes and bare feet.

Normal.

As he closed his door behind him, he heard the bearded guy say, "You going to go again? But after me, man. After me."

———

He hadn't been on his way to the bathroom the second time. He'd been waiting. Waiting for something and telling himself he wasn't waiting for anything at all. Telling himself he wasn't sleeping because he wasn't tired. It made him remember being much younger, every sound a sign his dad had come back. Stupid and hopeful. A year of broken sleep.

He kept checking the time on his cell phone, wishing he could see through walls, his door. Every so often he opened his door and looked down the hall. He also did this whenever he heard voices or footsteps, but so far it was just other students stumbling back from a party, some sort of takeout box in hand, laughing. The boys had gone. Would he have to wait until morning? Time crawled past him like something low-bellied and long.

Finally, just past two in the morning, he heard another noise in the hallway: a door opening, and then a quiet but clearly audible *thud*.

He darted into the hallway and felt his heart fail.

She was there. He'd known she'd be there, had been waiting all night for her to appear, like this was some dark fairy tale and she would be conjured into being at an appointed time. A yellow dress and bruises. He looked at her and she seemed to fill his vision, everything else falling away into nothingness. He couldn't breathe, seeing her lean heavily against the door, trying to get her feet under her. Still drunk. No coat. Her dress had an unnaturally high collar that couldn't be comfortable and then he saw the tag and it was like little fires were being lit inside his chest, each one a new orange-red realization.

He went to her. She ran away. And then her blood was on the underside of his foot and he smelled it like coins left out in the rain and he was banging on the door she'd come out of, hitting it again and again, hearing his hand like a drum even though it didn't seem to belong to him.

The room was dark, a slice of yellow sliding across the floor as the door was pulled open. It was the tall one with the beard.

Andrew stared at him, his bare feet shifting on the tile, feeling the wet slickness of her blood.

"What?" he demanded, and when Andrew didn't answer, he yawned. "I was sleeping."

"No," Andrew said. "You weren't."

The boy stopped midyawn, which might have been funny if his eyes hadn't turned shrewd. "You got a problem?"

"Who was she?"

"What?"

"The girl." He couldn't believe what he was saying. The entire night had the texture of a dream. "Who was she?" Then he took a step forward. He heard the boy protest, felt a shove against his shoulder, but he'd seen the coat in the glow of the hallway light, lying on the floor two feet from him by the mini-fridge and a discarded plastic cup. He reached for it, then stumbled back as soon as it was in his hand, looking up just in time to see the door slam shut. He stared at it, panting, wondering if he should knock again, but he didn't. Instead he turned, running to the end of the hallway and spiraling down the stairs, the coat trailing after him like a heavy black banner until he pushed open the front doors. They were cold against his hands as he stared around, eyes narrowed against the darkness, trying to see a flash of yellow, but the world was empty winter with no color at all. So he went back inside and sat on his bed with her coat in his lap, and when he found a driver's license in the pocket he stared at her picture for a very long time.

CHAPTER TWENTY-NINE

Andrew had replayed that night in his mind a hundred times.

If he'd only done *something*. And not even him, personally. He could have gotten the RA. Called the cops anonymously. Called Rick and asked him what the hell he should do. Anything. It would have taken two minutes. He could have changed everything.

It reminded him of the history credit he'd taken this past semester. Medieval History and the Middle Ages, which was a strange title because they were the same thing. The fifth to fifteenth centuries—the fall of the Roman Empire to the Renaissance—also called the Dark Ages. Joan of Arc was burned at the stake. Andrew remembered that probably most of all. He had a thing about fire. When he was around nine, about a year after his father had left, when he'd begun to sleep normally again, a neighbor's house had caught fire and they'd all gathered out on the street. It was an already warm summer's night and the fire made them sweat even at a distance. The sky lit up blaze-orange, sparks like fireworks, his mother's hands tight on his shoulders to hold him back from that childlike curiosity to get closer, reach out a hand, young eyes still half hypnotized by a world half understood.

Everyone got out except the cat. He remembered that even

now. Ginger. An orange cat the color of the fire. For weeks he had nightmares about it, his unconscious brain imagining the animal backed into a corner as the flames came at it.

Joan of Arc was burned three times. Twice more after the initial burning to make her nothing more than ashes. Her executioner later said he knew he was damned as soon as the first fire caught. That detail had stayed with Andrew. He found it strange the man didn't douse the fire right then, or at least protest, try to stop it. But now he thought he understood. You waited behind a door you'd closed behind you. You told yourself you didn't feel the heat of the fire or smell the smoke. That naive curiosity was gone, replaced with an adult knowledge of exactly what was happening, and you didn't want it, so you rejected reality. You told yourself it was fine, everything was fine, even though a part of you knew that if there was a hell, you'd now and forever deserve to be there.

Because there had been a fire. And you'd let it burn and consume a girl alive. More than once.

———

"James?" Bob asked him. "The preacher's son?"

"Yes," Andrew said.

"Huh," Bob said. He looked down at his lentil soup for a moment, then took a spoonful. "I smell bacon," he said to Minda, half turning.

"No, you don't."

"I do." He turned to Andrew. "She fed you, didn't she? Something good?"

"No," Andrew said.

"So it wasn't good?"

Andrew thought he was understanding more and more why Bob and Minda were married.

Bob pushed his soup away and gave Andrew an unusually piercing stare. "What's your gut telling you?"

"I don't know."

"Yes, you do."

"No, I don't."

"Think."

Andrew tried not to roll his eyes.

"Fine," Bob said, reading this expression clearly. "What if I tell you your gut is right?"

Andrew felt his eyes widen. "It is?"

"Well, partially right," Bob admitted. Minda took a seat next to him at the table and pushed his bowl back toward him. Bob gave her an aggrieved look before turning back to Andrew. "We're not looking at James Pechman for this, but he did have . . . an encounter with us recently."

"For what?"

"Like I'm telling you details when no charges were even brought."

"That's a detail right there," Andrew pointed out. "That no charges were brought."

Bob glared at him. "Too smart for your own good. I've said it for years."

"So he did do something," Andrew said.

"Define *something*."

"An attack. On a girl in the church."

Bob raised his eyebrows. "Where'd you get that from?"

Andrew said nothing, but Bob gave him a shrewd look.

"Just what exactly have you been getting up to? Because I can tell you right now, your information's dead wrong."

Andrew's heart was beating fast. He felt like he was about to get yelled at. Why was he even asking about this? This wasn't his theory. It was Catherine's. Catherine's and Henry's. He wasn't even in the picture at all.

But then he saw her again in the hall in the yellow dress and her bruises might as well have been burns.

Andrew sighed. "We heard . . . There might have been something about a cover-up."

"What kind of cover-up?"

"The police." Andrew took a deep breath. "Doing Pechman a favor."

All of Bob's irritation seemed to disappear. He actually chuckled at that. "Pechman likes to *think* we do him favors. Likes to throw his weight around. But that case—yes, I know the one you're referring to, though I'll admit I'm surprised *you* heard about it—it was a he-said-she-said in the simplest of terms. It was going absolutely nowhere, Pechman or no Pechman."

"Really?"

"Really."

"Fine." Andrew relaxed back into the chair. "So, if you're not looking at James, who *are* you looking at?"

"Tell you what. You tell me what she made you and I'll give you something in return."

"Carbonara," Andrew said, ignoring Minda's exaggerated look of betrayal.

Bob turned to her. "Carbonara. You must hate me."

"It's out of love, dear."

"Lentil soup is not love."

"You know, that would make a great bumper sticker."

He took a spoonful of soup. "Okay, it's not that bad."

"Oregano," she said, looking pleased.

"So if you're not looking at James," Andrew interjected, "is it that Eric guy? The one Catherine did the sketch of?"

Bob shook his head. "Alibi."

"A good one?"

"Considering he was raising hell at Barnes & Noble by refusing to leave at closing time and then spent the night sobering up in one of our holding cells, yes, it's a good one." He turned to Minda. "Salt?"

She shook her head. "Remember it's out of love."

"I want a divorce."

"You'd die in two weeks if I left you on your own."

"Fair enough."

"I have a question about alibis," Andrew cut in.

Bob sighed. "Go ahead."

"Well, they're based on time of death, right?" He was still thinking about James, about Henry. That nine-to-eleven window. "But how do you even know time of death so exactly? I thought it was usually a range, especially with extreme temperatures."

"Nine to eleven isn't a range?"

"It's a narrow one, from what I know about TODs."

"And here you told me you were going to be a journalist. Having second thoughts? I can wrangle another internship, if you like."

"No," Andrew said flatly.

"Suit yourself, but you've got a natural inclination to the profession, if you ask me. Anyway, to answer your question—there are a few reasons. One, the body was found shortly after death. This wasn't a case where the body is left for days or weeks and decomposition sets in and you have to get bug experts and soil technicians and all that. Two, she was a child. We don't have to guess her schedule, like a college kid out partying who wanders off sometime between the hours of ten and, say, midmorning, when her friends start sobering up and notice her missing. Or, even worse, an adult who lives alone. And because Amy was so young, we don't just know her entire schedule the day of her death—we also know the exact time, quantity, and content of her last meal because she ate with her parents. Coroner used stomach digestion to establish TOD. Amy's parents said she ate dinner at seven-thirty that night. A substantial amount of it was still in her stomach when she was killed. Ergo, it couldn't have been later than eleven, and even that's pushing it, according to the coroner. Amy's mom said good night to her at just after eight-thirty. So it's a pretty small window, which I'm not complaining about, believe me. Makes alibis easier to check. Like Eric Russell's, for instance."

Andrew considered this for a moment. "But you said you have DNA, too, right? Is that from . . ." He trailed off, shooting Minda a look. "I mean, I know you're looking at the registry."

"It was hair," Bob said flatly. "Pulled out by the roots. We found it in her hands. No hits yet, but DNA can take weeks."

Andrew said nothing.

"Listen," Bob said, leaning forward. "Someone can be flawed. *Really* flawed. Like our Mr. Russell. Doesn't make them pure evil, though. Doesn't make them a child murderer. There are levels to these sorts of things, you can't forget that—even if you're not going to join up."

"So, who then?" Andrew asked.

Bob took a few more spoonfuls of his soup, looking contemplative. "Someone she knew. So far, the evidence suggests Amy did sneak out to meet someone, so it was unlikely to have been a stranger, not to mention stranger killings are much rarer than people think. No, odds are she knew the person. Amy was active on social media, promoting her little bread business, and she did exchange messages with several people just before her death, so we're narrowing down that list right now." He smiled at Andrew's expectant expression. "That's all you get from me. Unless you saved some carbonara?"

"Nope," Minda said cheerfully.

Bob spooned some more soup into his mouth in silence and Andrew, sensing defeat, pulled out his phone.

> Bob says not James

> They're looking at her social media though

> She was selling her bread online?

Seconds later, his phone screen lit up: Catherine. Three dots blinking, blinking. Then—

> Forget James

> I know who did it

PART THREE

WORDS AND BLOOD

Haunt me then!
Be with me always—take any form—
drive me mad! only do not leave me in
this abyss, where I cannot find you!
—EMILY BRONTË, *WUTHERING HEIGHTS*

CHAPTER THIRTY

Her Instagram page was still up on the iPad. Her dad's iPad. Amy's Instagram. Catherine couldn't believe it. She'd been lying on the couch after Henry left, idly staring at the ceiling, all her past fervor and determination gone, leaving her exhausted, drained. Her mind started to drift in that way it never had before that night in the dorms, to something dark and dire. The iPad was on the coffee table, sealed neatly away in its black cover. She reached for it without getting up, put in the password—her birthday—and scrolled idly through Yahoo! News before typing *Instagram* into the search bar, wanting something mindless.

As she scrolled—posts and pictures—she realized it wasn't her own account she was seeing.

Amy was still logged in, from the day she'd come over with the bread. Catherine saw the sliding images of food and selfies, Amy's small circular picture at the top: blue ocean waters, sand on skin, a tongue sticking out. Amy at the beach last summer, a week Catherine got off. What had she done, while Amy was away with her parents? She couldn't remember.

Catherine's hand stilled. She was scared to click anything, sure the page would refresh itself, bring her to a login screen. How was the account still up? Her father, who didn't have an

Instagram, clearly hadn't been using the website. And hadn't Amy signed out of her account? But no, Catherine remembered. They'd gone right to YouTube. Comedians and food. Always back to food with Amy, always.

Maybe it was the iPad's settings. To remember passwords, to keep accounts logged in. But still, it unnerved her.

"Amy?" she said softly.

You have to look.

The page was glowing. The time in the corner read nearly five. Her dad was upstairs resting after his shopping, her mother due back from work within the hour. Slowly, as though waiting for the iPad to detonate, Catherine clicked on the icon that would bring her to Amy's direct messages.

The page didn't reset. Instead, the messages popped up. Catherine scrolled through them, looking for any messages sent before Christmas or right after.

Hannah is going insane over your bread. Even better than last year. How do you do it?

lol it's baking, like science

nah, you have a secret I know it

lol NO i just like baking

glad hannah likes it

i like it too.

> not ignoring me for lama hannah are you

> *lame I mean

>> i think lama hannah is better

> lol you may be right

> but seriously it's awesome

> i want more

And on and on and on. Catherine felt sick reading them. Matt Walsh. Sixteen years old. Flirting with a twelve-year-old who wasn't even *in* high school yet. Catherine swallowed against the bile in her throat.

Her phone buzzed. She tore her eyes away and read Andrew's text message.

And she felt so, so stupid.

Why hadn't she thought of Amy's social media? Why hadn't she realized how much danger that exposed Amy to? So much for her wariness when it came to Amy, her protectiveness or awareness or whatever you wanted to call it. She hadn't even *told* Henry and Andrew about running into Matt at Starbucks. And she'd been too casual about her encounter with Hannah. She should have made it clear exactly what Hannah had said about Matt, how weird it was, how *important.*

She texted Andrew back, then Henry, the whole time picturing Matt in the rain, the scratches up his thin, wet arms.

Catherine sat up straighter on the couch and read through the messages again. Things kept popping out at her with every new reading, little details that made her want to scream.

Like how he changed his tone to match hers, his first line more formal and then following Amy's the more they talked. Matt adding *lol*s and using less capitalization and punctuation with every line. Joking. Flirting. She could almost see Amy at her computer in her bedroom, typing and giggling, her heart beating fast even though she wasn't moving. Catherine had been twelve once. She knew what it was like. But her only interest then had been Henry, and they'd been the same age.

It's illegal, she thought. *Has to be.*

Flirting's not illegal, that stupid mean voice inside her said.

No, she said back. *But other things are.*

She shut the iPad off, snapped the cover closed. Forget James. Forget weird cryptic phone calls and prescription pills and pastors.

Amy's killer lived three streets down. Amy made him soup once. They'd boiled the broth all afternoon.

i want more

She was out the door in an instant, running down the road in the dark. No coat, her sneakers half on, the wind tearing at her throat like a hand.

—

Catherine thought her rage would get her there quickly, but it was cold and the Walshes' house was farther away than she thought. By the time she arrived at the house, she was panting, the skin on her face hot but the rest of her goose-bumped and shivering. She rang the doorbell before she could stop herself, waited a moment, then hit the door a few times until her palm stung. The porch light was on, and through a window she could see a clean, neat home with square rugs and pillows ramrod straight on a slim couch.

You were here. You were here this whole time.

The door opened, showing a wide entryway and a set of stairs. Hannah stood before her, already in pajamas. They had Disney princesses patterned on the blue fabric. The sight of them made Catherine want to cry.

"Is Matt here?"

Her voice was too fast, her question like a whip lashing out, and Hannah's eyes narrowed. She took a step back.

Hannah's mother suddenly appeared, a small dog on her heels, its nails clicking on the hardwood. "Catherine," she said, looking alarmed at the sight of her. "What are you doing here?"

"I came to see Matt."

"Matt?"

Catherine smoothed down her hair. She wanted to look normal and knew she was failing miserably. Even the dog was gazing up at her with its head tilted to one side. "Please," she said. "It's important. Is he here?"

Mrs. Walsh appeared to hesitate; then she said, "We were just about to sit down to eat—"

"No, we weren't. You still have to make the rice," Hannah

said, seemingly recovered. She'd picked up the dog and was stroking its white fur. She looked up at Catherine. "Brown rice takes forever. Plus, it's gross."

"I'll get him," Mrs. Walsh said, putting a hand on her daughter's shoulder. "Come on. Back to the kitchen."

Hannah gave Catherine one last look. "I miss Amy. I keep thinking I see her around, you know? And she'll come over to hang out. Like now, I thought you were her. Knocking to come in."

It was like the girl had slapped her. Catherine felt her face burn, her eyes smart.

"I—" she began, but Mrs. Walsh had already led Hannah away and called Matt's name up the stairs. The door was left wide, but despite the cold, Catherine waited on the doorstep until Matt came down the stairs toward her.

"Hello?" he said, eyeing her with some surprise. "What's going on?"

"Can you come outside?"

"Why?"

"Please." She nodded to the brick walkway. "It's important. It's—about Hannah," she invented wildly.

"What about Hannah?"

"Please. Just for a second."

She looked at him in the low porch light, wondering if Amy thought he was handsome. Maybe. Almost. And at twelve, almost was usually enough.

He joined her on the walk, closing the door behind him and crossing his arms over his chest, still looking uncertain. "What?"

"It's not about Hannah. It's about Amy." Her voice was shaking as well as her body. She didn't want that. She wanted to be calm, stoic even, so sternly indignant he would have to confess. Instead her teeth were chattering so hard she could barely speak.

It was the scratches on his arms, she thought. They made her want to lunge at him, break open the thin red lines with her own nails. Do what Amy couldn't.

"I don't want to talk about Amy—"

"But you talked to her. You—on Instagram. You talked to her—"

Her teeth bit down on her tongue and a burst of pain exploded in her mouth. She winced and put her hands to her lips, and by the time she looked back at Matt, his face was knowing and bitter, his eyes narrowed to slits.

"Instagram," he repeated. He raised his arms above his head and let his hands rest on his hair. The door was red behind him, the porch light small and pale and yellow. "Fucking Instagram."

"You t-talked to her." Her tongue felt like it was bleeding, like she'd torn a hole in it. "The cops, they already know—"

He shoved her.

It came out of nowhere. One second his hands were on his head and the next they hit high on her chest, his palms at her collarbone, toppling her backward.

She fell back onto the brick walkway with a cry she barely

registered, her hands coming behind her too late but scraping themselves to blood just the same. She stared up at him, dazed.

"Fucking Instagram," he spat at her. "You know how many times the cops already talked to me? Came here and freaked my parents the fuck out? Hannah wouldn't even talk to me. Still barely talks to me. Fucking Instagram," he said again. "I didn't fucking do it!"

He moved again, and she cringed back, her shoulder blades against the walk, but he just spun around to the door, slamming it behind him.

She could see the faint glow of the porch light past her feet. Her breath was shallow, her chest tight. Every part of her was vibrating with tension.

Then she was up, running, sprinting so fast up the street that when she got to her front door it had been a minute and yet an hour, her heart beating hard even though she felt her body like a hollow shell for something that had long since died.

The room smelled like smoke and something underneath it, something rotten, like food left out in the heat. There was a heavy weight on her chest. She couldn't breathe. Her eyes were closed. No, open. A dark room, then not; a flash of light. Dark again. Laughter. She groaned. Her throat was hot, bile creeping up her back teeth. Fever. Must be a fever. Sick at home. Medicine and blankets and a remote so she didn't need to move.

Mom. Mom. Mom.

Her legs moving. No, being moved. Too many blankets. Too warm.

She needed to pee, to vomit, to soak in cold water until her skin went from red to white again.

But everything was black except the eyes an inch from hers, rising up past her field of vision and then back down. Up and down. They glowed, those eyes, and she turned her head so she didn't have to look at them. There was a slice of light under the door. Then the door opened. She saw a face. Heard a low shout from the eyes above her, and the door closed again.

Everything fevered like a nightmare borne of illness and infected blood. Half real and half in shadow. It was a burning and a drowning. A death without the dying. A murder in the dark. But after, the corpse got up and ran away.

Still alive.

Still alive.

For now.

———

When she walked inside, her mother thankfully was still out, but the shower running upstairs told her that her dad was awake. She got her phone, kicking herself for not bringing it with her, and saw the texts, the missed calls from Henry and Andrew. She couldn't imagine what to say, couldn't make her hands type out so much as a word. She shut off the phone before walking upstairs, her mind full of that night, the knowledge of it suffocating all other thought.

Eyes. Pairs of eyes.

More than one.

She knocked over the table in the hallway. Small and round. Antiques of her father's. Collectables: eBay and auctions. Everything oiled and arranged. She wondered if anything was new from the sale he'd gone to earlier.

New. She bit back a laugh. New old things. Paying more for something that was brittle as winter branches, rusted through and rotting like a corpse—

She took the items from the carpet and put them back on the table, looking anxiously at her parents' closed bedroom door.

Nothing. But her hands were shaking, the objects knocking against the wood as she set them down. Fear like cold water, her fingertips pale purple, her mouth tasting of blood.

The last item was narrow steel, sheathed in leather. She held it in the flat of her hand, then curled her fingers around it. It wasn't fragile at all. Instead it was hard-edged, solid.

The bones of her chest felt bruised from where he'd pushed her. A girl flat on her back, staring up at the darkness.

Not again, she thought.

Not ever *again.*

CHAPTER THIRTY-ONE

She did eventually text Andrew and Henry. Scared they might get worried and stop by, she sent them both messages saying she'd explain everything at the funeral. Judging by their responses, they didn't want to wait, but she was too tired to even think of putting it all into words, either in texts or calls or in person. She was so drained she wanted to sleep forever.

She spent the rest of Wednesday almost entirely in her room, going downstairs only to eat dinner and try—in vain, she was sure—to reassure her parents that she was fine, just upset about the funeral tomorrow. They ate garlic chicken and pasta. Her mother was tired from work but then kept wanting to talk about Amy's mother. Her father, meanwhile, was distracted; her mother kept asking him to pay attention, and he would nod at her in agreement, which seemed to make her more upset. Catherine swallowed each mouthful of food thinking she probably wouldn't falter if the chicken morphed into cake, the pasta into almonds. Her mind had taken on a strange, severe focus quite unlike the distant, passive melancholy she'd gotten used to recently. She was seeing the world in dark lines and right angles. The way forward had never seemed clearer to her.

Her parents didn't ask her about the funeral planning meeting she was supposed to be at; she never told them she'd agreed to go, and they weren't involved in it, so it was simpler than it might have been otherwise to skip it. Yes, Pechman would be officiating the funeral tomorrow, but at least that would be a larger group. She could avoid him and any of his questions, let herself blend into the grief of the crowd.

She went to bed early. She kept what she'd taken from her father's table under her pillow, one hand clutched around it, so that when she woke up her wrist and hand were numb under the weight of her head. Her room was dark, but her curtains were open. The moon outside her window cast a white glow onto her bedspread. She blinked at the light, feeling dazed, a kind of disquiet you only get from broken sleep at odd hours.

Just past four in the morning. Thursday. Amy's funeral was in eight hours.

She wondered what she would do if Matt Walsh turned up.

She picked up the knife—an 1860s bowie knife from the Civil War complete with scabbard—with one hand.

Maybe it wasn't completely authentic, but she didn't much care. In the moonlight, free from its leather casing, it cast silver shadows across her face and throat, just above the faint bruises Matt had left on her.

—

The coffin was dark brown and gleaming in the stained-glass light. A framed picture of Amy sat on a table next to it, which was typically used to hold bread and wine for Communion. The picture looked like a school image, posed and professional, Amy's skin and eyes clear, her smile a little tense, her shoulders high. Catherine wished they'd used her Instagram picture instead.

Catherine sat with her parents in a pew toward the middle. Henry, with his parents across the aisle, kept trying to meet her eyes. Andrew was nowhere in sight. Pechman was talking. Actually, he was sweating a little; she thought if he took off his suit jacket, there would be stains under the arms.

Catherine shifted in the pew, pulling her dress down over her knees. She didn't like that the coffin was there. Part of her felt like any moment Amy was going to show up, telling her some joke about overly personal food blogs or Gordon Ramsay's crazy hair and being completely surprised at all the fuss everyone was making. *I've been here this whole time. Didn't you see?*

But she wasn't here, Catherine told herself. Her body was, in that coffin, maybe wearing a dress she and Catherine had picked out together, a thousand years ago. But Amy—who she had been, the very essence of her—was gone.

Because of Matt Walsh?

He hadn't turned up. She'd been looking for him since arriving at the church, brushing off Henry and staring around until her pulled-up hair started to strain against its pins. She saw Hannah and her parents, though; she wondered if they realized how conspicuous it was for them to be here when Matt wasn't.

Halfway through the service, it began to pour. She listened

to it, let it drown out the music, the preaching, and the prayers. She'd put the knife in her bag. It just fit, but she'd had to stuff a makeup bag over it, and for good measure, a scarf, just to keep it hidden from view. She kept checking to be sure it was there, her hand reaching underneath, not stilling until she touched leather, or the wood of the handle.

But the funeral progressed without a hitch. Without Matt Walsh.

—

The reception was where she started to unravel.

An unbearable almost-hour of standing dizzy in Amy's kitchen, which didn't smell like anything anymore, and making small talk that wasn't small. Andrew showed up to it, having missed the church service just like before, but Catherine hardly cared. Nor did she care that Henry's parents left right after the funeral, as they were going to their cabin in the Cascade Mountains. A two-plus-hour trip they couldn't put off any longer if they wanted to make their skiing reservation *booked weeks ago so sorry beautiful service, still can't believe it, yes thank you we'll be safe on the roads, this rain just won't let up will it?*

She could hear the tumult of the rain and Amy's mother sobbing, and people murmuring in strange, slow voices that made her want to shake them and make them talk like human beings. She heard the scrape of silverware on square white baking dishes and the listless trickle of fruit-flavored water from the decanter on the table. People milling around the hors d'oeuvres, their breath smelling of cold meat and deviled eggs.

I'm losing my mind, she thought dimly as Henry and Andrew asked her quietly what was wrong, who did she think did it, what had her text meant?

She looked at both of them, wanting to tell them that Amy's kitchen used to smell like spices and there were always thin lines of flour in the hardwood closest to the oven but now they were gone.

"Get me out of here," she said instead.

They did.

———

They went to Henry's house, since his parents weren't there.

"I still can't believe they left," Henry said as they settled themselves in the living room, shaking rain from their hair, their clothes. "Well, actually I can. Anything awkward, anything she can't control or throw money at, she'll bail, my mom. I knew she wouldn't stay for the reception. And of course Dad will do whatever she wants." He rolled his eyes as he flopped into the large armchair by the wall, Molly sitting by his legs with a yawn. "When I get married, I won't be such a pushover, I swear. Andrew, you can sit, you know."

Andrew, who had been hovering in the space between the kitchen and living room, gave a little start, then sat on the couch with Catherine, admittedly as far away from her as possible.

"Catherine?" Henry asked, leaning forward, trying to meet her eyes. "You okay?"

She closed her eyes and, to her horror, felt tears in them. Her mother had seen how upset she was. She hadn't liked the idea of Catherine's leaving the reception, but then Mrs. Lester had touched her arm to ask something and Amy's mother was crying in the background again and in the end, she had relented.

Catherine couldn't get that sound out of her head. That high, keening wail that was like an animal dying. It made her feel a sorrow quite separate from her own, one that carried guilt like a reminder: *You are not the only one who hurts. Or did you forget?*

That reminded her of hell again. Being flung into a tree by an angry God. And you were so lost in your own pain you couldn't see that you were surrounded by trees, a whole forest full of friends and neighbors—strangers, too. All around you, trees.

Catherine turned to Henry. "I want a drink."

"Yeah, okay. You want soda? There's some in the garage—"

"No," Catherine said. "I want a *drink*."

She felt Andrew looking at her, saw Henry raise his eyebrows, but she found she didn't care. If she didn't have *something* she wasn't going to be able to do this. Not after the silence of Amy's funeral, the scream of the reception. Not with bruises against her own bones again. She felt like she was one moment—one memory—away from shutting down entirely. But she couldn't do that. She couldn't be like Amy's mother, sitting and sobbing, unable to speak. She had to tell them about Matt Walsh, about the Instagram messages, about what had happened last night, about what she thought had happened to Amy.

And she would. She just . . . needed something to help her do it.

"I want a drink," she said again, and this time, Henry understood.

———

He came back with a large bottle of Dry Fly Straight Bourbon 101. It was a deep orange-amber color, and he poured them all generous measures into small, wide glasses he took from a high cabinet. She drank, trying not to think about the last time she had tilted her head back like that and let something burn its way down her throat.

She didn't intend to get drunk, but her muscles were softening, her thoughts slowing. The whiskey had warmed her, and the glass in her hand (her second, now empty) smelled faintly of vanilla and spices. It reminded her of Amy, in a good way. Not a coffin in her memory, but a comfort.

She told them everything. The messages from Matt. Her, going to his house. Him, yelling at her, pushing her down. She had Henry pour her a third glass. She was warm all over, her eyes watering not with tears but with tiredness, and found herself leaning back into the couch cushions, slipping off her flats and curling her legs under her. She took her hair down from its pins, feeling the tension leave her temples, her scalp. Her eyes closed. She wanted to disappear.

"This smells like her," she said drowsily, holding the glass up. "Like baking with her. God, we . . . we were always in the kitchen, making stuff, barely went out. Amy was so chill. I loved just . . . being with her. Hanging out. Baking. Her mom was mad about it sometimes. Not sad, like she is now. Did you hear her? How sad she was? But before, she was mad."

The boys were blurry watercolors before her. She felt Molly's head on her leg, a heavy, warm weight.

She stroked Molly's ears, her stitched-together neck. "Okay, not . . . mad. Upset. Amy getting sick. Throwing up." She put a hand to her mouth, wondering if *she* was going to throw up. "But it wasn't . . . wasn't my fault. Like Molly. Molly's sick, and that's not your fault. But her mom would text me at eight in the morning. . . . It wasn't . . . my fault. Was it? Because Molly—"

Henry took the glass from her. "Come on," he said.

"No."

"Catherine." He was kneeling before her, his hands on hers. "Come on. You have to lie down."

"It wasn't my fault," she said again. Her face was hotter now, burning. "Amy," she said, tasting salt in her mouth. *"Amy."*

"I know," Henry said, pulling her to her feet. "I know."

CHAPTER THIRTY-TWO

Andrew watched Henry half lead, half carry Catherine upstairs, presumably to lie down, Molly following them anxiously. He pictured it quite easily—Henry pulling the covers up to her throat, saying something close to her face. Henry, Andrew had discovered, was someone of action. In the maintenance closet, during that tense church meeting, Andrew had been too nervous to move, even after they watched Ken walk down the hallway and Henry's phone lit up. But Henry hadn't hesitated, darting into the hallway and into Pechman's office before Andrew could say a word.

If it had been Henry instead of him in the dorms that night, it might have been different. But Andrew? He just hid behind a door. Every goddamn time.

He knocked back the rest of his drink, then stood up from the couch just as Henry walked back into the living room.

"Going somewhere?" Henry asked him.

Andrew found it hard to look at him. Instead he nodded, glanced around for his coat, then realized he hadn't taken it off. "Home," he said, finally meeting Henry's eyes.

"Harper's place?"

Harper. Like Henry knew the guy. "No," Andrew said. "I

mean, yes, just to grab my stuff. But then I think I'll head back. Home," he added, because Henry was looking at him like he was speaking Japanese.

"O-kay," Henry said, dragging out the word a little. "Any particular reason why?"

Andrew said nothing.

Henry raised his eyebrows. "Are you even going to tell Catherine?"

Again, Andrew said nothing. He was beginning to think that for the past few weeks, everything he'd done, everything he'd said, had been a mistake.

"Right," Henry said, and now his voice was cold. "So you're going to leave me to tell her you bailed."

"I'm not bailing."

"Are you even going to tell Harper what Catherine just told us? About this Matt guy?"

"He already knows," Andrew said, slightly relieved to be able to answer a question. "The cops know about Amy's social media."

"Okay. But do they know about Matt freaking out on Catherine?"

"I'll tell him."

"And what about everything Catherine told us about Pechman? All the money shit and cover-ups. You sure they're not looking at James or his dad?"

"That's what Bob said. I can talk to him again, I guess."

"No offense, but you don't look up to talking to anyone

about anything right now. Actually, you look as bad as Catherine."

"I'm fine."

Henry sat back down in the armchair. Sitting while Andrew was standing should have made Henry seem smaller, diminished, but it didn't somehow. He looked up at Andrew with a steely smile. "Andrew Worthington," he said, and there was something soft and gentle in his voice that Andrew didn't trust at all. "I've been wondering about something. Maybe you can help me with it."

Andrew kept silent, still standing, hands deep in his coat pockets.

"This . . . church thing," Henry continued. "You didn't come to the service on Sunday, just the reception. And you didn't come to the funeral, just to Amy's house—"

"I didn't get an invitation."

"*No one* got an invitation," Henry said. He poured himself another drink. "It was open to the whole church, which admittedly you're not a part of, but Catherine did tell you to come. And it wasn't like they were checking tickets at the door. Still, you only came to the reception. In fact, the *only* time you came inside the actual church was when we broke in. Why was that?"

It was Andrew's turn to look confused. "Why was . . . what?"

"Why don't you like churches?" Henry asked.

Andrew stared at him.

"It's a simple question," Henry said. He downed his drink in one and poured another.

"Not really."

"I have a few theories," Henry said, as though Andrew hadn't spoken, and he actually wanted to—wanted to wipe that smug look off Henry's face and tell him that theories were based on observed facts or whatever and Henry didn't know shit about him—but Andrew stayed silent.

"One," Henry began, settling into the chair, full glass in hand. "Maybe you grew up in a terrible church. Were molested or something. *Two*," he said, more forcefully, because he saw the look on Andrew's face, "you're gay and it's not clear if we'd be cool with it." He gave another thin smile. "Or maybe you think the minute you step through the church doors for worship you'll be struck down by lightning."

"For being gay?" Andrew said, incredulous. "Which, by the way, I'm *not*—"

But Henry cut him off: "For being a sinner."

"I thought everyone was a sinner," Andrew muttered.

"Yes, but you're supposed to confess your sins to God and to the people you've sinned against," said Henry in a bored voice, as though reciting an old lesson, which, Andrew realized, he probably was. "Make amends. You know there's this part in the Bible where they'd make these sacrifices to God in this holy temple, but God told them they couldn't do that if they'd sinned against someone and hadn't made it right. He told them to leave the temple and go be reconciled to their brother—"

"Speaking of having something against your brother," Andrew cut in, "you know she thought you might be involved?

Before this Matt thing? Yeah, she thought you knew something about James and were protecting him. She told me."

Henry's face didn't change. "I'm not her brother. And I wasn't involved."

"Really?"

"Yeah, *really.*" Henry shot him an irritated look, finished his third—fourth?—drink and set the glass down hard on the glass tabletop, making it rattle. "Just stop. Stop for a second, okay? You know I didn't do anything to Amy. Because I was somewhere else, right? Unlike you, I might add—but that's beside the point," he said, waving a hand as Andrew opened his mouth again. "This isn't even *about* Amy."

"Then who is it about?"

"Catherine."

Andrew could tell he was trying to appear calm, but there was a hectic flush in Henry's cheeks that made him look fevered.

"You can tell me, you know," Henry said.

"Tell you what?"

"Why you look like you're carrying around a metaphorical cross all the time. You know you don't *actually* have to be miserable twenty-four-seven just because you raped her."

One second. Two. Andrew could not hear one single sound in the entire house, not even his own breath, or Henry's.

"Surprised I know?" Henry said, his voice soft.

Andrew stared at him. "You're wr-wrong," he said, his chest so tight the words came out jagged. "Completely wr—"

"I don't think I am. I've been thinking about it all week.

Watching how you look at her. Like you want to get hit by a car every time she smiles at you. It's eating you up. It's why you drove here to bring her stuff back." He adopted a fake-casual voice. "You don't live far away and just kind of maybe thought after Christmas you might as well—*bullshit.* You felt bad. So fucking bad you can't even go to a church service, not even a funeral for a murdered kid. Because what you did to Catherine is pretty much on par with what this guy—Matt or James or whoever the fuck he is—did to Amy. Maybe you get points for feeling guilty, but on the whole I don't really think so. Once she tells me the truth, I'll kill you just the same."

Andrew took a step back as though Henry had lunged at him, even though the other boy was still sitting down. "I didn't rape her." The words came out fast now, panicked. Jesus, he even *sounded* guilty. "I just—"

"You just *what?*"

"I knew!" he burst out. "I knew! I saw the guys in the hallway before, just standing there like they were waiting for something"—he saw Henry's eyes narrow but plowed on—"and I didn't say anything to them even though I wanted to know why they were just fucking standing there the night after finals when everyone else was out. And then a few minutes later there was a different guy there and the one from before, he—he asked the new guy if he was going—going to go again but it had to be a-after him and I just . . . I just walked back to my room and tried not to think about it. But I stayed awake and kept checking the hallway and finally she was there and I—I knew." He blew out a ragged breath. "I knew what I had done. And I knew it was my fault."

Henry said nothing. Andrew kept waiting for him to say something, *do* something. Hell, even stand up and try to hit him. But the other boy wasn't even looking at him. Henry was looking past him, and something dropped out of Andrew's stomach at the expression on his face. He turned to see Catherine standing feet behind him like a sleepwalker, her skin pale against her funeral clothes, her blue eyes wide, and Andrew saw something shift there as she looked at him, as clear a change as if they'd turned black or blind.

"You knew?" she said. Just then, Molly came down the stairs and trotted up to Catherine. She appeared not to notice.

"Catherine—" But he stopped. He didn't know what to say. She was Joan of Arc asking her executioner why, and he didn't have an answer.

"Get out," she said.

He didn't move.

"Get out!" Her face was turning red, her eyes spilling over, her whole body shaking. "Go—"

He went.

CHAPTER THIRTY-THREE

Catherine stumbled forward, felt her hands on the stainless steel of the Brisboises' sleek refrigerator, and let herself slide down it.

Henry was saying something. She tried to listen, but her mind sounded like a windstorm and nothing else was getting through.

He knew.

Andrew. He'd been there that night. Saw . . . them. *Waiting.*

She wanted to peel her skin off with her own fingernails, wanted to bleed until there wasn't anything left inside her. Wasn't that an old healing ritual, hundreds of years ago? Rid the body of impurities. Drain it dry.

But her skin was whole, all her blood inside it. Had Amy bled that night, in the struggle? Or was it just her breath that had been taken, and all her blood was left to thicken inside her, slowing to a stop inside her veins?

Catherine felt like hers was doing the same as she knelt like an invalid in Henry's kitchen, so far from the girl she used to be it was like that girl had died and all that was left was a ghost who drifted through the rain and made her grave in the trees.

Catherine raised her head. She tasted whiskey mixed with

the salt of tears. She thought if Henry left too she would fall through the earth. He seemed to her a tether keeping her from the depths of hell, a forest she'd never find her way out of. "I'm sorry," she said.

"For what?"

"For not talking to you. Last year. And the ones before it."

Henry reached out a hand, slowly, as though sure she'd shy away from him. But when his hand fell to her hair, she didn't move.

It cannot be helped.

She thought she knew now what her father had meant. It was as though something in her had latched onto something in Henry years ago, and they were fused into one. A connection formed in childhood that couldn't be changed, not after telling him about hearing her parents fighting, and vomiting on his bare feet after too many summer snow cones. And wrestling in the community pool, hearing the sound of whistles and laughter oddly muffled under the water, his hands on her shoulders, her legs.

He was her childhood, those laughing-crying-panting-breathless days when life had been so much simpler but also more concentrated in its intensity. And then she'd gone away, coming back changed, different—wary of anything childish or shameful, her mind remembering the kiss under garden lights, Mrs. Brisbois's rigid disapproval. She told herself he didn't fit into her life anymore. She told herself it was pathetic to be his shadow. How cruel she'd been. How senselessly cruel. Throwing them away—as careless as a suicide, a soul flung high to fall where it may.

Of course, he fit. He'd always fit. And if she was his shadow, he was hers as well. Time hadn't changed that. Her cutting him out of her life hadn't changed that. Even during senior year, just being in the same room with him again had been a struggle. It affected her. *He* affected her. She had allowed him inside her beating child's heart and years later, at eighteen, was surprised to find him still there, as though he'd been hidden away all this time.

She wouldn't cast him aside again. Andrew was gone. Amy was dead. She wouldn't lose Henry, too.

"Can you take me?" she asked him.

His hand traced its way from the top of her head to her shoulders, following her hairline so closely his fingers brushed against her tears on the way down. "Where?" he asked her.

"You know."

He helped Catherine get up, steadying her as she breathed shallowly for a minute before starting to walk. They went outside, Henry gently pushing Molly back before closing the front door. Catherine clung to him. His car was cold when he opened it for her. No music. The blur of the world outside: thin trees, the sun inching down behind them. Everything green and gold and entirely silent. He didn't have to ask her anything. She didn't have to speak.

Because of course, he did know.

Andrew hit his hand on the steering wheel, his lips pulled back against his teeth. His breath sounded thin, whistling, and even though it was only a ten-minute drive to Bob and Minda's house, it felt as though his mind and body had traveled a hundred miles to get there. He couldn't get that image of Catherine out of his head: like a ghost in her black clothes, the way her eyes changed as she realized.

It was just past four p.m. He could be back home in an hour. Out of this town for good. If Bob wasn't there he'd stop by the station to talk to him. But he'd grab his things now, leave a note for Minda if she was out too. Polite, even though being polite was the last thing on his mind. Manners and courtesy had been drilled into him at a young age: make his bed and open doors and please and thank you always and was that why he had done it? Gone back to his dorm room and waited in the dark for a sound that told him he was right even though a part of him already knew it? Scared to act, to cause any kind of confrontation. Don't make a fuss and don't make a scene and don't draw attention—lessons he learned as his parents' marriage broke apart. Meek and mild like that child—but he *wasn't* a child anymore. So why the hell was he still acting like one?

There was something bubbling up inside him as he entered the garage code and went into the house. He felt on the edge of rage. Like if someone said something to him, he'd shout a reply; if someone touched him, he might hit their hand away.

Minda greeted him from the kitchen. The sound of her voice rolled over him and he tried to master himself, rearrange his features into a face she wouldn't question.

"Hi," he said when he got to the kitchen. Minda was on her laptop at the table.

"Hi yourself," she said brightly. She was wearing her reading glasses, with narrow purple frames. "What are you up to?"

"I'm headed home, actually."

"Home?"

"Yeah. I, uh, think I'll grab my stuff now. Where's Bob?" Andrew had seen both cars in the garage.

She nodded her head. "He's upstairs, but he's on the phone. Very important stuff, apparently. *Cannot* be disturbed." She rolled her eyes. "Why? What's up?"

"Just want to talk to him before I go."

Minda set down the pen she was holding and leaned back in her chair, her eyes studying him behind her glasses. "What happened?"

"What?"

"What happened?" she repeated.

He tried to look confused. "Nothing. I'm fine."

"Uh-huh." She stood up and walked over to him, her expression shrewd. "You smell like alcohol."

He swore inwardly. "It wasn't—I was *with* people who were drinking."

"And you, what? Used it as mouthwash? Come on, Andrew—"

She reached for him but he jerked back. "Can you just get Bob? I need to talk to him."

She raised her eyebrows. "If you think he's going to be more relaxed about this than I am, I think you *may* be forgetting his chosen profession."

"I need to talk to him," Andrew said again. "Please."

Minda looked him over one more time. "You're not leaving tonight."

He stared at her.

"You're not," she said again, as though he hadn't heard her.

"I—Minda, you don't get it. I *have* to leave tonight. I can't stay here."

"Well, if that's not what all hosts just love to hear from their guests, I don't know what is. No, you're not leaving, Andrew. Not least because your mother would never talk to me again. How many drinks did you have?"

"One," he admitted, the word coming like a pulled tooth.

"Then you won't pass a Breathalyzer if you get pulled over. Not until very early morning."

He looked at her blankly.

"Alcohol absorption," she said. "There's a timeline. I'm a doctor, you know, in case you forgot my job as well."

Andrew disregarded this. "I'm below the legal limit *now*."

"Kid, you are eighteen years old. The legal limit for you is *zero*. And you won't blow a zero-point-zero-zero until"—she glanced at the clock—"two, maybe three in the morning."

"Then I won't get pulled over—"

"As opposed to all those people who plan on getting pulled over—"

"Don't talk to me like you're my mom. You're not even *a* mom."

The silence in the kitchen was a solid thing, pushing into all the corners; Andrew was almost surprised it didn't shove the table and chairs against the wall like a poltergeist.

"I'm sorry," he began. "Minda—"

"Sit."

"Please, I shouldn't have—"

"*Sit.*"

He sat.

She walked to the fridge, took out a whole roasted chicken, and set it in front of him, moving her laptop to the side as she did so. The chicken was store-bought, in a rounded plastic container that looked like a dome. Andrew could see drops of condensation clinging to the plastic.

"Eat," Minda said. She pushed her glasses onto her head.

Andrew gave her an incredulous look.

Minda undid the container with a snap. She tossed the top aside and it skidded across the table, almost to the edge. "With your fingers. No need for manners here. I'm not a mother, after all. I am a black woman doctor, married but happily child-free, so clearly I don't conform to any expectations. Why should you?"

"I said I was sorry," Andrew said, a little desperately. Looking at the chicken reminded him of that movie *Matilda* where a fat kid had to eat a chocolate cake the size of an ottoman. "I shouldn't have said that."

"Stop looking so terrified." Minda pushed the chicken toward him, but her voice had gentled a little. "You don't have to eat all of it. I'm not mad." A pause. "Okay, a little. You were being rude. But I think I know why."

Slowly, Andrew reached out and tore a piece of chicken off. It was cold but smelled good and tasted better. "Yeah?" he said, chewing.

"Yeah," she said. "Trauma. You have all the classic signs."

"I do not—"

"You're shaking and pale and look like crap. You're not eating or sleeping unless someone makes you, and you keep looking around like you're waiting for something to suddenly attack you. Classic trauma syndrome."

"It's not me," Andrew said, "who was traumatized."

"Trauma doesn't have to happen to you directly to have an effect."

Andrew frowned at her. "You deal with trauma? I thought maybe the ER or—"

"People think GI is all poop and vomit, and it is," she admitted. "But it's also emaciation and feeding tubes and feet of intestine removed to save someone's life. And sometimes patients die. Like this morning."

"I'm sorry."

She waved a hand. "We knew it was coming. Long time coming." She tapped her fingers on the table. "You're not eating."

He took more chicken. Almost despite himself, he was feeling a little better—but just barely. "So is this why you always feed people? Because you can't feed your patients?"

"And there you go with the detective stuff again. I wish you wouldn't fight it, you know."

"I'm not a detective."

"No, you're not. You're a kid with too much on his plate, and I'm not talking about food. Talk to me."

"I am."

"No," she said. "*Talk* to me."

CHAPTER THIRTY-FOUR

Catherine hadn't been to the clifftop since high school, but it looked pretty much the same.

A wide but unpaved road through the trees opening to a large semicircular expanse that ended at the cliff. There was a guard-rail that curved at the edge, maybe three feet high. In the fading light, it was hard to see. Catherine looked at the clock. Almost four-thirty. Sunset. So strange, how early it happened in winter. Full dark by five. Already the sun was falling, and she had to admit it was a brilliant sight: orange and red like fire across the landscape, the tops of mountains edged in gold, the sun cutting through tree branches, leaving amber shadows across the earth.

The strange, lone lamppost wasn't on yet, but even in its unlit state, it drew her eye as Henry parked the car.

Was that where it had happened?

Her heart started to race. She wondered if this was a bad idea. But a part of her wanted to see it—no, not wanted, that wasn't right. She didn't *want* to be here. But she needed to. She needed to stop hiding because eventually the terrible things came for you anyway: memories trickling back and coffins under stained glass and a confession like a slap in the face. She'd rather knock on the gates of hell than have them swallow her with no warning. And she felt Amy deserved more from her than cowardice.

"You cold?" Henry asked, his hand fiddling with the dials.

Catherine barely heard him. She was still looking past him, out the driver's-side window at the lamppost. There was no police tape. No indication a crime had happened there. It seemed wrong somehow.

"Someone should have brought flowers," she said.

"We can go back—"

"No. Later. We should stay." She blinked as the sun began to slip down the sky. "It's pretty here. Do you think—do you think they'll be able to get him?"

"Who?"

"Matt."

Henry blew out a breath. "I don't know."

The light fell. Her head drifted to the side, to Henry's shoulder. She felt him take her hand and she didn't pull away. Together, they watched the sunset fade, one last blaze through the windshield before sinking out of sight.

"Catherine," Henry said. His voice sounded strange.

"What?" She raised her head. His face was very close to hers, and in the coming night, his eyes seemed much darker than blue.

He kissed her.

———

Andrew looked at Minda, and to his surprise found he did want to tell her. He wanted to tell *someone*. That much was clear after

Henry's brief taunting had made him blurt out everything. And maybe Henry had had a point about the church; no, he wasn't really religious, but there was something about stepping over the threshold of a church with stained glass. Something about violins and a choir and old verses read aloud from pages so thin they crinkled like leaves when touched. He knew he couldn't handle it.

It was like years ago when he'd swum in the neighborhood lake even though his mom had told him a million times not to. When he got home he sprinted upstairs and tried to shower off the evidence before she saw him, using as much soap as possible, washing his skin until it hurt. But it was no use; he could still smell the lake on him afterward, a scent like sweat and rotten vegetables. Going to church would have been like walking down the stairs after that shower, knowing there were some things you couldn't wash off.

He shook his head. "I can't."

Minda gave him a swift, searching look. "Fine."

"Fine?"

She shrugged. "I can't make you talk. But I can make you listen. You'll have to give me something to talk about, though. I'm not doing all the work."

"I don't—"

"Ask me a question. Give me a launching pad."

Andrew blinked, taken aback.

"And you have to keep eating."

He took more chicken. His fingers were a greasy mess. After

he swallowed, he thought of something. "How'd you know when I'd sober up? I told you I had one drink and you said I had to wait until the morning or I wouldn't pass a Breathalyzer."

"I lied." She raised her hands in mock protest at his expression. "Like I was going to let you drive in the state you were in. *Mental* state, my friend, not physical. You had one drink? You'll blow a flat zero in max two hours, more likely one, but I don't want you driving when it's dark."

"Now you're sounding like a mom again."

This time, she smiled at him. "You're looking better. Would it cheer you up more if I tell you about how the body processes alcohol?"

"Not rea—"

"So the body processes alcohol at a standard rate of point-zero-one-five-percent blood-alcohol concentration per hour, and that's about one drink. Of course, there's variation, but alcohol actually doesn't stay in the body as long as, say, food. For instance, that chicken you're eating will probably leave your stomach in three, four hours."

"Good to kn—" He froze, a piece of chicken halfway to his mouth. He'd eaten almost all of the leg, and he could see the pink-tipped bone protruding from the torn flesh. "What if it didn't?" he asked.

CHAPTER THIRTY-FIVE

It was as though a bomb had gone off right in front of her. Catherine jerked back so hard she felt her head hit the passenger-side window.

"Jesus," she heard him say. "*Catherine.* Catherine?"

There were stars in her field of vision. Gingerly, she put her hand to her head, eyes screwed shut, feeling impossibly embarrassed.

"I'm sorry," she muttered.

"What?"

She sat back up but still didn't look at him. "Sorry. For . . . I just . . ." Her voice trailed off. She didn't know how to explain it. Even now her heart was hammering in her chest. "Maybe this was a bad idea."

He said nothing. Actually, he said nothing for so long that she turned to look at him. He was staring straight ahead, at the edge of the clifftop. "Why didn't you tell me?"

She stared at him.

"That you were raped? Why didn't you tell me?"

Catherine felt her mouth open, then close. "*What?*"

"Like, Andrew had to come, and then you told both of us. You could have just told me."

She didn't know what to say. Finally, she managed, "Henry, I didn't tell *anyone*. Not really, I—" She shook her head. "Listen, let's just . . . Let's just go home."

"No," he said. "Let's not."

———

"What do you mean, 'What if it didn't?'" Minda said.

"Like, are there variations?" Andrew said. "For stomach digestion. Can someone else eat this chicken and it go through their stomach a lot slower than it would mine?"

She tilted her head at him. "Why are you asking this?"

His heart was beating fast, each movement of blood bringing snatches of memory closer together in his mind.

He told Minda he was just curious.

"Uh-huh. You're not eating."

"If you answer my question I will eat this entire chicken, Minda."

Minda rolled her eyes. "I'll believe it when I see it. But yes, to answer your question. There are variations in how long it takes the stomach to digest food. Women tend on average to have slower transit time than men throughout the entire digestive system, including the stomach, but it depends on the food, too: certain foods pass to the small intestine more quickly than others. Carbohydrates are mostly absorbed in the small intestine, so they leave the stomach before, say, proteins, which are broken down almost completely in the stomach. Fats usually take the longest because they have to be emulsified by liver bile before moving down the digestive tract." Another pause. "Okay, so my job is a little gross."

"But are there variations in people?" Andrew pressed. "Not just women in general having slower digestions, but specific people—"

"You're asking about the girl," Minda said, her eyes widening. "Because she was found outside. In the cold. The rain. Can't depend too much on body temp with those extremes so you use stomach contents to establish TOD. Am I right?"

Andrew said nothing. He was hearing Catherine's drunken recollections about Amy, seeing Henry's raised eyebrows when Andrew had told him the time of death. And he was, like Minda, remembering his conversation with Bob, the explanation about how Amy's young age had been so *helpful* in determining the time of death. Her last meal, eaten with her parents. An exact timeline. Simple math.

"Hate to break it to you, kid, but what you're talking about is fairly rare. Delayed stomach emptying—or gastroparesis—isn't usually diagnosed until adolescence or later. And yes, it primarily affects women, but still"—she shook her head—"unlikely."

"Tell me about it."

You just want Henry to not have an alibi, a sharp voice inside him said. *That's why you're doing this.*

He ignored it.

To his surprise, Minda's face grew tight and solemn and she tapped her fingers on the table again. "My patient who died this morning had gastroparesis. Diagnosed four years ago. We tried everything. Nausea pills and Reglan and Dexilant and Motilium. Did the stomach pacemaker. Caused an infection. We had to remove it. Over the course of all this treatment she went from a hundred and forty to eighty. Pounds," she added at his expression. "We had to tube-feed her. Not through the nose. No point if the nutrients had to go through the stomach, where they'd just sit there and rot for two days before she threw them up again. We did a PEJ. Percutaneous J-tube. Inserted right into the small intestine. But . . . she was ready. She didn't want to live like that anymore." Minda trailed off, her eyes past him, distant. "She was twenty-nine."

"I'm sorry."

"So am I." She rubbed her eyes briefly. "It's a nasty disease. And half the time we're not even sure what caused it. Yes, you can get it from diabetes or a bad bout of the flu—what we call postviral gastroparesis—but so many cases I see are idiopathic. No known cause. Mind you, not all cases are as severe as the one I told you about. It's not . . . common to die from gastroparesis. It does happen, though. Nutrient deficiency leading to severe malnutrition leading to organ failure—but usually it's manageable. Some people go years before it gets bad enough to even warrant medical attention. They think they have IBS, reflux, or just ate something rotten. They avoid milk or gluten or go vegan. They have low energy. They say they have a *sensitive system* until the symptoms get worse and they're throwing up their dinners in the morning and then they come to someone like me and get a diagnosis." She gave a wry chuckle. "You know, it's funny—well, not funny, but interesting. One of the symptoms. It's not physical, but some of my GP patients get very interested in food, even before they know they're actually sick with a disease and not just drinking milk that's gone bad. Partly it's the diets they try to feel better, but it's also more than that. Some may get into cooking or watching *Cupcake Armies* or whatever it's called, studying food almost, as though their mind is trying to make sense of what's wrong in their body before they even really *know* something is wrong. One of my patients was even considering culinary school before she was diagnosed. It's not a conscious thing, I don't think. But it's interesting, you know? Andrew?"

CHAPTER THIRTY-SIX

Catherine looked at Henry for a long moment. "We're not . . . going home?" she asked.

He was very still, his eyes fixed on the windshield; then he shifted in the driver's seat to face her head-on.

"You never talked to me senior year," he said.

She stared at him.

"You never talked to me. You didn't even sit near me. One class we had together all of high school and you pretended I wasn't even there. You said sorry before, in the kitchen, but you didn't say why."

She shifted where she sat, feeling her purse scrape against her boots. Outside the car, the falling night was like a blanket being pulled over the earth. "Henry—" she tried, but he cut her off.

"Was it Josh?" he asked.

"Josh?"

"Your boyfriend."

Her heart twisted beneath her ribs. "No. No, it wasn't Josh."

"What, then?"

"It—" She licked her lips. "I was nervous."

"Nervous."

"To talk to you."

"I made you nervous?"

"No. Yes."

"Which is it?"

"I don't know!" she burst out. "Henry, I don't even know what we're talking about—"

"We're talking about *us,* Catherine. We're talking about us."

She didn't know what to say to that. She felt confused and impatient and a little dizzy with the sudden shift in conversation. Some part of her knew she should be more sympathetic, should offer him a reason, but she didn't know what to say besides an apology, and she'd already done that. Maybe it wasn't enough. Fine. But what did he want from her?

"I—I was wrong," she stammered. "I know that. I was stupid and fourteen and I didn't—didn't think about it. About us. I'm sorry."

Silence.

"Henry, can we just—?"

"Just what?"

"Go home."

She realized this was the wrong thing to say; something seemed to fall behind his eyes.

"I want an answer first."

She felt like she was about to cry again. "An answer for *what*?"

"Why you didn't tell me about what happened to you."

"I—*what*? Henry, why would I tell you something like that? We're not—I'm sorry, but we hadn't talked in years—"

"We talked at prom."

She gaped at him, caught off guard. "Yes," she managed. "Yes, okay, but for like a minute—"

"And whose fault is that? You know, I bet if I hadn't walked past your house before Christmas, you wouldn't have even thought of me."

"That's not true."

Henry turned back to the front of the car. She watched his profile, the curve of his eyelashes as his gaze darted. "I missed you," he said. "I missed you so much, Catherine."

—

Minda was staring at him, and Andrew knew something must have happened in his face, but he couldn't do anything about it. His mind was racing, facts spiraling like tendrils, reaching out and wrapping together, forming a conclusion that now seemed not just possible but likely.

Amy's bouts of vomiting. And not just vomiting, but *delayed* vomiting.

her mom would text me at eight in the morning

Andrew had gotten food poisoning before, waking up in the middle of the night after a seafood dinner to spew up oily sauce and shriveled bits of shrimp, his stomach churning. But by three in the morning there was nothing left to heave up, and he was resigned to gagging up bile and sweating through the T-shirt and shorts he'd worn to bed.

He'd never heard of vomiting so long after a meal. Throwing

up dinners in the morning. How long between the eating and the illness? Ten hours? *Twelve?*

Catherine had also mentioned that she and Amy didn't go out often, making Amy seem relaxed almost to the point of lethargy. Unusual, wasn't it, for a child to have such low energy she'd rather stay inside? But if Amy was sick, if her body wasn't processing food the way it should, of course that would affect her energy levels—except when it came to food. Because Amy had an interest in food that went beyond the norm. How many twelve-year-olds had their own baking business complete with online ordering and a seasonal bike-delivery service? More than a hobby even, it seemed to Andrew that Amy had been focused on food almost to the point of fixating on it.

studying food almost, as though their mind is trying to make sense of what's wrong in their body

"Say she had it," he said.

Minda was starting to look alarmed now, but he didn't care. He licked his lips. His mouth, despite the greasy chicken, felt exceptionally dry.

"Say she had it. The girl who died. Amy. Say she had gastroparesis and she didn't know, no one knew, and her last meal was dinner at seven or eight or whatever—could the time of death be wrong? Could they have opened her up and looked at what she ate for dinner and the food be so undigested that they thought she died just a few hours after dinner when really she was killed later?"

Minda gave him a pained look. "Andrew, if this is about that girl you were with—"

"Of *course* it's about her!" Andrew burst out. "But does it *matter*? Does it change the answer?"

When Minda spoke, her voice was flat, like a speaker at a lecture who'd gotten a question she didn't much like. "If the victim had undiagnosed gastroparesis, yes, the time of death, if based primarily on stomach contents and expected digestion time, could be off."

"By how much?"

Silence.

"By how much?"

"Hours," she said.

Andrew bolted from the table.

CHAPTER THIRTY-SEVEN

The lamppost just outside the car clicked on, and Catherine turned away from the light, blinking and slightly dazed. There were gold pinpricks behind her eyes that took a moment to fade. When she opened her eyes, Henry was looking at her.

"It's on a timer," he said. He was pointing to the car clock, which read 5:01. "You okay?"

"Yeah." It was strange, but she'd expected it to be later. "Henry, can we . . . can we go now?"

He said nothing. And it was strange, as well, that as she watched him, she heard Andrew's voice in her head.

If I were going to meet with someone about something illegal or horrible or whatever, I wouldn't get in a car with them. I'd want more control than that.

A way to get out, at least.

She reached for the door handle, even though she wasn't sure, even as her hand moved back, why she was doing so.

There was a plastic *click* from Henry's side of the car. Her hand pulled, but the door remained firmly closed.

"Trying to get out?" Henry said. Then, a beat later, he laughed. "Just kidding. Jesus, look at your face. Relax."

She watched his hand move on the armrest by his door. She heard two more clicks. The doors unlocking, then locking again.

"Henry." Her voice was soft, quiet. "I'd like—"

"Right. You'd *like*." The rancor in his voice took her aback. He seemed to notice this and exhaled, hard. "Sorry. Just . . . it's nice here. I don't know why you want to go. I mean, you were the one who wanted to come in the first place."

"Yes," she said, trying to keep her voice even. "But I don't want to be here anymore."

"So you changed your mind."

"I—yes. Yes, I changed my mind."

"Color me shocked."

She blinked. "What's that supposed to mean?"

"Nothing." His eyes flicked across her face and then away. "Why do you look like that?"

"Like what?" She realized how much his breath smelled of whiskey. She, however, had never felt more sober.

"Like you're scared."

"I'm not scared," she said, and it wasn't until the words left her mouth that she realized they were a lie.

She swallowed and looked out the windshield. It was raining gently, a light pattering of droplets across the glass, slowly obscuring the night. It made her think of another rainfall days ago, at almost the exact same time, an untouched coffee in the cupholder.

"Henry," she said slowly, still watching the rain. "What was her name?"

"What?"

"Her name. Your ex. You never told me what happened with her."

"Leyna?" He sighed bitterly. "She lied, okay? That's what I said. She lied."

"To who?"

Henry shot her a dark look. "To fucking everyone. Thank God no one believed her."

Her blood beat like drums, like a red melody. It was that word: *God*. It flashed across her mind like a sword, cutting through her, bringing with it an accusation she hadn't fully understood until now.

A teenager . . . was attacked by a member of this church.

This has happened before, when someone is valuable to you.

You've gone through this before, with James.

She heard the words again, as though she were inside the cabinet. Noticing, now, the pauses and nuances.

Before. With James. She'd thought Ken was referring to James about all of Pechman's cover-ups. But what if she'd been wrong? What if only the first time had been for James—with the prescription pills—and Ken was just using that as proof that Pechman would do it again? For anyone who was valuable . . .

"Money," she breathed.

"What?" Henry asked.

But she said nothing. She was seeing the girl in the grocery store, that look in her eyes. How had Catherine not recognized it? Fear. The kind when nightmares became real and you saw them during the day.

Be careful out there.

Don't want to get hurt.

A veiled warning. Too veiled. She'd missed it completely.

It wasn't James who Pechman had been protecting after all. At least, not only James. Because of course he would lose his reputation if James was convicted of a crime, like selling pills. But there was something arguably more important to Pechman than even his status.

Money.

Henry's mother donated so much to the church. Henry had told her so himself many times. Pechman would do anything to stay in her good graces. A favor, he'd consider it, and she'd return it without question. Anything for her son.

"Henry," she said. "Please take me home."

He must have read something in her face, because his own features twisted. His breathing picked up. "This wasn't how it was supposed to go. This *wasn't* how it was *supposed* to *go*. . . ."

"Henry—" she burst out, a note of real panic in her voice now.

But he cut her off.

"You know, you could at least give me some credit here. Like, this wasn't the first option."

She felt her lips part. "What . . . wasn't the first option?"

"I mean," he said, "I did *try,* you know. With Brittany. Leyna. Maybe that was stupid. Maybe that's why you're mad. Because I thought they could be you. But I *know* that was stupid, Catherine, thinking anyone could be you. But then, it's not like you gave me much of a choice."

And when she said nothing, he continued, his voice now fevered, adamant.

"I tried, you know. I mean, you must have known. How could you not? Even in high school. You must have noticed. Josh. I mean, really? *Josh Tyler?* He couldn't even ride a bike properly. Such a prick. Oh, like you didn't know. And it wasn't all my fault. Idiot never followed basic traffic laws, it was a matter of time before someone knocked him down. But then you go to college, right? And I think, I can handle it, I'll go with her. Only you fucked me up so much senior year I failed half my finals and didn't get into West Washington. Even with buying from James. It . . . it was a bad time. After prom especially. You came up to me in that dress, smiling and talking. I thought you were back then—that we were back—I really did. But I was wrong." His face tightened for a brief moment, then relaxed again. "Anyway, like I said, I did try other things. I visited you. Not sure if you knew that. Just a few times. I saw you one night, with this guy. I was so . . . angry. Too angry, I'll admit it. It wasn't fair of me. But it also wasn't fair of you. I mean, some *random* . . . But I saw you got my flower. You looked so happy."

He'd said everything very quickly, but his words seemed to come to her like a slow trickle of sand through closed fingers.

As she, by millimeters and minutes, absorbed all he'd just told her, her mind seemed to separate from her body, flattening and darkening to a void, narrowing by the second, until it disappeared entirely like something falling down a well.

She had no idea what to do.

CHAPTER THIRTY-EIGHT

Andrew ran upstairs. Yelled at Bob in his office to put down his phone. Explained his theory—yes, a theory, goddamn it—as Minda waited behind him, looking pained and dubious all at once.

"Andrew, I still don't think—"

"But why not?" Andrew half shouted, cutting her off, before turning back to Bob. He was going to give this another minute, and then he was going on his own. He didn't care anymore. "What harm could it do? To check? If I'm right, if the TOD's off, then he's alone with her *right now*."

But Bob was looking at him with the same expression as Minda. It made Andrew's desperation spike and he fought to keep himself under control.

"Okay, tell me this then," he said, his voice shaking just a little. "Have you seen Henry before we came to the station? Has he . . . been in before? For something? Does he have a criminal history?"

Bob ran a hand down his face. "Andrew, I'm not—"

"Yes or no?"

"Yes," Bob said reluctantly. "Not officially, but yes, we had a complaint."

"About Henry? For what?"

"I'm not going to tell you something like that."

"Why?"

"Because—"

"*Because no charges were brought?*" Andrew's breathing was so fast it hurt. "That's what you said, right? No charges. *A he-said-she-said in the simplest of terms.* So I'm asking you, what did *Henry* say? Or did you not even bother to talk to him?"

Bob said nothing.

Andrew gave a shaky laugh. "You've got to be fucking kidding me. I've been with this guy all week! *Catherine's* been with him! And you didn't tell me? I thought it was that James kid this whole time."

"Well, James did have trouble too," Bob admitted. "But that was for something else. I never lied to you, Andrew. About James, or Henry. There was nothing to tell. Nothing *happened* with Henry. Even the girl took it back, said she'd made a mistake. We almost went after her for a false report but decided not to. If anything, we were easy on her."

"Easy," Andrew echoed. He didn't recognize the man in front of him. "That what Pechman say to do?"

Bob shook his head. "This has gone far enough. Andrew, I'm telling you right now, *enough*. This is on me. I told you too much. Things you didn't need to know. I thought, with you showing interest again, maybe you wanted to be involved, be part of the team, but now I realize my mistake. Forget this, Andrew. We are handling it, do you understand? *Leave it alone.*"

Andrew's desperation was bubbling over now. He didn't have time to argue, to say he understood things a hell of a lot more tonight than he had in a long time. "You've always told me to trust my gut. You've always said I'm too smart for my own good and that I have the right instincts. Well, this guy has bothered me from the start and now he might not have an alibi and I fucking left him alone with her. So you can come with me or not, but either way, I'm going."

And he would go. Alone, if he had to. He'd thought it was guilt and penitence, not wanting to leave Catherine, agreeing to anything she suggested. But maybe it had been something more this whole time. The thought of her alone with Henry was making him shake where he stood, a fear so primal and basic it was like thirst or hunger. He couldn't let anything happen to her. Not again.

Bob sighed, but there was a flicker of something behind his eyes Andrew had seen before: a mixture of exasperation and pride that had always made Bob seem like family to him, even a father. But the recognition was blurred now, as though he were seeing Bob through glass, or rain.

"What do you even want me to do?" Bob asked.

"Get him away from her."

CHAPTER THIRTY-NINE

"The flower," Henry repeated. He was looking at her impatiently again. "A dahlia. You know what it means, right? Betrayal, but," he added quickly, "I didn't want you to take it that way. I wanted it to mean forgiveness, too, like I knew about what you did but was still giving you something to show we could move past it. Also, you hate roses. You used to say they were cliché, remember?" He frowned. "You did . . . you did like the flower, right? You got what I meant by it?"

"Yes," someone else said in her voice. "It was beautiful."

He nodded, looking relieved. "Right. I knew you would."

"You put . . ." She struggled with herself. Fought to be within her own body and mind and *think*. "You put a lot of effort into all of this."

He half laughed. "God. You have no idea."

She tried to laugh with him but it didn't work at all. "I'll bet."

"But I've always been pretty determined, you know that."

"Yeah."

"Enduring, right? Stubborn?"

Again, she tried to laugh. It was a little better this time.

"Like, with the cabinet," he continued, looking encouraged. "Going to the furniture store. Stuff like that."

"The cabinet."

"God, you were amazing with that. So incredible."

"Well," she said, clearing her throat. She put her hand against it. "That was your idea."

"I suppose it was."

"A . . . different idea, admittedly . . ."

He laughed a little again. "Yeah, I'll take that, it was weird."

"So . . . why the cabinet?" All she could think to do was keep him talking. She hadn't liked the glares he'd shot her before, in the silences.

Henry shrugged. "It wasn't about the cabinet. Or even Pechman, really."

"What do you mean?"

He flashed her a searching look. "What's the game here?"

"No game," she said, which was true enough. Whatever this was, it didn't feel like a game. "We're just talking."

"But you're upset."

She forced herself to breathe. "Because you know more than I do. And I always hated that."

He grinned at her. "Tell me something I don't know. But I'll give you this: I always knew Pechman was shady as hell. How could he not be? God, it was so obvious. But a little too obvious, you know? James made so much more sense."

"Really?" she asked as something seemed to fall away inside her.

"Well, yeah," Henry said, as though this were all perfectly clear. "Connection to the victim through the church. Previous criminal history with selling at the high school—Pechman was all over that, and James told me everything, how his dad got rid of the charges, smoothed it all over, but still—it doesn't hurt that the cops would recognize his name. And James is such a homebody. Just plays video games all the time. His alibi any night would be his parents. His mom, who is a total pushover, and his dad, who . . ."

Henry looked at her expectantly.

She stared at him, lost. Disbelieving.

". . . would be under investigation for . . . ," Henry prompted.

". . . financial crimes," Catherine managed. "With the church."

"Making any alibi he provided . . ."

". . . worthless."

"Well, maybe not totally worthless," Henry amended, "but certainly a lot less credible. It would either be us who brought it to the cops or Ken would have eventually. Still, that whole part was just extra, really. The DNA was the important part."

"DNA," she echoed. She could feel the right armrest digging into her back. A fleeting image came to her of twisting around, unlocking the door, and running—but she knew he would catch her. "Henry . . . whose hair was on Amy's body?"

"Whose do you think?"

And the awful thing was, she did know. Because whatever twisted path his mind had led him down, she was following it.

"James's," she said softly.

"Why?"

"Because . . ." Her hand shook against her neck. It felt made of bones, but that wasn't right, was it? "Because he liked her—"

"Because he was *obsessed* with her. Saw her all the time at the church and finally she agreed to meet with him but then she rejected him, so . . ." His voice trailed off.

"Silly of him," she said faintly. "To leave DNA."

Henry shrugged. "It's amazing how easy it is to pull some hair. James trips all the time, he's such a klutz."

She could picture it, too: Henry play-shoving James, or waiting for him to stumble, then reaching forward just a little too high, grabbing scalp instead of shoulders. Apologizing as James glared and rubbed his head, then shoved Henry back, who laughed . . .

"Don't get me wrong," Henry said quickly. "Just because it's James's hair doesn't mean he'll go to prison. It's more there to exclude anyone else. James is probably going to be fine. Not like his DNA's in the system, not for pills that aren't even on his record anymore." He gave her another of those searching looks. "Can I ask you something?"

She nodded against her hand.

"Why did you say you were going to transfer and then back out?"

She stared at him. He raised his eyebrows, impatient again.

"Oh, come on, you say college sucks and you're going to transfer to Falls to be with me and then you just change your mind. Like overnight. Then you yell at me and message me to leave you alone."

She said nothing. His frown deepened.

"I just want to know why girls do it," he said.

"Do . . . what?"

"*Change their minds.* Why do girls *always* change their minds?"

"I don't. . . ."

"You do, though. You must. *Why do girls lie?* Like how Brittany tried to come off all smart but within ten minutes of our date I could tell she was an idiot. Even when she saw her dad she was like, *Oh, whoops, yeah, I kind of didn't tell him I was going out,* and I was just sitting there and freaking out. Or Leyna saying she wanted to be with me and then deciding randomly one day that she actually didn't want to? Like, why do girls do that? Is it a compulsive lying thing? Do they do it because they know they can get away with it? No, don't look like that. I genuinely want to know."

Catherine didn't say a word. She felt the overwhelming instinct to stay as still as possible.

"Sorry," he said. "I just . . . get frustrated. But I know it's a lot, all of this, all at once. Anyway, I don't want to talk about any of that. Brittany or Leyna. That's all in the past now, and I don't want to get lost in it. I mean, you remember what we studied senior year? Like, talk about a cautionary tale, right?"

The change in subject jarred her. Her mind already spinning, she just shook her head.

"But you know the book?"

After a moment, she realized he wanted her to answer. "What . . . Which one?"

"*Which one?*" he echoed, and now he sounded almost disgusted. "Which one do you *think*?"

Her mind raced even faster. What had they read? Dark books. Gothic. She cast her mind back, to castles and torchlight. But no titles came to her.

"*Wuthering Heights,*" Henry said, cutting up the word, stretching it out. "*Wuth-er-ing Heights.* Please tell me you at least read the fucking book, Catherine."

"Of course."

She hadn't. Not a single page of it.

"Then you know!" he said fiercely. "You get it. You *must* get it. Catherine. I mean, God, you have her name."

"Catherine," she said, her voice very faint.

"Yes," he said. "Exactly."

He was speaking a language she had never heard before and didn't understand, but something inside her brain was telling her to be slow and soft, to agree with him. That same voice that had told her to keep him talking. It was like being in that dorm room again, her hair over her face as she pulled on those brown ankle boots, her mind putting a divider up inside her thoughts, only letting certain ones through and pushing the other ones back.

Abandon all hope, ye who enter here.

No, no, wrong book. *Fuck.* What was so important about *Wuthering Heights*? What was he even talking about?

"I wasn't going to be like Heathcliff," Henry was saying, and she tuned back in to him with a sense of complete unreality, the absurdity of it all so strong she was almost tempted to laugh. "Fucking Edgar. You think I was going to let you be with him? After *Josh Tyler* and the random guy at college?"

Again, looking at her as though genuinely wanting an answer.

"Edgar?" she said blankly.

"Andrew!" He waved an arm and she flinched. "Fucking Andrew! You wanted to be with him. You were *going* to be with him before today, it was obvious. I was going to tell you, by the way. Even if you hadn't come down and heard him. I was going to tell you what he'd done. Hadn't done. Whatever. I'd never keep something like that from you. Not like how you kept stuff from me."

Jealousy. So simple it almost relieved her at this point. *This* she knew. *This* she understood.

"Andrew?" She gave a small, light laugh. *Ridiculous,* that laugh said. "I wasn't going to be with An—"

RING!!!

RING RING

Her phone going off in her purse. The high chime of bells, the plastic vibrating so hard she felt it through her bag.

She reached into her purse, pulled it out.

"Who is it?" Henry demanded.

Catherine closed her eyes.

"Who is it?"

CHAPTER FORTY

"Hi, you've reached Catherine Ellers. I can't come to the phone right now, but if you leave your—"

Andrew shut it off, then immediately redialed.

"Not picking up?" Bob asked. He was parked down the street from Catherine's house, waiting with admittedly limited patience for Andrew to tell him where to go next.

They'd gone first to Henry's house—empty, Henry's car gone from the driveway, an absence that seemed to drop Andrew's stomach into his feet—then to Catherine's. Andrew rang the doorbell as Bob waited down the street. It had been Bob's idea and Andrew didn't argue; he couldn't blame Bob for not wanting to sound the alarm for something that might be nothing.

Please let it be nothing.

"No, Catherine's not here," her mom said with a frown after she answered the door. "I thought you all were at Henry's?"

Andrew shook his head, trying to mirror her expression, then checked his phone. "God, I'm an idiot. She texted me ten minutes ago to meet them for dinner. Guess I didn't hear it."

But her mom's frown deepened. "Bit of an early dinner, isn't it?"

"Looks like we're getting coffee beforehand," Andrew said,

still pretending to scroll through the message. "Anyway, sorry to bother you—"

"Wait."

He turned back to her, his heart beating very hard.

"Can you tell her to come home?" Her hands were pressed together in front of her, so tightly the fingers were white. "I'd tell her, but, well, lately . . ." She trailed off. "Tell her we want her home tonight. It's been a hard day, what with the funeral and all. . . ."

"Okay," Andrew told her. Promised her. "I'll do that."

But now he had no idea where Catherine even was. Had Henry taken her out to dinner? To a movie? To one of the fifteen coffee shops in town? Or had he taken her somewhere else, somewhere more private?

Hands shaking, Andrew put the address in the GPS on his phone because he'd never actually been there. "Go straight," he told Bob. "Then left at the stop sign at the end."

After just two more turns, Bob looked at him. "What is this?" he asked Andrew, though his tone was still calm, almost kind, like Andrew was a child to be indulged. "Do you think he'll return to the scene of the crime? That's TV stuff, you know. Doesn't always happen."

Andrew said nothing.

CHAPTER FORTY-ONE

"That's him, isn't it? *Isn't it?*"

His hands grabbed at her but she cringed, trying to shove the phone down between the seats, but her hands were slick with sweat and panic and his were like pliers pulling her fingers back. He wrenched the phone away.

She watched his face as he looked at the screen, silent now but still glowing with another call; then his eyes flicked up to hers.

He hit her.

Not a slap, either, but a fisted blow to the left side of her face, phone still in hand, the hard plastic cracking against her skull.

Her face snapped to the side, slamming into the passenger-side window. She flung her arms over her head, her eyes shut against the pain. When she opened them again, the world was a small oval edged in red. Dazed, she blinked blood out of her left eye; she could smell it, like rain on metal, and taste it on her teeth.

"Jesus, Catherine," he said, panting. She heard the window grind down, saw the arc of his arm as he threw her phone into the grass. "Why are you doing this?"

Those sentences again, everything backward, locks with no keys. Nothing that made sense.

The window was still open. The cold air hit her face and seemed to hiss there along her cheekbone, where everything was swelling heat.

And with the pain came clarity. Something falling inside her mind. A wall coming down and every thought trapped behind it rushing to the front: Leyna's warning and James's hair and Henry's alibi—but that last part didn't matter. She was sure, even though she didn't understand. The pain *made* her sure, took away her confusion and her doubt. It didn't matter why he'd done it, or when. She was seeing them both as though from outside the car: a boy and a girl who looked like each other, and one was bleeding and the other one had locked the doors and she had been so, so stupid.

Again.

Amy, telling her to look. Screaming at her to see.

Now she was looking. Now she knew.

"God, I'm so sorry," he said. "I didn't mean to do that."

What was he talking about? He hadn't meant to kill Amy? But then his hand was on her hair, touching the blood in it, and she realized: he was apologizing for hitting her.

"It's okay," she said. "I'm fine." That voice again, telling her what to say, her restraint coming back to her by millimeters, like a slow pull of rope. Before she could make herself move, to do something, anything, his hands closed around her wrists. At his house, he had held her hands, but this grip was harder, different, and she fought not to fight back. Not yet.

"You're not." He looked upset, even regretful. "I didn't want to do that."

"I know."

"I just got . . . so angry."

"I know."

"You do always know me." His fingers stroked the inside of her wrists, down to her palms and up again. "I knew that was all that needed to happen, really. You, knowing me again, like when we were kids. See, that was the problem with Heathcliff and Catherine: they drifted apart. *We* drifted apart. I know it's a little weird, the book, thinking of us like that, but she had your name. It seemed like a sort of . . . sign, don't you think? And now, seeing you again. Being near you again, after all those years away. It was like the book was trying to tell me something. I couldn't let you go away, not again. So I knew I needed something to make you stay, make you want to be around me. Not my own loss—I didn't want your pity—but one of yours. I didn't want to wreck you completely, but I knew it needed to hurt. So I could help you through it. A Goldilocks kind of grief, I guess you'd call it. Not enough to kill you, but enough to make you stay." A pause. "Also, I thought a child would be easier."

Outside the car, the rain had shifted to snow. She saw the slow drift from her right eye, but even that was red at the edges, as though each snowflake had been dipped in blood before falling through the night.

"I saw Amy after I ran into you," he was saying. "She was

on her bike. I went to my house, got a piece of paper. I left it on her bike. Then I went to James's house. I still . . . wasn't sure, though. I mean, I had the hair, the note, I knew she'd meet me, but still . . . Then I got your text message, and I knew I had to do it. I already had plans that night and really, I should have canceled them. But then I thought maybe that would look bad, later, canceling plans. So I went. When I realized Brittany's dad was a cop . . ."

He shook his head. Catherine watched the movement of his hair across his forehead, his temples. She couldn't stop staring at him. It was like looking at Henry and, at the same time, like looking at a stranger.

"You have to understand. I didn't know how far Leyna had gone. I knew she'd gone to the cops and they'd sent her away. My parents told me that much. But I didn't know Pechman knew. I almost had a heart attack when you told me what you'd overheard at the church; thank God you thought it was James. I'm so done with the police at this point. I hated even going to the station, having to make a scene outside your house so you'd come out. God, all the risks I took for you. But I couldn't make it seem like I was nervous around the cops, like I was avoiding them. How weird would it have looked if I didn't want to come to the station with you? But actually, everyone was pretty chill about me being there. Maybe that was Pechman, though honestly, they probably saw Leyna for what she was and didn't care what she had to say. I guess Grant was the exception because I made the mistake of taking his daughter on all of one date.

Dads, right?" Henry sighed. "So I came home. Then I went out to meet Amy. I can't explain the time thing, though. That was a bonus I didn't really need but I wasn't going to complain, you know? Anyway, I want you to know, I didn't *do* anything to her. I wouldn't do that. I mean, Jesus, she was just a kid. Not that I think what happened to you, like, ruined you or anything," he added quickly. "You being raped didn't change how I feel about you. You've always been the same to me."

For whatever reason, it was at this point she remembered the knife in her bag.

"I understand," she said.

"You do?"

"Yes. Now you explained it. I understand. Thank . . . thank you for telling me."

"Yeah. And you have to admit, it did work, right? We've spent so much time together lately. It's been nice, hasn't it?"

"Yes."

"I did it because I love you. I wouldn't have done it if I didn't love you."

The snow was light, dusting, scattering across the windshield. The left side of her face still burned where he'd hit her, her cheek-bone swelling up to her eye. His hands were still around her wrists. "I love you, too," she said.

He smiled at her then, a Henry smile she remembered from years ago. It made a thin flame of hope spark inside her chest. He believed her. He'd take her home. He'd let her go.

"Catherine," he said. "Don't lie to me."

CHAPTER FORTY-TWO

The road leading to the clifftop was dark when they turned onto it, and Bob drove slowly, grumbling about there not being enough streetlights here. Andrew didn't reply. He was very aware of the crunch of gravel under the tires; it sounded indecently loud.

He'll hear us, Andrew thought.

And then what? Henry thought he had an alibi. Hell, he *did* have an alibi. He wouldn't be spooked—

He would, though. Andrew knew it with the same certainty he'd felt when he hit the door in the dorms again and again, his palm on fire, panic making him pant. Because people—criminals, murderers—*did* worry about getting caught. If they saw a police car coming up behind them, chances were they'd do something desperate.

"Stop the car," Andrew said.

"What?"

"Stop the car. If he sees your cruiser, he'll panic."

"If he's even here."

"He is," Andrew said, with more conviction than he actually felt.

Bob stopped the car and turned to Andrew. Snow was falling

gently onto the windshield, melting on contact and running down like tears. "Well, I'm not letting you go on your own."

"I thought you said this was nothing."

"It is. There is a ninety-nine-percent chance this is a complete waste of time."

"But not one hundred."

Bob frowned at him, then took out his radio. "This is Officer Harper. I've got a possible ten-fourteen at Lookout Point. ETA two minutes. Requesting backup."

After a moment, the radio crackled. "Ten-four, Bob. Ten-seventeen. ETA five." The radio crackled into silence again.

"What's ten-fourteen?" Andrew asked him.

"Report of a prowler," Bob said. He pointed a finger at Andrew. "You're staying here."

"I'm not staying—"

"*Then I will handcuff you to this car.* I'm waiting for backup, and even when they get here, you are staying the hell out of this. Whatever it is."

CHAPTER FORTY-THREE

"I'm not lying," she said.

"You are. You think I don't know when you're lying to me?"

"I—"

"Kiss me."

She opened her mouth, closed it.

"If you love me, kiss me. Unless you don't—"

She leaned forward and pressed her mouth to his. He opened his mouth at once and she shut her eyes, feeling his hand creep up her face. She wondered if he'd leave fingerprints in her blood.

She made herself wait, then broke away.

"There—" she said, trying for light, playful.

But he pulled her toward him again and she flinched as she felt his tongue between her teeth and one hand tight at her waist while in her mind she pictured two children in a backyard and, one by one, every summer garden light around them went dark.

"Henry," she said.

But his mouth was over hers, taking her words and swallowing them. He smelled like night air from the open window, tasted like whiskey and ice. The pressure of him kissing her was like a knife into her bleeding temple and a white-water current of adrenaline was crashing endlessly and the black terror of it all was so much she thought she would break in two along the fault line of her heart.

He pressed her back, his mouth still on her, his hands moving down her body, and it was like she was made up of separate parts all screaming together.

She tried to make herself relax, make her muscles limp, let him arrange her the way he wanted. She'd never be able to respond, could never bring herself to give him anything close to that, but maybe she could manage a kind of submission. Would that be enough? She pictured him moving her, pulling off her clothes, her underwear, parting her legs, pushing the seat back so she was flat underneath him. Tried to tell herself it wouldn't last that long. That he'd be inside her for minutes, then it would be over.

But the whole time she'd have to stay under him. The whole time she'd have to not cry. Not scream or push back or fight. He'd kiss her neck, pull down her bra. She'd feel him on every single part of her and she'd have to pretend that was okay, or he'd—what?

Kill her? Wrap his hands around her throat the way he'd done to Amy? She pictured that, too, the pressure of his thumbs under her jaw, her hands scrabbling uselessly before dropping to her sides again. She held those two images in her mind like weights as he pushed her back, his hands sliding up her shirt, his fingers touching the bottom of her rib cage: the placid, prone girl, or the one who got to scratch and claw and scream. It wasn't even close.

Then kill me, she thought. Almost dared him.

Because I'd rather die.

She pushed him off her.

"Don't," she said, cringing back, one arm twisted behind her, a sudden thrill of dread rolling over her. "Henry—"

Henry sat back in the seat and rubbed his eyes. "Catherine," he began.

Her finger felt along the door handle. But he'd hear the lock click up, wouldn't he? She began breathing harder, more through her mouth. She was supposed to scream now, lash out, fight back, but the light behind his face dazzled her eyes, scattering black diamonds across her vision, and she couldn't do it.

"I didn't want this to happen," he said.

"Right." Her breath, panting, five fingers moving, pressing. "No, of course not—"

"But I thought it might."

"Okay." Keep talking, making noise. Tears slipped down her cheeks. She ignored them. "Henry—"

"You have to be realistic about these things, you know?"

Her hand froze. That had to be the lock. *Had* to be. She waited for him to speak again, one finger braced.

"I knew if I told you, you wouldn't understand. You say you do, but I know you don't. Just like I know right now you're trying to get out of the car."

Her heart fell, then jolted back up in panic.

"You're not getting out, Catherine." He reached for her and she cringed but he seized her hands again, his grip fierce, brushing against the edge of pain. "I had a plan, just in case. Because I know life sometimes *is* like the books. Not just you having her name, but being like her too. Betraying your own heart. It's why I didn't want to tell you. I knew you wouldn't be able to handle it. But now . . . There's no going back after this, is there?"

A sudden gust of wind scattered snow through the open window. She thought of her father on the front porch. *Smells like snow, doesn't it?* It had landed on her jeans, her face, her open eyes. She couldn't say anything. Terror had stolen every word she'd ever known.

He sighed, as though her silence was an answer he had long expected. "When you left for college, I did something stupid. But I regretted it. Absolutely and totally regretted it. I . . . I went out alone. In the woods. I wanted to lose myself in the trees the way we used to do. I thought I wouldn't mind if I died there. And then I did mind. Because I was alone. Fading. And all I could think about was you. I realized then I couldn't go without you coming with me. I didn't *want* their ending. I won't let it happen that way. I won't let you leave. I *can't* let you leave. Because I know what it's like living without you, Catherine. I've done it for four years and I can't do it anymore. I can't live without my life. I can't live without my soul."

He looked away from her then, out the windshield. The night was black and endless, the outline of the mountains drawn in faint gray. She waited for him to say something. This whole night was a question, a looming blank she had to fill, like children creating the monsters that would haunt their closets, and poets building hell like a house. Because nothing was as bad as not knowing.

When she looked at him, his face was in profile, the lamp-post haloing him from behind, lighting the edges of his face, the snow caught in his hair.

Demons were angels once, she thought. *Then they fell. Fell into hell and reigned there.* Wasn't that how it worked?

He put the car into drive, put one hand on the wheel, kept the other on her. He smiled with kindness, a look she remembered, and as the car crept forward, she realized he had given her as good an answer as any.

She screamed.

CHAPTER FORTY-FOUR

They both heard it.

Andrew turned to Bob, about to yell at him that they had to do something, do something *now*, but Bob had already slammed his foot on the gas, Andrew's seat belt snapping against his chest at the sudden acceleration. Bob was speaking rapid-fire on the radio, codes Andrew didn't understand and barely heard. His heart was beating in his ears, everything else strangely muted.

"You're staying in the car," Bob said to him again as they sped up the road, lurching on the uneven gravel. "You don't fucking move a muscle, got it? *You stay in the car.*"

They came out of the trees to the clifftop, which was like a negative image: white snow and black night, a single car at the guardrail, so close to the edge it seemed to bleed into the sky.

CHAPTER FORTY-FIVE

It was the headlights that did it.

That arc of color across Henry's car, the backseat, the windshield—he couldn't help but turn in surprise, his mouth half open, his foot easing off the gas.

Catherine dived for the purse between her feet. She'd just gotten one hand inside it when she heard Henry say something, and by the time her hand—scrabbling, frantic—felt the sheath of the knife, he'd grabbed her by the hair and yanked her back with such force she felt some of it rip from her scalp. But she didn't care. It meant she was free for one more second, her other hand wrenching off the sheath, and then she was turning too quickly to even see, lunging blind until she felt the sudden pressure against her hand as it sank into him.

Into his stomach. She'd wanted higher—his chest or throat—but missed. Still, she felt the blood well up under her hand and jerked back, against the passenger door, her wet hands sliding across the buttons, unlocking the handle, and then she was out—falling to the ground—and when she used her hands to push herself up, they left red prints in the snow-dusted grass.

"Help!" she screamed, at the car, at the headlights that had just pulled up. She gave a little cry of relief as she stumbled forward, trying to run. *"HELP!"*

She was down before she knew what had happened, Henry's breath at her ear, calling her a *fucking bitch,* panting, his hands on her as she fought, kicking, still screaming. For a moment he let her go and she thought it had worked, but then she felt his hands on her legs, her ankles, dragging her backward.

She couldn't fight. He was holding her legs up as he pulled, her shoulders and head against the snow, her face to the sky. Almost upside down. She tried to kick but nothing happened and her arms couldn't reach him. She began to claw at the ground, trying to grab at something, but everything was snow, the grit below it driven so far under her fingernails it hurt.

Someone was yelling, but she couldn't see. Then Henry was over her, dropping her legs and pulling her upright, against him, her back against his chest, and as the world righted itself, she realized he had dragged her to the guardrail. They were only feet from the edge.

"Henry," a voice called from across the clearing. Catherine squinted into the darkness. There was someone there. But she could barely see them; the world was a wash of black and red.

She felt something at her throat. Something thin and wet. Her father's knife. Henry was holding it to her neck, pulling her harder against him. She could feel the place where she'd stabbed him; his blood getting onto her, soaking through her light jacket, onto her skin.

"Come any closer and I'll kill her!" Henry said, and it was like a slow drip of poison, knowing this was real.

The person across the clearing was saying something, but Catherine couldn't hear what it was. They seemed very far away to her, so far away she knew the exact distance didn't matter. They were out of reach. No help at all.

"Henry," she said. Her voice was hoarse. "Henry."

But he wasn't listening. He was trying to step backward, over the guardrail. The knife trembled at her throat. His left arm was across her stomach, locking her arms to her sides. She felt the metal of the guardrail through her jeans, on the backs of her legs. He was panting, trying to pull her over after him, his arm lifting under her ribs, and she felt a sudden heat at her back as more of his blood seeped onto her.

I'm so sorry.

I didn't mean to do that.

"Henry," she said again.

He was pulling her harder now, up and back. She could feel the press of the guardrail against the backs of her knees, her calves, her boots barely brushing the snow, and she knew there wasn't time.

She thrust her neck forward, into the blade of the knife.

She felt it slice into her skin, parting it, and the pain was like a sudden line of fire at the side of her throat. Blood fell to her shirt collar, but she didn't care.

What she cared about was Henry's sharp intake of breath, his hand dropping the knife, his arm loosening around her for a fraction of a second, and that was all she needed.

She jerked herself away, forward and down. The moment her face and palms hit the ground she heard the explosion of a gunshot cut through the night, felt it move the air just above her.

Another shot, then two more. The air on fire. The taste of ashes in her mouth.

One second.

Two.

Or maybe more. Maybe infinitely more. Her ears ringing, her whole body frozen in the snow, feeling it seep into her coat at the elbows while a gritty warmth flowed down her throat to her chest.

At some point, she started to move. Not up, but forward. Crawling on her elbows like a soldier. Someone tried to grab her arm. She screamed and clawed at them. They said something she couldn't hear and then someone else was there, a low, kind voice that seemed to reach her through the blood and the pain.

Fingers against her neck, then something heavy. It fell over her face for a moment, then was pulled away. Something was at her throat, a pressure that made the pain there spike. More voices. She blinked the blood out of her eyes, sat up despite the hands on her shoulders, and looked.

She saw him as though through a telescope the wrong way, stretched out and distant. He seemed very small to her against the sky, his front half slumped forward over the guardrail, unmoving, his hair and hands in the grass.

He hadn't even made it over the edge.

And with that thought came blackness, swift, like a curtain pulled at a window.

PART FOUR

SHADOWS AND SOLID THINGS

Time will change it . . . as winter
changes the trees.
—EMILY BRONTË, *WUTHERING HEIGHTS*

CHAPTER FORTY-SIX

What came next was fragmented, as though someone had taken a sledgehammer to each hour, each minute, and it was up to her to make sense of it.

White walls and white sheets. A bed they could move up and down. Taking more blood after they finally got the blood to stop coming out of her. There was a needle, then more. Talk of surgery. Talk of no surgery. Maybe a different surgery. Asking her to stand up. A blood pressure cuff like a python at her upper arm. Sit down. Pressure, a hissing-snake release. A nurse's eyes flicking between the numbers. Look here. A face unblinking an inch from hers. At the light. Left. Right. Are you thirsty? Police officers marching in and out. Telling her story, over and over and over again. Her mother crying. Her dad white as the hospital sheets. When she told the officer about the knife, her dad ran his hand over his face and then reached for her, his shaking hand on her shoulder, and it was the first time he'd touched her since she'd come home.

"That probably saved you," one officer said, a short, broad man with red hair. "He lost a lot of blood from that wound, from what I saw. You weakened him. Made it harder for him to pull you over the guardrail. Gave you the chance to get away."

Eventually, they left her to sleep. Rest, they called it, as though that were possible. As though ghosts could rest. Her mother sat in a chair by her bed. Her father had gone to talk to the doctors yet again.

"What time is it?" she asked her mother.

"Four."

"In the morning?"

"Yes."

Catherine blinked up at the ceiling. The room was bright. Her mother kept asking if she wanted her to turn off the light. She didn't. She remembered, as though from a different life, asking her mother not to turn off the light in her bedroom the first night after she came home, not to draw the curtains.

"Catherine?"

She turned. Her mother looked sick in the hospital light, lines of exhaustion around her eyes and mouth. Catherine knew she couldn't look much better, with that massive bandage around her neck and blood still in her hair. A plastic surgeon was coming to look at her tomorrow—today—which she found hard to believe. Like she was getting a nose job. But it was standard practice, they said, for wounds like hers. To cut them open again and stitch them thin and neat and clean.

"What can I do?" her mother asked.

"Just stay."

Minutes passed. Neither of them talked. Catherine propped herself up in bed, her shoulders and spine hard against the plastic headboard behind her. She didn't want open air at her back.

Her fingers danced around the blanket, seizing it in her fists until her knuckles turned white before letting go. Her mind kept flashing back, sending out half-second bursts of terror that were like little electric shocks. She kept letting out these stupid small cries in her throat that made her mother flinch and reach for her.

She wanted to explain something to her mother. It was very important: the night of the rape. Why she had called her.

I wanted to hear your voice. No, not want. Need. Like I was lost in the dark looking for something safe and I knew it had to be your voice and nothing else.

She opened her mouth, but the words didn't come. Her eyes were closing, the lids heavy. She felt herself sinking down, her hands fisting in the sheets again, her body tensing for a moment before collapsing into sleep that was broken into a million tiny pieces, each sliver a different nightmare.

—

She was awakened after a few hours to meet with the plastic surgeon and two more police officers. Tired and shaky, she found herself getting things mixed up. She talked to one officer like he was Bob and had been there and heard herself tell the plastic surgeon examining her wound that Henry hadn't stabbed her.

She shook her head to clear it and the plastic surgeon pulled back from her. "Wait, sorry. I stabbed me. Myself. After stabbing him. But I don't think I did it that well. Stabbing him, I mean."

More tests. Thin needles. Pressure cuffs. Look here. Move

this. Lie still. She was glass splintering under the weight of all they were doing to her, all that had happened. She could feel her brain struggling to right itself like a newborn foal lunging and trembling on too-long legs, thin as spindles.

The surgery didn't take too long, her parents told her. The stitches itched like crazy. She asked when she'd get out of there. Soon, they said. Her mind jumped from subject to subject, her hands always moving like insects across the hospital blankets. Her mother brought her clothes—sweats mostly—but anything at her neck was unbearable. The skin there felt like a rash, like it would be red if she could take off the bandage. But she wasn't allowed to.

At some point a different doctor came in and asked her if she wanted to kill herself. She was very proud of her response: "You know, I did try to get away from the edge. Want to see the scar? They're trying so hard to make it pretty." Trying to take off the bandage, hands on her, pushing down, her own half-hysterical laughter. She felt like a shallow pool of fizzing, hissing water, a geyser about to erupt, everyone just waiting for it to happen so they could smother her back down again.

The doctor gave her pills. They blurred time, made her sleep almost whole. She slept for a long time, stirred briefly to gulp down some water, then slept again. When she woke up, she stretched, blinked, ran her hand over the bandage along her neck, felt the panic that came with waking. She took a breath. Another. Her room was empty, but the door was open, a spill of light across the floor. Darkness outside the window. She stood up, walked to the sink by the wall. Her mother had brought her stuff from home, a stiff plastic toiletry bag it took her three tries to open.

Slowly, she brushed her teeth. The mirror was slightly clouded, as though polished with a thin film of water that had long since dried. She found a hair tie and pulled back her hair, mindful of the left temple that was still crusted with blood from when he'd hit her, a bruise spreading purple down to her eyebrow.

She turned her head to look at the bandage at her throat: wide and white, about six inches long, it ran from the right side of her neck, below her ear, to almost the center of her throat, secured with a line of Band-Aids like ladder rungs across it. She touched it lightly with one finger.

Henry.

Henry.

Had they buried him yet? Where were his parents? What would happen to Molly?

Slowly, knowing she wasn't supposed to, waiting for someone to yell at her from behind, she slid her finger under the Band-Aids one at a time, peeling them off her skin and letting the bandage fall into the sink. There was something underneath, a thin, glossy material that reminded her of cling wrap. She pulled that off too and made herself look.

The skin around her cut was rash-red and swollen, the wound slightly raised, as long as a finger: a thin purple line secured with a smile of black stitches, slathered in some kind of clear ointment. She could see the knots in the stitches like thin barbed wire.

She looked at it for what felt like a long time, wondering what she should feel. Upset about the wound or proud she'd been able to save herself. Mad she'd been in that situation at all or thankful she'd survived it. She had a map of roads inside her that ran every which way but they all seemed to stop in the middle, so she hitchhiked across her own mind, looking in whatever direction seemed promising at the moment.

Finally she walked away, feeling the air move across her neck. She called out into the light of the hallway, to the nurse standing outside her room as though waiting for her.

"I want to shower," Catherine said. "Do you need to rebandage it first, or after?"

The nurse beamed at her.

—

The girl came into Catherine's hospital room slowly, as though expecting to be doused in hot oil at any moment.

It was Sunday morning. Catherine was being discharged that afternoon, but right now she was sitting in her hospital bed, clothed in sweats, her hair clean and almost completely dry now, all the blood scrubbed away by careful hands. A small bag sat to the side of her bed, holding the few things her parents had brought from home. Packed and ready.

But there was one more thing she wanted to do, before she left.

The girl didn't sit. Instead she stood just a few feet inside the room, the door still wide behind her.

"Hi," Catherine said.

"Hey," the girl said. Her blond hair was down and ridiculously shiny. She had long eyelashes and winged liner and was wearing jeans and a black sweater. Catherine found she missed this: looking at a girl her age and noticing her makeup, what she was wearing. Not quite judgment. Just observation, as natural as a greeting you said without thinking.

"I wasn't sure you'd come."

"Yeah, well." The girl shrugged. "I got your message. I heard what happened. I wasn't going to not show."

Her name was Leyna Wollard. She was eighteen. She went to Falls and had a white cat named Sir Coconut and nearly nine hundred Instagram followers and had responded to Catherine's message with just three words: *tell me when.*

Her eyes flicked to Catherine and then away. "They said he tried to kill you and throw you off the cliff."

"Actually, he was going to kill me *by* throwing me off the cliff. With him."

Slowly, Leyna nodded. "So you killed him."

"The cops killed him. Cop." She hadn't seen Bob since it happened. Or Andrew. She was trying not to think about what that might mean. "Is it on the news?"

Another nod. "Yeah. People keep texting me. People who know I knew him. Asking me stuff. Stuff I can't answer." She looked at Catherine again. "Someone was saying he cut your face. But you look okay."

"My neck." She turned her head. After her shower, the nurse had put on that plastic material again and another bandage held in place with Band-Aids. "I wanted to talk to you."

"Yeah. I figured." After a moment, Leyna walked forward. She sat in the chair but pulled it a little away from Catherine's bed.

"I was wondering," Catherine said, "if you could tell me what Henry did to you."

Leyna's eyebrows shot up. "How do you—? Did he—?"

"No," Catherine said. "He didn't tell me. But I . . . I heard something. About an attack."

Leyna said nothing.

"You went to the cops," Catherine continued.

"Yeah. Very productive, let me tell you."

"They didn't believe you."

"No." A pause. "I met him at Falls, at the library where he worked. We dated for a few months. But he was . . . intense. It was too much, too fast. He wanted to be around me all the time and if I canceled plans or wanted to hang out with other people . . ." She sighed. "So I broke it off. He was upset, but he seemed to take it well. At the time. I thought that would be the end of it. I had no idea, no clue, what would come next."

Another silence. Catherine waited, watching the other girl's eyes, the way they went distant and dark.

"I was walking back to my car one night after an honors council meeting. He was there, waiting for me, just standing in the parking lot next to the driver's door like he was going to take me home or something. I asked him what he was doing and he was acting very . . . it was weird. Like he was trying to act like we hadn't broken up. Like I was still his girlfriend. I didn't . . . I was kind of mean. I was tired and it was late and I just didn't want to deal with him anymore. I told him to leave me alone."

Leyna shut her eyes.

"He grabbed me. My arms. Pulled me toward him to hug or kiss me, I don't know. I kind of froze and then tried to pull away and he—he didn't like that. He kept saying I couldn't leave him. It was incredible, how strong he was. I remember trying to get away from him and realizing I physically couldn't do it. Then he called me Catherine." Her eyes opened. "*Catherine, Catherine, you can't leave me. Catherine, no.* Just over and over. I was fighting, pushing, and then—I don't know if I tripped or what but I was on the ground and he was pulling me. Then someone drove into the lot and parked really close to us, and he seemed to . . . I don't know . . . come back to himself. He let me up, anyway, kind of dusted us both off. My cheek was scraped and bloody, all that crap from the pavement in my hair. He was really upset about that. Kept apologizing. I finally tried to get in my car and he went to stop me but then I told him I'd scream and that other car was parked just a few spaces away and . . . he let me go. He was crying, but he let me go." A tremor rolled across her shoulders. "If that other person hadn't showed up . . . I don't know. I try not to think about it."

"At the clifftop," Catherine said slowly, turning her head so Leyna could see the bruising at her temple, "he hit me. That's how I got away. It was how he looked at me after he hit me. There was blood and he was . . . surprised by it. Like he hadn't meant to do it. He actually said that: *I'm so sorry. I didn't mean to do that.*"

"*This is awful, please forgive me,*" Leyna said in a flat little voice. "*Let's just get out of here, get something to eat. You hungry?*" She sighed bitterly. "I went to the police right after, shaking, like a total wreck. They did absolutely nothing, even when I showed them my arms—I don't know, I'd wiped a lot of the blood off and the bruises weren't that bad yet. But then I got kind of panicked and desperate—I wasn't sleeping well and I kept seeing him around—and I remembered Henry was really involved in his church, super close with the pastor, and I thought that might be something. Not going to him directly, but to someone else Henry wasn't friends with."

"Someone who could kick him out of the church?" Catherine asked, trying to understand.

"No," Leyna said. "More like . . . be aware of what was going on. Watch him. I think I just wanted people to know. And the church is so big here, I was hoping . . . Anyway"—another sigh—"I was on the church website awhile, trying to figure out who to go to. And when I Googled that guy Ken, I saw his wife was a therapist. It seemed like a good idea. I figured, they're religious and know about stuff like this so they'll feel compelled to do something. . . ."

"I think they tried," Catherine said.

Leyna looked uncomfortable at that. "He left the church. Because of me. Ken and his wife. They're freaking moving out of town. I went to the cops after, tried to retract my statement, but it didn't matter by that point. God, I feel like I messed everything up. I should have told you. I'd seen you with him at the store, and then I heard your name—Catherine—at Starbucks and you were talking to that girl about Henry. . . . I *almost* told you. But I couldn't. I don't know why. I just felt stupid, about everything."

"No," Catherine said. "You weren't stupid. That wasn't your fault. None of it was. And there was more going on in the church than just Henry. Ken would have left anyway."

"How do you know?"

"I was in a tree once. I heard things there."

Leyna was looking at her like she was insane, but Catherine didn't mind. She stared right back at the other girl and thought she felt someone else, too, a smaller presence off to the side, just on the edge of her vision: a red coat and the smell of spices. It made her wonder if you had to be young to be believed, or if you had to have a certain number of bruises, a wide-enough bloodstain on the snow. Or maybe you just had to die. It made her think of that Bible quote, the famous one about the mustard seed she'd had to memorize for Sunday school all those years ago, how the smallest amount of faith could move mountains.

She wondered if doubt was just as powerful—if it could cement everything in place, keep it exactly how it had always been, so that nothing ever changed.

"I wanted to say I believe you," Catherine said. "That's why I wanted to talk to you. To say I'm sorry, and that I believe you."

Leyna burst into tears.

CHAPTER FORTY-SEVEN

She was released just shy of three days after what the papers were calling "The Clifftop Showdown: Attempted Murder-Suicide at Lookout Point." Her parents tried to hide the paper from her, but she had the internet. Emails. Instagram and Snapchat. Dozens of messages she didn't answer.

Her parents hovered. Her mother seemed to want to talk about Amy. She was a nurse, after all, and she'd spoken to Minda Harper about what might have been wrong with Amy. But Catherine didn't want to talk about Amy. She didn't want to talk at all, most of the time. Her father was better. He sat with her in silence, and even though it wasn't completely comfortable—nothing was—she could look at him now, and he at her. She kept the curtains open in her bedroom, watching the soft motions of the trees, the birds scattering pine needles and the last dustings of snow. She listened to the rain from the front porch. Saw a moving truck swallow furniture and boxes from the Porters' house. She asked her parents about Amy's parents, what was going on, if they'd talked to them. Their responses were sad and vague and that was fine because the answer was obvious, inevitable.

She asked them about Henry's parents too, and about Molly.

She worried about Molly, pictured the dog dying at Henry's house, forgotten in a room, Mrs. Brisbois stepping over her with an impatient, nasal exhalation. Catherine's mother didn't like when she asked about anything having to do with Henry, but her father shot her considering looks every time she said Molly's name.

She slept a lot, but not well, falling asleep on couches and chairs and rugs. Her doctors weren't worried, though, said it would help the healing. She wondered if that was actually true. She found herself waking at intervals with a start, feeling first panic, disorientation as the nightmares faded—then guilt.

Because she was literally doing nothing. And there were things she had to do.

Three days after she got out of the hospital she called Amber, who swore fluently over the phone before crying for a minute straight. The next day, she listened to the voice mails Andrew had left her. She didn't answer them, but she didn't delete them either. She responded to her professor but didn't do any actual work on the paper, and the day after that, the doorbell rang and her mother asked her if she'd like to come to the door.

Catherine got up from the couch, a blanket wrapped around her, and slowly walked with her mother to the entryway.

Bob was standing on the front porch. With Molly.

"Hi," she said, dumbfounded.

Bob had a sheepish look on his face and Molly was struggling on her leash to get to Catherine.

She knelt down, blanket still around her shoulders, and

stroked Molly's face. "Hey, girl," she said. She looked directly into the dog's eyes, even though she knew you weren't supposed to do that. Molly looked back at her, panting a little, and licked her neck, just to the side of her wound, now covered with just a large Band-Aid.

Catherine stood back up. Bob was watching her closely, his normally pink-white skin almost red at the cheekbones.

"Thought I'd stop by," he said. "Hope that's okay."

"Why do you have her?" Molly was standing closer to Catherine now. She could feel the dog's body heat against her legs.

"I, uh, might have overstepped a bit."

Catherine was very aware of her mother watching her. "It's okay," she said, still looking at Bob. "I'm fine."

Her mother nodded, then went to the kitchen. Catherine heard the water running, and she returned a moment later with a bowl, which she sat at Molly's feet. The dog sniffed the water, then turned, knocking it with her tail. Catherine's mother made a noise and went back into the kitchen, presumably for paper towels.

Catherine rubbed idly at the Band-Aid, then made herself stop. "You overstepped?"

"Somewhat," Bob admitted, tugging Molly back from the spilled water. "Though with Celia Brisbois, I'm not sure how that can be avoided."

She gazed at him curiously as her mother returned to mop up the spill.

Bob sighed, pulling Molly back again. "From what you told

us, Henry planted James's hair on Amy Porter's body, but when we submitted it for DNA testing, the lab let us know some of the hairs weren't human. Along with the hairs that ostensibly belong to James—though the DNA will take weeks to confirm—there were microscopic dog hairs." He nodded at Molly, who was trying to sniff the paper towels; Catherine's mother shooed her away.

"So you wanted to see if those belonged to Molly," Catherine said, watching her mother's futile attempts to push away the Labrador.

Bob nodded. "It would definitively link Henry to the killing. But when we came to collect the hair, I believe the exact words were, 'If you want her, take all of her. Get her out of this house.' Bear in mind, the Brisboises' house has been searched thoroughly, and that can be fairly . . . disruptive. I guess the dog was the last straw." His eyes softened, and he looked past her. "And I got word you'd been asking after her."

She turned to see her father leaning against the wall just by the stairs, his arms crossed across his chest, looking pensive.

"Richard," her mother said, rising to her feet, damp paper towels dripping from her hands. "You can't be serious."

"She doesn't have much time left," Bob cautioned. "From what I understand. We can always take her to the shelter—"

But Catherine had already held out her hand for Molly's leash.

"Richard," her mother scolded, now walking past her, to her father. "A word, please?"

Catherine heard their footsteps recede to the living room,

caught her mother saying something like *didn't even bother to consult me on this?*

Smiling, she watched Molly lap up the remaining water in the bowl.

"Thank you," she said to Bob.

"Still think I'm overstepping a bit. I was surprised to hear you wanted her, to be honest," he admitted. "With her previous owner being, ah . . ."

"I want her."

He nodded. Bounced on the balls of his feet. "You know, Andrew never told me how you all knew about Pechman."

"What?"

"John Pechman. Andrew asked about him. His son as well."

Catherine said nothing.

"I don't know if you're aware," Bob said, "but Ken Itoh came to us after the . . . incident. At Lookout Point. Very keen to talk to us about Henry, and John Pechman." He gave her another searching look.

She wondered if Pechman had discovered his books all out of order, the shelf no longer screwed into the sides. Though maybe he had more pressing matters on his mind now.

"What's going to happen to him?" she asked.

"The case has been transferred to the higher-ups. Seems people thought it best, on the whole, to leave local law enforcement out of Pechman's dealings. I believe there's an audit of the church going on as we speak." A pause. "I'm sorry," Bob said. "I don't know if I've said that to you."

Catherine looked up at him. "You did kill him. You did save me."

"That was Andrew," Bob said. "All Andrew. He says he's been trying to get in touch with you."

"I haven't . . . really been up for it."

"No, of course not. I'm sure he understands that."

"Can you—?" She broke off.

"What?"

She swallowed. "Tell him to give me some time."

"Catherine," Bob said. "I think that boy would give you several lifetimes if you asked him." Then he cleared his throat, looking awkward. It made him seem younger somehow. And in that moment she saw him in a way she hadn't been able to that night: standing across the clearing in the gently falling snow, aiming past her, elbows locked, waiting for an opening, his heart racing just as fast as hers. She wondered if he had nightmares like she did, if he woke up breathless at strange, dark hours, his mind full of how it might have ended.

"Well," Bob said, taking a small step back from the doorway. "You sure your parents are going to be okay with this?"

Catherine looked at Molly, who was now belly-down on the hardwood, head on her paws. She could just hear her parents in the living room:

". . . a reason for being, for getting up in the morning. *Ikigai,* they call it—"

"I swear to God, Richard—"

Catherine smiled and put her hand on the door. "Yeah," she said. "We're good."

———

It took Molly all of twenty-four hours to completely exhaust her. She went to the pet store and set up a vet appointment and her parents bickered over what the rules should be, where Molly should be allowed to go in the house. Catherine's mother thought Molly shouldn't be let in the living room, but by nightfall she was reading on the couch, absentmindedly stroking Molly's head, which lay on a pillow in her mother's lap.

"Told you," her father teased.

Her mother pretended not to hear.

The next morning Molly woke her up at seven to go outside. Catherine stood shivering in the cold, sleep still in her eyes, as Molly leisurely made her way around the front yard as though this was a very important decision.

"Oh, come on already," Catherine said.

A bark sounded in the distance, high-pitched, almost a yowl.

Molly whirled and ran out of the yard.

"Molly!" Catherine shouted, watching her disappear down the sidewalk. *Why didn't I put her on a leash?* "Molly!"

Catherine ran, finally catching up to her a street or so down. Molly was wagging her tail furiously at a small white dog as a teenage boy looked around with a bewildered expression on his face.

"This your dog?" he called. Then he recognized her, and she, him.

She froze on the sidewalk, not sure what to do, but Molly was circling the smaller dog, who clearly did not share her enthusiasm, and she didn't want the situation to escalate.

"Molly," she said, and walked forward. She took hold of the collar, her breathing fast. "Sorry."

"It's fine."

Matt wiped his nose. "Ours isn't really trained either."

"She's trained," Catherine said, a little defensively, though she actually wasn't sure that was true at all. Silence fell as they looked at each other; then Matt cleared his throat nervously.

"How's Hannah?" Catherine asked finally, realizing as she said it that she genuinely wanted to know.

Matt shrugged. "Okay, I guess. School started, so she doesn't think about it as much."

"And you?" she asked before she could stop herself. "You think about it? About her?"

Her heart was beating very fast and Molly was whining and the small dog was growling now, little teeth bared.

"I didn't do anything to her," Matt said, tugging at his dog. It leapt up at him and dragged its way down his arms, pulling at the sleeves.

"You knocked me down, though."

His eyes darted to hers. "I fucked up. Seriously. I just . . . I freaked. Getting called down by the cops, asked all these questions. My parents yelling at me, looking at me like it was possible I actually, like, *killed* someone. Thinking about going to jail. I mean, I watch the shows. It doesn't take much, does it? To send someone away? Then you came to my house and you were starting it all up again, saying what the cops were saying, and I just . . . lost it. After, I felt like shit about it, about everything. Then I heard what happened, at the clifftop. I thought I should apologize or something, but I figured you probably didn't want to talk to me anyway."

"Why were you even talking to her? *Why?* She was twelve years old. Can't you see how bad that looks?"

"She . . . was nice to me." His voice was quiet, his eyes wet. "That was all. I liked it, that she was nice to me. How is that so bad?"

She realized how very thin he was, how young and nervous-looking. No wonder he'd liked talking to Amy. She almost . . . felt bad for him. But she was angry at him at the same time. She couldn't figure him out, where to put him in her mind.

Was he a threat? Was he like Henry? The boys in the dorms? *Could* he be?

She felt like the world was made up of all these horrible possibilities now, and she fought with herself on the sidewalk, tried to make her blood slow and her mind quiet. It worked. Sort of.

She let go of Molly's collar so she could stand up straight, but still blocked the dog with her leg. "Just because you didn't kill her doesn't mean you didn't do anything wrong. Stick to girls your own age, Matt. Or at least in your own school. And the next time you think of hitting a girl, even shoving her, think of me. Last guy who did that? I stabbed him." She pointed to his abdomen, her fingers an inch from his ribs. "Right around here."

And she turned at that, pulling Molly down the street, thinking that even though she probably could have handled that better—with perhaps fewer threats of violence—she also could have done a hell of a lot worse.

———

A few hours later she was sitting on the porch with Molly and a cup of coffee, her laptop just off to the side. She sipped and squinted and scrolled, a blanket wrapped around her legs, Molly's head on her knee. She wanted to finish the edits to her essay before she left for school next week. Her heart flew into her throat at the thought but she forced it back down.

One thing at a time. One page at a time. She scrolled down, looking at the comments in the margins.

A movement in the corner of her eye. She looked up. A car was rounding the median, coming to a stop in front of her house. She recognized it, and her heart moved again as the boy got out of the car—no hazards this time—and walked toward her.

Molly ran to him, but Catherine was slower as she rose from the porch steps. There was no snow on the ground at all now, and while it was raining, the rain was light, like an exhale from the sky. It dampened Molly's fur, though, and dotted Andrew's shoulders, his hands.

She'd called him last night as Molly settled into bed with

her and she found herself staring for so long the dog began to blur and waver like something underwater.

"I'm sorry," he'd told her before she'd even said hello. "I'm a total coward."

"You are," she said. "But you're also not."

He told her how he'd come to the hospital, how they wouldn't let him see her. How Bob had been so busy with the fallout he was constantly at the station. How his mother had heard what had happened and freaked out and demanded he come home right away. How his brother even came home for a few days afterward.

She didn't blame him, she told him.

"You should," he said. "You really should. A million, million times over, you should blame me."

"Come back," she said.

"When?"

"Tomorrow."

He sat next to her on the porch, Molly between them.

"I bought flour," Catherine said, twisting her ring around her finger. She couldn't see the mark on Andrew's face at all.

"Flour."

She nodded. "To bring to Amy."

A pause.

"Flour. Instead of flowers."

"I haven't been to the grave yet. But when I do, I wanted to bring something."

Andrew drew back a little to look at her. She felt his eyes

linger at her throat. She was still wearing a Band-Aid over it. The doctors wanted her to have something covering it at all times for at least another week, and then for a month whenever she was in the sun, to prevent further damage.

She pulled the Band-Aid off. "Here. I don't care. You can see it."

"I don't—" he began, but she turned her head, baring her neck, her face in profile. After a moment, she drew back, sticking the Band-Aid back into place with some difficulty.

"It's not that bad," he said.

"I feel like it's on my face sometimes, the way people act around me. Like I've been marked."

"I didn't mean to—"

"No, not you. Or at least, not just you. Anyway, I didn't want to meet up to complain."

The rain was picking up. The porch was covered but she could see it now, falling in broken lines to the grass, the asphalt.

"Do you ever wonder why they call it West Falls?" Andrew asked her.

She raised her eyebrows.

"Seriously," he said.

She shrugged. "It's west of the Falls Creek Falls."

"So why not West Falls Creek Falls?"

"Because that sounds stupid."

"So does Falls Creek Falls, and that doesn't seem to have stopped them."

She smiled. The rain was pattering. She pictured a graveyard she'd never been to, the headstones gleaming. A place of ghosts, but not in a bad way. She'd leave the bag of flour against Amy's resting place and she'd shake and cry and maybe kneel, but then she'd get up and go home and walk Molly and work on her essay and pack, and for what felt like the first time she saw the stretch of time and it did not make her want to die.

She pulled the loose Band-Aid off to feel the air on her healing skin. "I'm going back to school," she said.

"Really?"

"Yes, really. And actually, that's why I wanted to talk to you. I need to ask you a favor."

"Okay."

"What were their names?"

Andrew stared at her. She watched his shoulders tense, his eyes darken as he looked away from her. "I thought you didn't want—"

"I didn't. But now I want to know. I have to know."

Nightmare meant one who lay down with the sleeper.

Well, she was awake now.

Not a sleeper in the dark or a girl who bled into a boy when he kissed her in a summer back garden. Past black sleep and innocence. Outside of every single tree. Her soul uprooted, not preyed on by harpies or Henry or anyone else. It was her own, soil-stained and bloody, half savage and free.

But she had to know their names. It was the first step out of hell. The key to the gate guarded by something shadowed and crouching. And you had to know the name to get out—because monsters lost their power when you knew what they were called.

So he told her. Told her how he'd learned one name—the guy who actually lived in that room, on his hall—then found the second on an online forum for an honors course; Andrew had recognized that boy from the class, which had only twenty students in it. The third he'd tracked down on the first one's Instagram, searching through a hundred pictures until he found that last face and name.

He told her what they were called: six words. Syllables like heartbeats, like rain.

A long silence. She put a hand to her cut, felt the roughness of the scar. Remembered.

"I'm going to report them to the police," she said.

Slowly, Andrew nodded. "Okay."

"I don't think anything will happen. I'm kind of expecting it not to. But I'm going to go to the police and tell them the names you just told me and I want you to come with me."

He blinked at her. "You do?"

"Yes."

"As, like, evidence?"

"Yes."

A pause, then—"Okay."

It was her turn to look surprised. "Okay?"

"Yeah. Why not?"

"Well, because—they'll be pissed. Other people too, probably."

"Yeah," Andrew said mildly. "I think I'm okay with people like that being mad at me."

In a different story it would be bright and warm, her mind a landscape of flowers instead of graves. But this was her story, and it was gray rain and headstones and the sharp edge of a cliff.

But that was fine.

Because she could feel the texture of her broken skin, knew blood beat just beneath it. So alive she felt like screaming, each breath a kind of bitter triumph. She had been inside something stiff and unyielding, and it had told her she belonged there, would in fact never leave. But she was gone, out, had pried herself from the ground like a long-buried thing, shaking leaves from her feet, roots from her hair. Running. And there was a fierce and defiant freedom in it, as she trailed blood and branches, leaving wide-spaced footprints in the earth that had once held her.

ACKNOWLEDGMENTS

This book is not mine alone. My gratitude goes to many but to Greg first, because he is the only part of my life I have never been able to put into words.

A good book needs a good team behind it: a million thanks to Random House and my editor, Emily Easton, for taking me on, showing me the ropes, and believing this story could be great. I am also tremendously indebted to my agent, Victoria Sanders, and all at Victoria Sanders & Associates for sticking with me for four years while I tried to write a book (or three). Thank you for giving me the time to learn how to do it right.

Thanks also to Justin Rizen, who helped me get across the finish line. You are a true friend, Justin, and your feedback was invaluable. Here's to Panera lunches and brutal honesty.

Rosie and Kelly shared their knowledge and personal experience with me during the editing process, ensuring this book was true to life, and to trauma, while Kevin allowed me to shamelessly take advantage of his law-enforcement connections. As my understanding of police work comes solely from *Law & Order*, this input was especially important.

A special shout-out to the staff at the Christiansburg Library, who likely created the most positive work environment in the world.

I miss you all, not least because there are only so many people who will tolerate my continuous talk of Harry Potter and serial killers.

Endless gratitude to my family: Dad, I can talk to you for hours about anything and come away better for it. Mom, you have a good heart and read all my drafts no matter how gruesome. You and Dad being proud of me means more than you can know. Chris, I love you and Robert and your little Hufflepuff; I'm glad we're all Texans together now. To Greg's family: Thank you for welcoming me into your life so many years ago and making all those horror stories about in-laws seem completely implausible. I also must thank Grandma and Grandpa for being arguably two of my biggest cheerleaders, and Papa (and Nana) for their prayers and love. "Youth cannot know how age thinks and feels," Dumbledore tells us, but I have been incredibly fortunate to hear and see the wisdom of age through my grandparents.

Credit also must go to Alice Sebold for her memoir *Lucky*, which has haunted me for ten years, and to Emily Brontë for writing in a time when women were told they should not. You and your sisters used male pseudonyms to ensure your words would be read at all. It's better, a little, these days. I wish you could see it.

To all victims of sexual assault, regardless of age, race, gender, orientation, drinking/drug habits, sexual history, or clothing choice: None of it matters. Any actions on your part before or after the attack do not negate the crime done to you. It was not your fault. You encountered a monster along the path of your life and survived. This book is for you, and also for those who did not make it. I believe all of you, even the ghosts.

ABOUT THE AUTHOR

MONICA RODDEN is a Virginia Tech graduate who lives in Austin, Texas, with her husband and a dog that enjoys terrorizing the local squirrel population. She has worked in the public library system for over five years. *Monsters Among Us* is her first book.

Underlined

A Community of Book Nerds & Aspiring Writers!

READ

Get book recommendations, reading lists, YA news

DISCOVER

Take quizzes, watch videos, shop merch, win prizes

CREATE

Write your own stories, enter contests, get inspired

SHARE

Connect with fellow Book Nerds and authors!

GetUnderlined.com • @GetUnderlined

Want a chance to be featured? Use #GetUnderlined on social!